Praise for Fuminori Nakamura's *The Thief*

A *Wall Street Journal* BEST FICTON OF 2012 SELECTION
A *Wall Street Journal* BEST MYSTERY OF 2012
A *World Literature Today* NOTABLE TRANSLATION
A *Los Angeles Times* BOOK PRIZE NOMINEE

"*The Thief* brings to mind Highsmith, Mishima and Doestoevsky.... A chilling philosophical thriller leaving readers in doubt without making them feel in any way cheated."—*The Wall Street Journal*

"An intelligent, compelling and surprisingly moving tale, and highly recommended."—*The Guardian*

"Nakamura's prose is cut-to-the-bone lean, but it moves across the page with a seductive, even voluptuous agility. I defy you not to finish the book in a single sitting."—*Richmond Times Dispatch*

"Fuminori Nakamura's Tokyo is not a city of bright lights, bleeding-edge technology, and harujuku girls with bubblegum pink hair. In Nakamura's Japan, the lights are broken, the knives are bloodier than the tech, and the harujuku girls are aging single mothers turning tricks in cheap tracksuits. His grasp of the seamy underbelly of the city is why Nakamura is one of the most award-winning young guns of Japanese hardboiled detective writing."—*The Daily Beast*

"*The Thief* manages to wrap you up in its pages, tightly, before you are quite aware of it."—*Mystery Scene*

"Nakamura succeeds in creating a complicated crime novel in which the focus is not on the crimes themselves but rather on the psychology and physicality of the criminal. The book's power inheres in the voice of the thief, which is itself as meticulously rendered as the thief's every action."—Three Percent

"Fascinating. I want to write something like *The Thief* someday myself."
—Natsuo Kirino, bestselling author of Edgar-nominated *Out* and *Grotesque*

"*The Thief* is a swift piece of crime noir, surprisingly light on grit but weighted by existential dread. It's simple and utterly compelling—great beach reading for the deeply cynical. If you crossed Michael Connelly and Camus and translated it from Japanese."—*Grantland*

"Surreal."—*Sacramento Bee* "Page-Turner" Pick

"Nakamura's writing is spare, taut, with riveting descriptions…. Nakamura conjures dread, and considers philosophical questions of fate and control…. For all the thief's anonymity, we come to know his skill, his powerlessness and his reach for life."—Cleveland.com

"Disguised as fast-paced, shock-fueled crime fiction, *The Thief* resonates even more as a treatise on contemporary disconnect and paralyzing isolation."
—*Library Journal*

"I was deeply impressed with *The Thief*. It is fresh. It is sure to enjoy a great deal of attention."
—Kenzaburō Ōe, Nobel Prize–winning author of *A Personal Matter*

"Nakamura's memorable antihero, at once as believably efficient as Donald Westlake's Parker and as disaffected as a Camus protagonist, will impress genre and literary readers alike."—*Publishers Weekly*

"Compulsively readable for its portrait of a dark, crumbling, graffiti-scarred Tokyo—and the desire to understand the mysterious thief."—*Booklist*

"Like Camus' *The Stranger*, Nakamura's *The Thief* is less concerned about the fallout of a particular crime than about probing the nature of human existence…. The story is fast-paced, elegantly written, and rife with the symbols of inevitability."—*ForeWord*

"The drily philosophical tone and the noir atmosphere combine perfectly, providing a rapid and enjoyable 'read' that is nonetheless cool and distant, provoking the reader to think about (as much as experience) the tale."
—International Noir Fiction

"Both a crime thriller and character study, it is a unique and engrossing read, keeping a distant yet thoughtful eye on the people it follows…. [Nakamura] may be looking at his story with a cold eye, but the warmth he sees is real and all the more poignant because of its faintness. It's a haunting undercurrent, making *The Thief* a book that's hard to shake once you've read it."
—Mystery People

"[An] extremely well-written tale…. Readers will be enthralled by this story that offers an extremely surprising ending."—*Suspense Magazine*

EVIL AND THE MASK

Also by Fuminori Nakamura

The Thief

EVIL AND THE MASK

FUMINORI NAKAMURA

Library of Congress Cataloging-in-Publication Data

Nakamura, Fuminori, 1977–
[Aku to kamen no ruru. English]
Evil and the mask / by Fuminori Nakamura.
p. cm
ISBN 978-1-61695-212-9
eISBN 978-1-61695-213-6
1. Family secrets—Fiction. 2. Corruption—Fiction. 3. Japan—Fiction.
I. Title.
PL873.5.A339A7713 2013
895.6'36—dc23
2013000545

Interior design by Janine Agro, Soho Press, Inc.

Printed in the United States of America

10 9 8 7 6 5 4 3 2 1

EVIL AND THE MASK

Detective's Diary (Extract)

While that big case was moving towards an unexpected solution, the fact that several unnatural deaths surrounded it was barely mentioned. Their exact relation to the case is still unclear, and now that the most important evidence has disappeared it will be impossible to uncover the truth. I was only responsible for investigating one man, but in retrospect it should have been a couple, a man and a woman. Even though I was just a single member of the inquiry team, I wondered at the time if our solution was acceptable. Maybe I was operating under a serious misconception all along. Reflecting on it now, I can't help thinking that perhaps by some chance I alone was the closest to the truth about that entire sequence of events, which could have been linked but never were.

I still don't fully understand that couple's relationship. Right from the beginning, however, I was obsessed with a single hypothesis. If he offered to explain everything he knows about those mysterious events and about his own life, I'd love to hear it. Not so much to solve the case—I'd love to hear it as a fellow human being.

As a detective, I've always been involved in other people's lives. Looking back, I've hardly lived my own life at all. I've spent my career prying into their affairs, sticking my nose in, prodding their lives in the right direction. It may be an odd way of putting it, but the main character has always been the criminal. I've spent more time thinking about them than about my own life. In that sense, I've allowed other people to take the lead and I've been merely an observer.

If this case were fiction, I would obviously have a supporting part, appearing only rarely, a genuine bit player. But still, I'd like to talk some more with that man, who was born and raised in that peculiar family and who, if my guess is correct, ended up choosing the wrong path in his life. Now I want to know everything about him.

Not as a detective, but as a man. As a man who, in spite of being a detective, has always borne a grudge against society.

PART 1

PAST

1 PAST

"NOW I'M GOING to tell you some important facts about your life."

I was eleven, and my father had called me to his study. In his black suit he leaned back heavily on the leather sofa, perhaps because he was already an old man and standing tired him. A ray of the setting sun peeped through a crack in the curtains. With the orange light behind him, his face was in shadow. Clutching a red, radio-controlled car, still with dirt on its tires, I was aware of how small I was in the center of the large, cold room. Father's breath smelled faintly of alcohol.

"About your education. This does not mean, though, that I hold any great hopes for you. It's just that I intend to leave a 'cancer' in this world. Under my guidance, you will become a cancer. A personification of evil, you could say."

I couldn't see my father clearly, but it was hard to imagine that he was smiling. No doubt his face was as immobile and expressionless as ever.

"My other children are already adults, occupying important positions in society. That is because they came into the world uninvited, and were free to choose their own paths. Your life, on the other hand, I created on purpose, when I was already past sixty. This is something of a practice in my—no, our—family."

I still couldn't see his face.

"By 'cancer' I mean a being that will make this world miserable. That will make everyone wish that they had never been born, or at least make everyone think that the light of virtue does not shine in this world."

There was a knock at the door, and at his signal a young servant girl entered. Her lips and nose were narrow, her eyes large and clear. I thought she was probably my father's type. On our estate there were at least seven domestic servants. When she whispered something to him he nodded. "Send her in," he muttered, then turned back to me. "The most recent recorded example was in the Taisho era, almost eighty years ago."

The servant left the room silently.

"Our ancestor revived the custom when he was over sixty years old—the custom of delivering a cancer into the world. He seems to have realized that his own life was nearing its end, and that even though he would die, the world would carry on.

That was something he was unable to forgive. In his life he had obtained everything he wanted and he was arrogant, as I am. If his life was going to end, then everything must perish. So on June eighteenth, nineteen fifteen, a young woman gave birth to his child. To bring this world to an end—no, to be precise, to be a negative force, to make the world as unhappy as possible. He raised that child to be a cancer on society, and the boy was excellent. He turned into a creature who was destined to make many peoples' lives hell, who was destined to increase the number of people who believed that life wasn't worth living. They say that when the old man was on his deathbed, he was no longer afraid. He thought the unhappy people created by that cancer would create more unhappiness, and cancer would spread like gushing foam. If that continued, the world would begin to fail. Well, he thought, at the very least I have been able to create a person who will spread a stain over the light of the world in my stead after I am gone. In his bed, the old man heard the news of the outbreak of the war in the Pacific. That cancer had nothing to do with the events leading up to the war, but as a high-ranking officer he committed all manner of atrocities—so much evil that God covered his eyes."

The door opened and a girl I had never seen before entered. Cold air from the rest of the house flowed in, and she walked toward us on skinny legs. Her face was immediately flushed with the slanting orange sunlight, and her large eyes stood out vividly in her face. I caught my breath, confused, as though I was threatened by the unexpected presence of those eyes, as though they were going to vanish into the light. I was careful not to show it, however. My father gave no reaction to the girl's entry.

"With our wealth and power that have been passed down through the generations, we can use this life to do whatever we want. Then when we feel that our time is running out, by breeding one of these cancers we can mask the fear of death with amusement at the entertainment it provides. Of course this custom is not observed in every generation. From time to time, however, it is remembered and put into practice. I have revived it once more. A number of years ago a religious group occupied a nuclear power plant. When their plan was foiled by Public Security, they all committed suicide. While that group was in the process of turning into a cult, one student from Tokyo University played a leading role. His roots can be traced back to that cancer clan. Namely, he was the son of that soldier, from a lesser branch of our family tree."

The girl was about my age, wearing a white dress and carrying a large bag. She stared at my father and me in wonder. I looked idly at the nascent bulge of her breasts. Even after I turned back to my father, his face still hidden in shadow, the image of her white dress, tinged with orange, stayed in my mind's eye.

It was not just me and Father that she seemed to find strange, but everything around her. The room, spacious and unheated. The deer's head mounted on the wall, antlers spread wide on either side, its coat covered in dust as if it had turned to stone. The enormous black desk, the sofa where my father was sitting, the countless books and earthenware pots placed carelessly on the ancient shelves.

"First, you need to become competent."

My father's lecture was not finished.

"In this world, you must be powerful, because when an able person becomes a cancer, he is formidable. I hear you are highly intelligent. That, however, is thanks to your education thus far. The differences between people are not as great as the differences between humans and apes. Talent is simply the ability to work harder than other people. At present, you have the habit of diligence—in other words, perseverance and willpower. From now on you must also form the habit of resisting the temptation towards inertia or resignation. To purge from your soul any tendency to give up. You must also form the ability to communicate, to manage human relationships shrewdly. Last week a young man was going around assaulting people at random in the streets, but I don't want you to limit yourself to trivial crimes like that. Under my tutelage, you will become a brilliant man. Intellectually you will be greatly in advance of your years, and then when you turn fourteen, I am going to show you hell."

Still he did not move a muscle. He must have been well into his seventies, and his legs were spindly. The girl continued to stand beside me, forgetting even to put her bag on the floor.

"A hell which will make you want to reject the world. A cruel, devastating hell. This girl will play an important part in that torment. At that time, as you are entering adolescence, under the surface your psychological balance will be upset, causing major neurological disturbances. You will be engulfed by that evil, and you will feel a need to use it to influence the people around you. That is just the beginning, however. When you turn fifteen I will show you hell once more, and twice when you turn sixteen. Then at eighteen you will learn another truth about your life. All this has already been determined. It cannot be altered."

My father shifted position slightly, and for a moment his head moved out of the shadow. I caught a brief glimpse of his face, still completely without expression, and then it was hidden again.

"You will become part of the nerve center of this country, or else the nerve center of some organization that is fighting against this country, and you will foment evil. I will leave you a greater share of my wealth than my other children, so that ideally this world may be brought to an end."

He sighed heavily. The girl's frightened eyes were still illuminated by the glow of the setting sun.

"Why am I telling you this now? There are three reasons. One is that I am exceedingly drunk. The second is that you are still young and will not remember this conversation for long, because you are still in short pants and holding a toy car in your hand."

I thought he might laugh at this, but he didn't.

"And the third reason is that your mother was a good woman. She spent nights with an old man like me and gave birth to you. She waited patiently for a chance to bring out the goodness that I rejected my entire life—no, which I couldn't even comprehend. I respect that. But you will soon forget this talk. Probably you don't even understand a word of it. It will be like a tale heard in a dream."

My father stood. With the light behind him, his body looked like a black void that had appeared in the air.

"This girl will live here with you. From now on the two of you must become close. For the hell that you will see in the future, so that you will become a cancer. However, you and this girl will not live happily ever after. Never. Now go to bed. You are still a child, and there is nothing so foolish as a child."

Father turned his back and took a book from the shelf as though he had already forgotten us. Then he went through the door to the adjoining room at the rear. Whenever he opened a door, it never made a sound. The girl in the white dress was staring intently at the stuffed deer's head.

But my father was wrong. I was already a cancer. The only reason I was carrying a radio-controlled car was to deceive him. I was always thinking of ways of exterminating him, and I had been fantasizing about those plans for a long time, every day it seemed.

2

AT THAT TIME I did not know how many rooms there were in the mansion.

The hill behind the house was like a forest, and in the garden were two ponds surrounded by stones. The hill was untended and wild, but the ponds were stocked with carp. Usually carp live to a ripe old age, but for some unknown reason on our estate they never lasted long.

Apart from the young servant girls, there was also a quiet, middle-aged woman called Tanabe who was in charge of all the domestic staff. At first I thought she was my mother, but that wasn't the case. I had no idea where my mother was. No one had even told me if she was alive or dead.

The girl in the white dress was named Kaori. Not even she knew her original last name. She was adopted into the family from a children's home and given the same surname as me, Kuki. Our gloomy house was on the outskirts of Nagoya in Aichi Prefecture. The building is still standing, but no Kukis live there anymore.

Kaori and I went to the local public elementary school. Normally I would have expected to attend a private school like my older siblings, but my father wouldn't hear of it. He thought that a public school was better for coming in contact with people from all levels of society. To make me a cancer I had to learn to mix with a wide range of people. That was probably what he had in mind.

Most of my schooling was done by three home tutors. I've largely forgotten what they were like. There is only one, a young man, I remember well. Although he was only there for a short time, he became a bright spot in my joyless daily routine.

He was very muscular, and behind his back the servants and I called him the Muscleman. When he heard this nickname he took a fancy to it and started using it himself. Physically, however, he was so weak that it made me wonder what those big muscles were for, and he moved ponderously. He also had a tendency to say tactless things—for example, he once told a servant whose eyes were too far apart that she was lucky to have 180-degree vision. Usually I laughed at his jokes just because that's what children were supposed to do, but sometimes my laughter was genuine. For some reason, at those times I would feel sorry for myself.

My school life was uneventful. All I had to do was make some effort to hide my depression from those around me. I couldn't afford to let them discover that I was the kind of boy who regularly threw lizards and other small creatures off the cliff on the hill out the back. Nor that I used to pick up hair and fingernail clippings that had been dropped around the house and store them in a box, on the theory that at least some of them must be my mother's. Even without those eccentricities, a boy who lived in an obscenely big house and was good at nothing but studying was unlikely to fit in at school. I decided to trick them by concealing myself in a cloak of laughter. I think the other kids were more at ease with me that way. He might be a Kuki brat, they'd think, but he likes a joke as much as the rest of us, and he's more frivolous than serious.

For instance, our homeroom teacher was so fat that he always seemed in danger of bursting. He also had the habit of saying, "To give a concrete example," and then following up with an explanation that wasn't concrete at all. I christened him "Concrete Bomb." During lessons I would count how many times he said, "To give a concrete example," and tell my classmates. The big blob's lectures were full of statements like, "To give a concrete example, the numerator and denominator are like curry and a sweet bun." We had gotten it into our heads that if he used the phrase more than forty times his stomach would explode, so we were always keyed up in his classes. I felt terrible about deceiving people around me to hide my darkness, but later I learned that many people actually live like that when they are young.

Kaori was in the same class as me. Since she was tall with large eyes, she attracted a lot of attention. Concrete Bomb told the class, falsely but thoughtfully, that she was a distant relative of mine. On her first day there we did the high jump. When she leapt higher than all the other girls, a small cheer went up. But I was less interested in the height of the jump than in her white legs sticking out of her gym shorts on top of the blue mats. I was still young and felt a deep shame at my lustful urges. If my father said we had to become intimate, that was a sure sign that we shouldn't. I looked away, but a child's will is weak, and before I knew it I was staring at her again.

Kaori and I went home from school together. Since Father had dismissed the estate's driver, it had become my habit to walk home.

"It must be great being rich," Kaori said on that first day.

"No, it's not."

"It must be. And I hear you're good at studying too? I'm hopeless."

She laughed innocently, showing her teeth. With her long limbs, I couldn't imagine a girl who would look odder wearing a child's school bag than her.

"Even if I am rich, it's not like I earned it. And the only reason I am able to study is because I've got a tutor. There's nothing impressive about it. Not at all." In those days I had the habit of forgetting to pretend and rebelling against even the smallest things.

She looked pensive. I had to keep talking so she wouldn't think I was being perverse.

"So I've got to grow up. If I can do something for myself, that will be impressive." I didn't really believe this.

She gave me a puzzled look, and we walked in silence for a while. Then she laughed.

"But weren't you the one who gave Concrete Bomb his name?"

MY FATHER HAD five other children—my older brothers and sisters—but at that stage I'd never met any of them. Most of them lived in Tokyo and never came near the mansion—they hadn't even come to see me when I was born. My father's name was Shozo, but none of my siblings, not even the eldest son, had inherited any of the Chinese characters in his name. Twenty-five years separated me from my oldest brother; from the next, twenty-three; from my oldest sister, eighteen; my third brother, fifteen; my second sister, twelve. I also knew that the Tokyo University grad student my father had talked about, the one who was in the cult, had a son the same age as me. I wondered if he had become a cancer, and vaguely expected that I'd meet him sometime, along with my brothers and sisters.

When we reached the gloomy house, the Muscleman was standing outside the gate. He grumbled that I was late, but then he noticed Kaori. Immediately he held out his hand and introduced himself, using his nickname. She hesitated before shaking his hand, perhaps intimidated by his physique, perhaps put off by the fact that he was sweating even though it wasn't hot.

"You said I was late, but I've still got five minutes, haven't I?"

"Well, I don't care," he mumbled. "But my muscles do."

He wiggled his pecs. Laughing in surprise, Kaori cried out, admiring his pointless muscles. Then, with his usual lack of tact, he looked at her and said, "Maybe you and Fumihiro will get married." I was struck dumb, but Kaori turned to look at the dark buildings.

"If I do, I'll live like a princess, won't I?" she said and laughed carelessly.

From a distance it would have looked like a happy scene. And who knows, maybe at that time we were still happy.

THAT NIGHT, OR perhaps the next, my father summoned me. It was the first time he had called me since the day he told me of his plans for my education. Until then, he had never shown the slightest interest in me. When I heard that he wanted to talk to me again, I was certain it would be more on the same subject. And even if it wasn't, just meeting him was enough to make me nervous. Stifling my panic, I took a bunch of stickers from my desk drawer and clutched them in my hand.

The room to which I was called was large, with a long table, a television and a carpet of a dull purple-red. Here Father always dined alone, and he had decreed that Kaori and I would eat with the servants in another room.

There was no answer to my knock, so I opened the door quietly. Father was sitting in one of the six dining chairs, smoking and watching TV. His face was blank, and I couldn't tell what sort of mood he was in. This time too he smelled of alcohol. It occurred to me that he never used to drink that much. The room was dark, but I could still make out his face. With a big nose and abnormally narrow eyes, he was quite ugly. Half of his left ear was missing, I didn't know why.

"My second son is involved in this war," he said, still gazing at the screen and not looking in my direction.

The news was showing a report on a civil war in a small African country I knew nothing about. The anchor was reading out the number of deaths.

"You should remember this. They're calling it an ethnic conflict, but that's a lie. Someone is stirring up trouble between them. My son's got the rights for postwar reconstruction. I don't remember raising him as a cancer, but somehow he keeps acting like one. I need to do something about that."

He turned to me and gestured slightly with his fingers. I didn't understand what he meant, but he pointed at my stickers.

"Put those in the ashtray. Don't bring things like that in here."

My legs went weak and my heart was racing. As instructed, I put the bundle of stickers in the clear ashtray, and Father placed his half-smoked cigarette on top of them. He didn't stub it out, just rested it there, still smoldering.

The surface of the stickers scorched and then caught fire. Small, red flames flickered in the noise of the war report on TV. Looking at the orange glow, I couldn't prevent my brain from going foggy. I was unable to gauge my father's thoughts, whether he was burning the stickers because I valued them or because the cheap, sparkly things offended him. The flames grew larger, and a curl of smoke rose from them. When the stickers started to give off an unpleasant odor, Father doused the fire with the liquor from the glass he was holding. His expression didn't change. I realized that he wouldn't even register the smell, the price of his own spite. My stickers turned to wet, black ash among the cigarette butts. I thought of the hell that Father had promised to show me someday.

The stickers weren't important to me, though. I was only carrying them to make myself look childish, and the flames caused me no pain at all. I looked away from him, my mind in a whirl. My father was wrong. I was beyond his control. But straight after that I thought of Kaori.

"That's enough," he said softly. "Go. What are you so upset about? You're even forgetting to act childishly. You still haven't perfected your role. Fool. There is nothing so foolish as a child."

I left the room and headed for the hill out the back.

Carrying a flashlight, I went out the back door, crossed the garden and crawled through the hole in the fence. The trees rustled in the breeze as though moving of their own volition. Insects brushed against my cheeks and when I heard a dog barking I halted. There was faint moonlight, but the night was dark and cold. Until then I'd always climbed the hill in the late afternoon, while it was still light, but I had to conquer my fear.

My earliest memory was of Father. The servant girls were chasing me and laughing. I was laughing too as I waddled away from them, always on the verge of toppling over. I felt like I was floating in mid-air, perhaps because I'd just started walking and didn't have full control of my legs, and because my line of sight was suddenly higher. On the dirt wall I could see a large green circle, an after-image of some kind. I tried to move forward once more but ran into something that felt like a pillar. I raised my eyes, and there was Father. Somehow I knew who he was. Stony-faced, he swept me aside with his foot, as if it was a nuisance even to kick me.

My flashlight illuminated the dirt path through the weeds. I was relieved. If I'd come this far, the hole was nearby. I shouldn't have been afraid, though, because it was my mountain. I remembered the first time I'd found my father's underground room. The house had an enormous cellar and over the years a huge hoard of furniture and other old junk had been stored there. When I was in fourth grade I got lost in there, and since then I'd explored it in secret. In the basement I'd discovered an entrance to an even deeper level. After moving aside some worn tires and lifting an ancient cloth that looked out of place, I found a square hatch in the floor. When I opened it I could see a narrow set of stairs with a door at the bottom.

My instincts immediately told me that this was bad. This was a place I should not enter, I felt. If I went in there my life would change forever. The door handle was almost entirely free of dust. I held my breath and pushed down the lever. There was no lock.

Inside, I was hit by an overpowering darkness. I'd never seen such an impenetrable black. Its density, actually heavy enough to feel, continued to bombard me, the intruder, even after my eyes had grown accustomed to it. It reminded me of my father. He was purely the embodiment of terror, and whenever he spoke my hands, my feet, my heart, even my temples went numb. I was a thing to be brushed aside with his foot, and as such I could be crushed by a change in his mood as easily as I could crush an insect in my hand. Out of the corner of my eye I could faintly make out a white switch in the darkness. When I turned it on, blades of light struck my eyes. Beyond the glare, in the center of the room, stood a bed.

My mother was sleeping. That was the first thought that popped into my head. No one was there, though, and the empty bed was the only furniture in that confined space. It had a white quilt and pillow, and sheets covered the mattress. Even though, like the door handle, the room was almost free of dust, it felt deserted. On top of the bed were four long ropes. Clumps of old hair were strewn on the pillow and duvet, an extraordinary amount.

I didn't know what it all meant, but I sensed that this place was the center of something. A side of my father that I wasn't supposed to see. I didn't have the courage to touch the ropes or the hair. From that day on, that bed in that black room haunted my dreams. Sometimes I heard a woman's voice coming from underground, but that was impossible. The room had been soundproofed for some reason, and no matter how much noise was made inside, it would never be heard.

Perhaps the reason I started making regular trips to the mountain was to fight back against that darkness in some way. To protect myself by building up my own darkness. At that age, however, I hadn't formed such a theory. Still, I think I went there with that vague idea in my head.

On that day, when I was climbing the hill with a flashlight in my hand after my stickers were burned, I still couldn't have put those thoughts into words. I just forced my feet to move, telling myself that I mustn't be afraid of the darkness. In front of me I could see a hole in the cliff, covered in wire netting. I didn't know what it was for. Feeling the menace of the darkness and the surrounding trees, I tried to convince myself that I was calm.

I walked along the fence, moved aside a sheet of plywood in the thick foliage, and picked up a small, concealed cage. Inside were lizards and snails that I had captured before. I grabbed a lizard, reached through the fence and abruptly opened my hand. Without a sound, it was swallowed up by the darkness. I didn't hear the noise when it hit the ground, but I imagined it. I took a snail, reached through the netting again and dropped it too. Through their sacrifice, I believed, my own darkness would become deeper. Deeper than my father's. Bigger and stronger than that terrifying, incomprehensible figure.

3

THE SERVANTS DRESSED Kaori in an assortment of clothes. A yellow, patterned cardigan, blue denim shorts, a plain white skirt, a cream coat. A pink hooded sweatshirt with pale blue pinstripes, a thick white sweater. Kaori always said that she didn't want expensive clothes. She preferred to wear the same as her classmates. She was using a dirty old bag and umbrella until the servants noticed.

We entered sixth grade.

I watched her in her various outfits, looking away whenever she seemed about to catch me at it. After my tutor left she always came to my room, never noticing my discomfort. She would sprawl unguardedly on the bed, her legs sticking out from her skirt. Let's play cards, she'd say, laying them out on the covers. Looking at her while trying my best not to, I found it hard to breathe.

Once she found my porn magazine. When I came back from the bathroom she was in my room, and the large drawer of my desk was open. The magazine was chock-full of pictures of naked women, and I'd gone to a lot of trouble to get a hold of it. Kaori was studying it earnestly, and she cried out when she saw me. Usually I put it inside a city directory at the bottom of the drawer, under an atlas, a name list for the kids in my class and a pile of thin files, but on that particular day I hadn't hidden it properly.

I was confused and ashamed, but Kaori laughed and called me a dirty old man. Suddenly I thought of a boy named Iijima who sat next to me at school. I put all the blame on this poor kid, making up a story that I'd borrowed it from him, that he was the real pervert. Kaori pointed at the breasts of one of the women in the photos, exclaiming how big they were. Then she cupped her hands in front of her own chest.

"So, you're interested in things like these?"

"No."

"Do they turn you on?"

"No."

She looked at me, grinning.

"You never lift up the girls' skirts like Yazaki and the others, so I thought you were a nice boy."

It was true I didn't do that, but I always had a good look when Yazaki and his friends did.

"So, do you want to lift mine, then?"

She laughed again, raising the hem of her own skirt.

IT WAS ABOUT three months later that she found my box of hair and fingernail clippings, when she was looking for my porno mag again. Kaori had gone into my room without telling me, and when I came back she was staring at the open box with a puzzled frown.

It was filled to the brim. The tangled old hair was bone-dry and the nails were shriveled and curled. Their color had changed to a dark red as they dried, as if to show that they once were human. Even from where I was standing in the doorway it was obvious that it wasn't all old stuff, that some of it had been harvested recently.

I was surprised how shocked I was. It was only natural that I was upset that my secret was revealed, and by Kaori of all people, but I didn't know what to say or do. More than feeling humiliation, more than wanting to hide my shame, all I could do was wish that it had never happened. I snatched the box from her and went to throw it in the trash, but I couldn't. That disturbed me more than anything. I had no idea where to look. Kaori was right in front of me, and at that moment our eyes met.

"It's nothing," I said when I came to my senses.

But I didn't know what to say next. Kaori was wearing a white sweater and white jeans. I closed the lid of the box and put it back in the drawer. I was thinking that I'd just have to walk out when she spoke in a soft voice.

"What is it?"

"Nothing."

"But . . ."

No matter what Kaori thought, for the moment I just wanted to get away from her. I needed time to come up with a plausible explanation, but she didn't look like she was going anywhere. She just sat there, gazing up at me.

"It's none of your business, is it?"

"That's true, but what is it?"

She wouldn't leave me alone. She was determined to find out what it was.

"My mom."

Once I started, I knew I'd end up telling her the whole story.

"I pick them up because I think some of them might be my mother's. I know they can't be, but I collect them anyway."

My throat was tight.

"Even now. Of course I know that there won't be anything of Mom's in what I'm picking up now, but I still can't help myself. If I don't, I feel like they'll be gone forever."

Kaori looked away.

"I even end up picking up the servants' stuff too. If I don't do it I get scared. Really scared. That might sound gross to you, but to me it isn't at all. The servants kind of know about my habit. It's embarrassing, so they clean the house every day."

I couldn't look her in the face. At the back of my mind I saw the mass of dried, discolored hair and the purple shreds of nail she'd just been looking at.

"You must have some," she said suddenly. "There must be

some of your mother's in there. Definitely. So you must never throw them away."

She spoke seriously, with a childish expression, but I was still a child myself. Her long hair was tied back, and her large eyes looked straight into mine as I stood there. That was probably the moment I started to fall in love with her. It was only some time later that I remembered she was an orphan.

AFTER WE FINISHED elementary school, Kaori and I were enrolled in the local junior high. Once again we were in the same class, but this time I thought Father might have had a hand in it. By the time we started, Kaori was only slightly taller than average, while I had shot up.

She was still a bit better at sports than the other girls, but no longer stood out as much as she had when she was younger. Since she was cheerful she had plenty of friends, but she wasn't the center of the class. As always, schoolwork was the only thing I was good at, so I wrapped myself in jokes and frivolity. At the time, that was pretty close to my true personality. I hadn't discarded my box of hair and fingernails, but I'd gradually stopped picking up new ones, and I'd also given up throwing living creatures off the cliff behind the house. I also liked telling jokes, and the lessons, mere repetition of what had already been drummed into me by my tutors, were simply boring. During classes I mucked around with the kids sitting near me, so the teachers often told me off.

I thought only of Kaori, fantasizing every day about our future. Marrying her, finding a job, I didn't care what. If she wanted to work she could, and if she wanted to stay home that was all right too. If we had children, perhaps I'd be able to give them what had been missing in my life. To make her happy, I'd be a thoroughly decent person, and the malevolent strain that ran in my family's blood would stop with me. I'd work hard and buy a house with a nice view, by the sea, maybe. It wouldn't matter if it was small. In the evenings we'd go for walks along the beach. When we quarreled I'd always apologize, and if I thought she was in the wrong, I'd just keep my mouth shut. Maybe even then I'd be the one to say sorry. For me to marry Kaori, however, I'd have to be good enough for her. I wasn't sure exactly what that meant, but for the time being I persevered with my tedious, day-to-day studies. I took pains with my appearance, and thought up stories to make her laugh. I squeezed my darkness into this tiny piece buried deep inside me. All my pent-up energy, which had been trapped by my depression, burst forth directly, even obsessively, towards Kaori.

Almost every night I imagined having sex with her. If I could do it for real, I thought, that would be the happiest thing in the world. Seeing Kaori's body, touching her all over, entering her. It seemed like a miracle, and it never occurred to me that most adults were enjoying the same pleasure. I thought it was only for me, in love with Kaori. Just as she had been in elementary school, she was listed as my relative, but for some reason walking home together had started to feel awkward. She joined the volleyball club, so we left school at different times and went home separately, but she still came to my room every day.

My entire happiness was right there in front of me, and I

couldn't touch it. Still, at least it was close by. While it was trying at times, all in all it was a good thing. It was enough to fill the mind of a junior high school boy like me. Gazing at her body as it grew soft and round, at the swelling of her breasts, was painful, but at the same time I was happy. My thoughts were fixed solely on her, to the almost total exclusion of everything else.

Kaori teasing me by hunting for my adult magazine became a regular game. I hid it in the bookshelf. I took volume Sa-Su of my encyclopedia out of its case and put the magazine in the box in its place, so she never found it. But I hardly needed it any more. My youthful sexual desires were fixated entirely on her.

"I know you've still got it, and I'm going to find it," she said as she opened the closet, still in her school uniform.

"I don't."

"Aren't you interested in girls anymore?"

"That's not what I mean, but it isn't here."

That's how we spent the year before I turned fourteen. Before Father was going to show me hell.

"YOU DON'T LOOK much like your father, Fumihiro."

I don't remember exactly when she told me that. She was staring at me intently, and I felt quite uncomfortable.

"Maybe not. His face is horrible." I turned away, unable to look her in the eye.

"Yeah, you could say that."

We were walking along a dirt road one evening, just after the rain had stopped.

"Somehow I feel like his face isn't his alone."

She was beautiful when she was thinking.

"It's like there's a whole lot of history and other people's faces piled one on top of another. Sometimes I get really scared when he just looks at me. Like all this stuff, Kukis from the past, ancient events, come floating to the surface, all mixed up. It's so freaky. I'm sorry, it's just really scary somehow."

She suddenly lowered her eyes, as if she was afraid. I noticed again how long her lashes were. If I was her boyfriend, I thought, at times like these I could put my arm around her. In reality, though, I couldn't even touch the tips of her fingers.

"YOU'RE ALWAYS STARING at Ms. Yoshimi," said Kaori, just before the summer holidays in our first year of junior high. "You like her, don't you?"

Ms. Yoshimi was our music teacher. She always wore tight-fitting clothes, so all the boys liked her. Based solely on her dress, we'd already decided that she was a slut.

"I don't stare. Why'd you suddenly bring that up?"

I was tall by then, and I had to look down slightly to see Kaori's face.

"Mari is sad. She can't compete with Ms. Yoshimi, and she looked like she was going to cry."

She was watching me with a grin.

"What are you on about?"

"Well, it looks like Mari's going to tell you she's got a crush on you, so you should go out with her."

Mari was a quiet girl who was always drawing. Once when we were cleaning the classroom after school, the bucket she was carrying was about to tip over, so I carried it for her.

"No, I won't. Sorry, but . . ."

"What? Do you like someone else?"

Still smiling, Kaori was looking right into my eyes. Her face, bathed in orange sunlight, was lovely. I was still too young to be able to face her directly.

I was in a turmoil. I remembered the girls' comics Kaori read, TV dramas. Couples were always breaking up because of misunderstandings, or missing each other through bad timing, or going at it all wrong. I hated them. Before I knew it, my body went rigid.

"I can't go out with her because I like you."

In those days I was probably a little odd. Kaori was startled. I was also taken aback by my own words, but I couldn't unsay them.

"I don't mean I want to go out with you or anything. What I mean is, I planned to tell you when we were older, so I hope we can put it on hold till then, carry on the same way we've always been."

"Carry on the same? That's impossible. But you're so brave."

She sighed admiringly. Then she said that if I liked her I should kiss her. Noting my surprise, she corrected herself, telling me that she liked me too, so I should kiss her, please.

We walked to a nearby shrine, hand in hand and staring at the ground. After waiting patiently for a drunk lying on a bench to leave, we kissed, just a little. I felt like I was entering an unknown world. As we walked back we kept holding sweaty hands until we saw the gates of the estate. It was six months until my fourteenth birthday, when my father had promised to introduce me to hell.

4

AFTER THAT SEVERAL things happened far, far away from me.

In line with the Western powers' hidden agenda, the civil war ended in the small African country where my father's second son—my brother, in other words—had been working to make money through reconstruction. The Japanese government announced a large aid budget. The surviving members of the religious cult that had occupied the nuclear power plant and then committed mass suicide appealed against their sentence. A shadowy citizens' group was holding demonstrations outside the courthouse, calling for the death penalty for those involved in planning and preparation. These events sailed quietly over my head. Father had gone to Tokyo and wouldn't be back for quite a while. Kaori and I passed the time lost in our own little world.

Every day after school she came to my room. We turned on some music so that people wouldn't wonder why it was so quiet, and then we'd kiss. We spent hours in each other's arms, tongues locked together, me touching the bulge of her breasts, though without removing her clothes. I felt that maybe we were still too young to be doing this, but I didn't care what anyone else thought.

Before long I managed to undress her and kissed her nipples. Then she started sneaking to my room every night. Naked under the bedclothes, we explored each other's bodies with our fingers and tongues, full of curiosity and desire. The only reason we didn't go all the way was that Kaori was scared to, but for me it was more than enough. To my immature mind, the reality of sex was overwhelming. While the news was causing a stir in the rest of the world, we were alone in my tiny room. I came many times in Kaori's hand, and I often kissed her and licked her private parts. We smothered our cries, soaked with sweat in my little bed. Over and over she told me that it felt good, as though I was filling a gap in her life, and I told her the same. Until then she had been moved from one institution to the next and had endured many things, wearing a mask of cheerfulness. Her urgent fingers and tongue touched me delightfully all over and, copying what she must have seen or heard somewhere, she took my penis in her mouth.

Several of the girls a couple of years older than her in the volleyball club, and one girl who was only one year ahead, had already had sex with their high school boyfriends. With them as her guide, Kaori told me that we could do it the following year. But for me, I didn't care if we actually had sex or not. What we were doing was the height of happiness.

Kaori wanted me with her whole body.

"I'm only happy when you're here," she said, touching me with her hands as though checking my shape. "When you breathe like that, when you're thinking, just because you're there."

For the first time I felt that I was allowed to exist without excuse or darkness or distortion. Apart from the hours I spent with her, everything was a waste of time. The TV news, lessons, my classmates' conversations, all forms of entertainment, they all seemed dull and didn't touch me. But as long as Kaori was there, as long as she was in the world, that was all right. If I had her glossy, black hair, her small face with large eyes and narrow lips, her budding breasts, her slender legs and ankles, her voice, our idle chatter, that was all I needed.

One day, however, Kaori didn't come. I thought this was strange and went to her room. She was asleep and I didn't want to wake her, so I returned to my own bed. The next day, too, she was sleeping. On the third day I couldn't stand it anymore and I roused her with a whisper. I kissed her, feeling that I shouldn't but unable to resist. At first she responded, but soon she suggested quietly that we'd better not do it that day. She was trembling slightly, and I got the impression that it was because of me. Dumbfounded, I had no idea what to do. I apologized over and over, and then left, wondering if I'd done something wrong. When I finally got into bed my head was churning, reviewing my recent behavior for faults. Even though I was still bewildered, I found myself growing hard. I dealt with it, imagining Kaori's body, and then lay there vacantly. Whatever the reason, I thought, I had to know, and once again made my way hesitantly to her room. She wasn't there.

I waited, but she was away too long just to be in the bathroom. Perhaps she'd gone into the garden. I went into the hall and headed towards the back, careful not to wake the servants. Recently several cats had made their home in our yard, and Kaori often fed them from the kitchen door. For some reason I paused outside my father's room. He had come home about two weeks ago. Heart pounding, I quietly opened the door. The yellow light from the desk lamp was shining on Kaori, standing there stark naked, while my father lay fully clothed on the bed some distance away, staring at her.

I nearly cried out, thought I actually did cry out, but somehow no sound came out. Kaori stood shaking in front of my revolting father. When he told her to open her legs, she sat down where she was and did so, face averted. On the table beside the bed was a bottle of whiskey. He ordered her to look at him and she obeyed with a shudder.

I couldn't move. This was the fear I had forgotten. My pulse grew painful, my arms and temples went numb, my legs became horribly weak. But I had to overcome this terror and kill my father. I didn't know how, but I had to kill my father right now. With a sudden feeling of hatred that I'd never experienced before, I opened the door. No, I thought I did, but in reality my arms didn't move. Just as I was wondering why it was still only open a crack, even though I was sure I'd pushed it, Father told Kaori that was it for tonight, and she started getting dressed. I didn't understand what was happening, but I stood rooted to the spot.

She finished putting her clothes on and I came to my senses and fled, leaving the door ajar. I intended to go back to my own room, but plucked up my courage and waited in Kaori's instead. When she saw my face she climbed into bed without a word and hid under the covers.

"I saw," I said, but there was no answer. "I couldn't believe it. What's going on?"

It was like I was talking to myself.

"What is Father . . . ?"

Underneath the bedclothes Kaori was weeping.

"What is he . . . ?"

"I don't know," she said in a small, tearful voice.

"He calls you to his room, makes you strip?"

"Mm."

"What else?"

"I don't know," she replied, and started sobbing violently. "Now it's just taking my clothes off, but I don't know what's going to happen next. I think he's going to . . ."

"But so far you just strip and he watches you?"

"Mm."

"Mmmm."

Wrapped in the futon, Kaori's body looked tiny.

"His face, that blank face, suddenly it fills with lust, and I get even more scared, but I can't move, and your father's face gets uglier and uglier, and all the time, he's staring at me."

I could hardly breathe.

"Do you remember? What Father said the day you arrived? He said he was going to show me hell."

Kaori raised herself a fraction in the bed and shook her head, still crying.

"When I turn fourteen. Six months from now."

My heart was beating so fast it hurt.

"Then my father said that you would play an important part. An important part in showing me hell. So that's it, that's what he meant. I knew it, he's mad, crazy, completely insane."

Apart from the desk, bed and closet, Kaori's room was completely bare. She had never asked for dolls or trinkets or anything.

"He's planning to do even worse things to you. He's already old, so maybe he'll hire someone, maybe even a whole lot of people. And he's going to make me watch?"

Kaori was looking at me, tears streaming down her face.

"But I won't let that happen."

I looked directly into her eyes.

"Even if I have to kill him."

5

THE PROBLEM OF how to murder someone without getting caught has puzzled many people throughout the course of history. Now I was contemplating it too. I'd fantasized about killing my father for ages, but when I was eleven my ideas were just childish. Even though I was still young, in my first year of junior high, now I had to come up with a detailed, viable plan.

What else could I have done? In the face of the old man's madness, what could a child like me have done? Even after it was all over I kept on thinking about this. Maybe I could have gone to the police and told them that half a year from now Father was going to show me hell? If I'd done that, I'd have been taken into custody as an emotionally disturbed minor. Or maybe I should have got a video camera and taped him watching Kaori. Then I could have sent it to the police or the orphanage where she was raised and asked them to take her back into their care. That might have worked. But those were all just "what ifs."

The orphanage's main benefactor was a company in the Kuki Group—my father, in other words. I remembered two cases where firms related to the family had been accused of minor irregularities, and the local police had hushed them up. Even so, it still might work in this case. Perhaps Kaori could go back to the institution, beyond Father's reach. But even if she could, would he give up? There was no way that this affair on its own would be enough to send him to prison. No matter how much I wanted to believe it might, the likelihood was far greater that it would not work out. And even if she did go back to the orphanage, it wasn't beyond the realm of possibility that he would hire some people and come up with an ingenious plan to get her back—basically to abduct her. For him it was no longer just the enjoyment of taking me to hell. He'd also started to develop an obsession with Kaori herself. I was only given a tiny allowance, much smaller than you'd expect in a rich household like ours, so if Kaori and I ran away together he could easily track down a couple of penniless teenagers. And if my various schemes failed, things could turn really bad. If he discovered my treachery he might speed up his plans. In his usual detached manner, he might set things in motion immediately. The safest thing for us would be if my first act of rebellion could put an end to it—that is, if he disappeared. As long as he was alive, Kaori and I were always in danger.

Was it always wrong to kill someone? Was it a crime to kill someone who was absolutely determined to harm you and the person closest to you? Was this just our selfishness? Weren't we being forced to break the rules to protect ourselves from this powerful madman? Perhaps society would tell me no. You shouldn't kill your father. First of all you should tell people about his wickedness, even if that's unlikely to succeed, you should appeal for help to the police and the child welfare service. That you'll both be taken straight to hell if you fail, that's just your imagination. Perhaps your father will take your rebellion to heart and be reformed. You're too quick to make judgments, to dismiss other possibilities. That's what society would probably tell me. Maybe they'd say that I was the evil one. But I didn't care.

The most valuable thing in my life wasn't virtue or society or God, but Kaori. I didn't care if it was wrong to protect the most precious part of my world. Maybe I was misguided, but I believed that the things of greatest value must transcend ethics and morality. If your new-born baby was about to be killed, would you just watch and do nothing? If you could kill the person who was threatening your child, wouldn't that be okay? Even if you could get away without killing them, wouldn't it still be acceptable if it made the baby safer? Even if it was wrong? At least that's what I thought at the time. If my father died unexpectedly it could cause chaos in the Kuki Group and spread ripples through the wider community, but of course that didn't bother me at all. I proceeded with my plan.

My first idea was poison. It was hard to get hold of, but among the many mushrooms on the hill out the back was a deadly variety called East Asian brown death caps. When I was eleven I'd looked them up in an illustrated book of plants, thinking I could use them if I needed to get rid of Father. But it would be tricky getting him to eat them, and even if I put them in his drink to make it look like suicide, there was no guarantee that the dose would be lethal. If he received immediate treatment, he would very likely survive. If he didn't die and if the police discovered that the substance came from poisonous fungi, eventually they would find out that those mushrooms were growing nearby. Then it would be obvious that the perpetrator was someone in the household.

In Father's study was a hunting rifle. I considered using that to shoot him. Of course if I chose such an extravagant method everyone would know straight away, but perhaps that wouldn't matter. Brazenly shoot my father with his own gun in his own room, like it went off of its own accord. If I shot him from an unusual angle, maybe it would look like I shot him by mistake when he was showing me how to use it. The only person in the house who knew of my murderous intent was Kaori, and no one would think I'd done it on purpose. Even if they were suspicious, they couldn't arrest me unless I confessed. The only proof would be hidden inside my head. What's more, by law they couldn't prosecute a child of fourteen. Even if the whole story came out I wouldn't go to jail. The worst that could happen was that I'd end up in juvenile detention. In this country anything a minor does is not a crime, and they can't be punished for it. In the eyes of society, guilt is exonerated by youth. That fact gave me courage. If I couldn't think of any other method, I decided to use the rifle.

In the end I came to the conclusion that I wouldn't kill him, but rather leave him to die. How about locking him up in that secret underground room? By moving some heavy furniture on top of the hatch when he was inside, for example, or tampering with the door so that it couldn't be opened from the inside. I turned over many possibilities in my mind. Then I could throw in a handful of death caps. When he got hungry enough he'd eat them, even knowing they were poisonous, either out of a will to live or to take his own life to avoid starvation. Down there he couldn't get quick treatment. If it happened like that, if he was ever found it would look like Father had gone to the hidden basement room and killed himself. If I estimated when he would be dead and repaired the door and removed the furniture from the hatch, no one would know that he'd been imprisoned there. And even if he didn't eat the mushrooms, since he couldn't get out he would eventually starve to death. If his body was discovered later, surely it would be treated as a bizarre, mysterious death? At least there would be no evidence pointing to me.

This method had other advantages as well. Father often left the estate without telling the servants or anyone else where he was going. Sometimes he stayed away for up to a month. The staff was scared of him and would welcome his absence. No one would worry about him, assuming that he was up to his usual tricks, and it would be at least a couple of months before anyone started asking questions. By that time he would already be dead, either through lack of food or by his own hand. As long as I cleared away all traces of my handiwork, I'd be home free. And on top of that, there was high turnover among the servants, so not one of them knew there was another room beneath the vast cellar. Ever since one of the maids stole some old jewelry from a cupboard in the basement many years ago, they had been forbidden to set foot down there. The housekeeper Tanabe might have known about it, but something had happened and she'd left and found another job.

Lately Father had got into the habit of visiting the underground room about once a month. He went alone in the middle of the night, without a servant to accompany him. What he did there I didn't know, but he had told Kaori that next month he would take her somewhere. Probably he meant this room, I thought.

One problem was what I'd do if, for example, he had an appointment with someone from his company two days after he died. When he didn't show up they'd contact the house. Then they'd learn that he had vanished and the police would be called. They'd search the house and garden in case he'd collapsed somewhere. If they decided to check the basement as well, I'd be in trouble. I decided to take extra steps to make doubly sure.

After he was safely confined, I would leave the window in his room on the ground floor closed but unlocked. Then I'd go out the back door wearing adult-sized shoes, leave footprints from the end of the gravel path and climb in the window. I'd leave a little bit of dirt behind on the carpet, not too much, and go out the window again. Next I'd put on a different pair of shoes and repeat the process, sometimes retracing my steps. Hopefully they'd think that several men had been in the room. I'd also leave all the drawers of Father's desk shut, but empty one of them, so it would look out of place. Basically, my plan was to plant some subtle clues, things that wouldn't be too obvious but would be noticed once they started to look closely.

There were some shadowy figures lurking behind my father. He had some influence with several people with yakuza connections. His disappearance would be strange but somehow typical of him. Maybe he had surprised some burglars, who killed him, went through his papers and took the body away with them so it wouldn't be discovered right away. Or perhaps they had intended to kill him from the outset, and for some reason wanted to delay discovery. Certainly no one would suspect his thirteen-year-old son of locking him in an underground room, because at school I was regarded as a bright, cheerful boy. At least, I thought I was.

6

WEARING THICK RUBBER gloves, I picked five brown death caps on the hill, put them in a case and sealed it. I took the train all the way to Mie and bought two large pairs of mass-produced sports shoes. While my father was out I went into the cellar and studied the mechanics of the knob on the door to the secret room. It was the common lever type, with a handle that you pushed down to open. That meant that if I put a piece of furniture or something under the handle on the outside so it couldn't move, the door wouldn't open. Perhaps I could make it look like some of the furniture on the stairs had somehow tipped over and obstructed the door entirely by chance. Among the junk stored down there I found the remains of a broken air-conditioner that was exactly the right height. When I tilted it forwards from the steps, it fit so snugly under the lever I could hardly believe it. It blocked the handle completely, so no matter how much you shoved or pounded, the door wouldn't open. And if I placed a cloth over the hatch at the top of the stairs as camouflage and dragged a piece of furniture on top of it, there was no way it could be opened from below. I planned to scatter tires and old plywood around the furniture. No one would ever think there was another flight of stairs beneath it.

I made my preparations, rehearsed the process several times, and then kept my ears open. The next time my father went to the cellar, that would be D-Day. But one night, after waiting for several days, I heard Kaori's bedroom door open.

If Father summoned her before I killed him, she would have to go to his room. Foolishly, I had overlooked this vital fact. In my nervousness about committing the murder, my judgment had deteriorated markedly. I didn't know what I was going to do, but I left my room, rushed along the corridor after her.

"You don't have to go!" I called.

"But . . ."

Her back and shoulders were unnaturally stiff.

"You don't have to. From now on if he calls for you, tell me first."

Taking a deep breath, I headed towards his room. Maybe all my schemes were about to come tumbling down. I was too panicked to come up with a better plan. If the game was up, I might as well kill him now. That's how I felt in my desperation, and my fear prevented me from thinking clearly. Many thoughts raced through my mind. Uppermost among them was that nobody could punish me, because I was only thirteen. Surely the old man would die if I strangled him. Any method would do. If he was gone, all my problems would be solved. Confused, unprepared and gasping for air, I knocked on his door.

Even when he saw that it was me and not Kaori, his expression didn't change. The light over the bed was on and he was reclining in his dressing gown, sipping whiskey. Glancing at me and then looking away in disgust, he raised his glass to his dark red lips. My heart was thumping and I could hardly breathe.

"I've got something to ask you. I'm sorry, but could you please raise my allowance?"

My voice quavered as I uttered this ridiculous request. Father turned back to me as though he knew exactly what was going on. I didn't care. I was beside myself, but even in my turmoil I knew I was going to kill him. It didn't matter how. I would conquer him. As for what to do afterwards, I'd cross that bridge when I came to it. What happened next would depend on what he said, I repeated to myself.

"Fallen for her, have you? The girl?"

His voice was slurred with alcohol.

"Obviously you have. How trite. But that's fine. You . . ."

I was sure he must be able to hear my ragged breathing.

"In two months we're going to the villa in Shizuoka. You, me and Kaori. Your fourteenth birthday will be just around the corner."

He stopped speaking, gestured for me to go. I left the room

with my head in a whirl. At any rate, I thought, Kaori was safe for the next two months. But time was running out. To murder him I would have to overcome an even greater fear than that I had just experienced.

When I went back to my room, Kaori was waiting for me. As soon as I saw her I began to cry. I asked for a kiss and she gave me one. We remained locked in each other's arms for a long time. She started to say something, faltered, tried again and then closed her mouth.

Three days later, in the middle of the night, my father left his bedroom. Clutching my backpack, I crept silently after him towards the underground chamber.

PART 2

PAST/PRESENT

1 PRESENT

THE WHITE LIGHT was hazy. I was lying face up on a soft bed. My head was still fuzzy, probably because the anesthetic hadn't worn off yet. A faint smir of rain was hitting the window. It occurred to me that the same cold rain was also soaking the expressway away in the distance. Inside the room, however, it was warm. I realized I still had no feeling in my face.

"I've got a daughter," the doctor said as soon as I opened my eyes. "Now she's old enough to understand what I do, and she keeps pestering me to fix her too."

He laughed softly.

"That's tricky," I replied, but my mouth wouldn't move and my words didn't come out properly.

"You still won't be able to talk very well. I'd like you to stay here for a bit longer."

He was looking out the window. On the cabinet beside my bed was a peculiar doll, its arms and legs too long for its body. I noticed vaguely that it was wearing a white dress. The green outlines of the potted plants shimmered in the light. I spoke to his back.

"I remembered some things from a long time ago."

"Yes?"

"More than ten years ago. My first love, this gloomy mansion I was living in, different stuff."

He turned around slowly.

"That often happens to people who've had major facial reconstruction, before they wake up. They're trying to remember details of things they've lost from their past."

The rain kept falling.

"It was a time when I was still happy, happier than I am now. A time when I had everything, when joy and despair were strangely mixed up. It's like the other me was working its way through my memories to tell me the story."

"But here you've gained a new life."

I smiled faintly. Or more precisely, I tried to. My cheeks and lips were numb.

"An unorthodox plastic surgeon like you must be able to tell that's not why I changed my face."

"It's not so you can make a fresh start?"

"Nothing's going to start. There's nothing to start."

I took a deep breath.

"How long before I can see my face?"

"Two or three days. It's going to be fine. It looks exactly like Koichi Shintani's. You've taken on a dead man's identity."

THE HOSPITAL WAS in an ordinary residential area in the suburbs of Tokyo.

At first glance it looked like a private house, but the inside was a clinic for illegal plastic surgery, used by people who wanted to change their faces for nefarious reasons. Mobsters and the like came here, but the doctor didn't have the air of desperation of other social outcasts. The interior was clean and quiet.

On the day the bandages were removed, the doctor watched with a smile. In the silver-framed mirror was another face. Confused, I moved my right arm in a meaningless gesture. When I opened my mouth, the man in the mirror opened his.

"You might be a little uncomfortable for a while," said the doctor. "Your brain is disoriented. It'll take some time before it accepts the face it's seeing as normal."

"I guess so."

He returned to his chair and drank his tea.

"But it's made you a little older. You were in your twenties, but now you're thirty. If you're going to use this Shintani's identity unchanged . . ."

I nodded.

"The two of you have similar bone structures, very similar. For ID photos and things you'll look the same, I think, but if you meet someone who knows him well they might think something's not quite right. That's how human faces work.

It's certainly a handsome one, though. Do you still think you have no future?"

"Are you still going on about that?"

The doctor smiled. A strong, thin beam of sunlight shone through the window.

"What's your story?" I asked. "The other day you were talking about your daughter, and you look like you've got a wife, too. Yet you're doing this. You can't get many patients, but your fees are enormous. Despite that, though, you don't wear expensive clothes, and your watch and your car are average too. That's been bugging me ever since we first met, for some reason, and now that I've had the chance to talk to you several times, it interests me even more. Nothing seems to hurt you, no matter what anyone says to you, no matter what happens. It's like nothing touches you."

He sipped his tea again. Looking at his bland expression, I felt compelled to continue.

"Are you just pretending? Pretending to have built a loving family? That's how it seems to me. While you pretend to love your wife and your daughter, you're simply going through the motions."

"You're quite talkative today. But perhaps you're right."

His lips twisted and he lit a menthol cigarette.

"I like to watch people who are starting their lives over. A thorough villain—what sort of life will he lead afterwards, thanks to me breaking the rules? Because some lives aren't governed by the normal rules, but by a separate set."

"Do you really believe that?"

"Partly," he said, and smiled again.

Leaving the cunningly disguised clinic, I caught a cab, made a phone call and headed for the Imperial Hotel. Circular Route 7 was very crowded and the inside of the car was too warm. The taxi crawled forward at walking speed, a meter at a time. I gazed at my reflection in the window.

I've disappeared, I thought. Other people recognized me by my face, and it was gone. My outward appearance had vanished from the world. All that remained was my inside, clinging to its memories, but no one could see that. My real self was invisible. That assumed, however, that my real self would continue to exist.

When I entered the lounge, the man was already there. He was dressed in an unremarkable suit and unremarkable shoes, but his eyes were piercing. I approached him, smiling, and he bowed slightly. It felt strange, another person responding to this face that wasn't mine.

I ordered an iced coffee and he asked for the same. Until the drinks arrived I observed him silently, but the silence didn't bother him. I waited until the waitress had gone and then spoke.

"There's something I'd like you to do for me. I believe you know an elderly gentleman called Shozo Kuki. He was the head of the Kuki family."

The man's expression didn't change. He looked to be in his forties but was probably older.

"I don't know him, I'm afraid."

"That's not true," I said, and lit a cigarette. "What did Shozo Kuki get you to investigate? That's what I'd like to know. Sorry to speak so bluntly, but your business is going downhill."

Outside the window a fine rain had started to fall.

"That's because nobody knows where he is and you've lost your connection to the Kukis. His children don't know you at all, so they aren't giving you any work. Also, your rates are too high. You're ignoring the competition. A private eye's main work is spying on unfaithful spouses, right? The average housewife can't afford your fees. That's why you can't keep your business going."

I brought out a silver briefcase.

"There's fifty million yen in here. I want to know what you were doing for Shozo Kuki and I want all your material."

"I don't know him," he replied flatly. "Really, I don't. As far as I know I've never heard the name Kuki. If I knew, for that much money of course I'd tell you."

He grinned.

"That's perfect," I said, taking the case off the table. "I was just testing you, because I can't trust someone who will sell information for money. For various reasons, I know that you worked for Shozo Kuki and were heavily involved with him. I also know that you're an excellent investigator. Now I've got a real commission for you. I'll pay you three times your normal rate."

He looked at me. Smiling, I reached into my pocket and took out a driver's license.

"This man, Koichi Shintani, I want you to find out what sort of person he was. His background, what he was good at, his personality, everything."

His face gave nothing away, even when he realized that the photo on the license was me.

"That's right. I want you to investigate me. Depending on how this job goes, I plan to ask you to do some regular work for me. Looking for a woman, and once you find her, reporting on her life. The fee will be big enough so you won't need to take on any other clients. Alongside that, I may also ask you to look into various other matters."

"I understand."

The man looked directly at me, but his face was still unreadable.

"I like you," I said, as I rose from my seat.

Name: Koichi Shintani

Date of Birth: 2 August 1979

Blood Type: A

Family: Father – Takashi Shintani (dec. 1992)
Mother – Kanami (dec. 2008)
Paternal grandfather – Kenjiro (dec. 1985)
Paternal grandmother – Sanae (dec. 1986)
Maternal grandfather – Yoji (dec. 1990)
Maternal grandmother – Chihiro (dec. 1978)

Academic Background:
Kakurabashi Nursery School
Minagawa South Elementary School
Minagawa South Junior High School
Kogurazaka Senior High School
Economics Department, Hosei University

Employment History:
2002 Joined Shintaka Shibaura Realty Co., Ltd.
2005 Resigned
2005 Established Earthnic Corporation
2008 Resigned

Qualifications: Standard Driver's License
Practical English Proficiency Test Level 1
Real Estate Appraiser's License

Residential History:
Setagaya 8-61-17, Setagaya Ward, Tokyo (at high school graduation)

Menzell's Mansion 201, Shimotakaido 9-1-23-20, Suginami Ward, Tokyo (at university graduation)

Taurus Condominium 703, Misono 6-15-31, Itabashi Ward, Tokyo (at resignation from Shintaka Shibaura Realty)

Klim Ciel 1102, Roppongi 12-13-40, Minato Ward, Tokyo (at time of disappearance)

Report (in progress)
[Koichi Shintani]

Real parents unknown. Adopted by Mr. and Mrs. Shintani from Sakurazaka Orphanage at approximately one year of age. For the same reason his actual date of birth is also unknown. Entered in the family register as August 2 for the sake of convenience. Class leader in 4th grade and 5th grade at elementary school. Belonged to basketball club in junior and senior high school.

Personality cheerful but somewhat suspicious, tends to have a limited circle of friends. Apparently cried at mother's funeral but was composed at father's. Hobbies include film (especially French and Italian movies; at university belonged to film society for approximately two years), bicycles, to a lesser extent collecting cigarette lighters. No particular favorite food, but likes Chinese noodles, often chews gum. Smoker.

In high school started dating classmate Mie Arakawa, broke up when entered university.

At university dated Sae Suzuki (died in a traffic accident after they split up), Sakiko Nitta, Ayano Togawa. Stayed with Togawa until one year before his resignation from Shintaka Shibaura Realty, but separated without getting married. The speculation (from his work colleagues) is that Shintani was afraid of commitment.

It appears that after establishing Earthnic Corporation Shintani had no lasting female relationships (needs further investigation).

People seem to die around him, but there has been nothing to indicate foul play.

As well as his university girlfriend mentioned above, he also lost a high school friend (Masao Yaeda), a university friend (Takayuki Isoi), both parents, and his direct supervisor at Shintaka Shibaura Realty (Mikio Suzuki).

The reason he left Shintaka Shibaura Realty was to set up Earthnic Corporation with some acquaintances. It was started as a venture company investing mainly in stocks and land. Two years after Shintani's resignation it was acquired in a friendly takeover by the Clarunal Corporation and ceased to exist.

Shintani's resignation from Earthnic is believed to have been due to exhaustion. Then he travelled abroad.

Went to Mexico via the USA, then further south. After that information about him stops.

He was probably abducted for ransom and killed by a crime syndicate based in Chile. Then his identity seems to have been sold on the black market. Since his relationship with his family was always weak, and most of them were dead, he was never listed as missing.

One year after Earthnic Corporation was founded, he was already having constant problems with other employees (for names, see separate sheet), and none of them kept in contact with him.

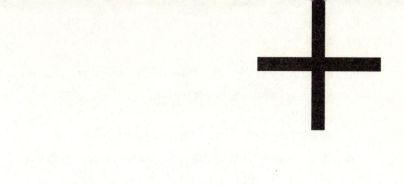

2

LOOKING AT THE report on Koichi Shintani, I found it mildly refreshing that a person's whole life could be summed up on two A4 pages.

In our room at the Shinagawa Prince Hotel, the investigator was sitting upright on the sofa, watching me read through the document. On the table were Shintani's graduation albums from elementary, junior high and senior high school, the class registers for his university tutorials, the membership list for the film society and the employee register for Earthnic Corporation. I looked at the detective and forced a smile, then put the papers in my briefcase. Almost all the information I needed about the man I was becoming was in there.

"We're still not certain about his relationships after he set up Earthnic Corporation, but my guess is that he didn't have any lasting girlfriends."

"This is enough."

I drank my coffee. As before, the other man's suit was plain, and I thought that he could easily get lost in a crowd.

"For such a short time, this is very impressive. At first I said I'd pay you three times your normal rate, but let's make it five. I'd like to ask you to do something else for me. It's a long-term job, a job with no end. Actually, maybe it would be a good thing for me if it did have an end."

I showed him a photograph.

"I'd like you to find this woman. Her name is Kaori Kuki. She's the adopted daughter of Shozo Kuki, your former employer."

The investigator glanced at me briefly.

"Born April 8, 1982. She took the name Kuki when she was adopted, and no one knows her original surname, or if her parents are alive or dead. She was left outside an orphanage called Kusunoki Nursery in Nagoya. Then she was transferred to the Kusunoki Children's Home next door, and when she was eleven she was adopted by the Kuki family. All I know at the moment is that she's working in a club in Tokyo. I don't know where, nor whether it's a high-class club or a floor show or what. This photo's very old."

He studied the picture closely.

"I want you to find her, and then give me regular reports on her life. I don't care how trivial it seems. Her day-to-day life. What she eats, what she wears, where she goes, any insignificant details. If you can get photos or video, that would be great. Also whether she's married, or if there's a man in her life."

I felt a bit jittery. I could still get rattled, I realized.

"Then I want you to find out her dreams. What she wants to do with her life. What job she wants to do. What vague visions she has for herself ten years from now. Her hopes for her life. That will need care and discretion. Have you got a woman you can ask to get close to her, become her friend? I'd like her to get close to Kaori and find out her secrets. Is that possible?"

He nodded slowly.

"Maybe you think I'm crazy," I added.

He was observing me calmly. The ceiling fan continued silently slicing the air. He paused a beat before answering.

"Is there anyone who isn't?"

"That's a tricky question."

Finally he picked up his coffee.

"Our job involves looking at things that people usually can't see."

His voice was slightly hoarse.

"People ask us to find out things which can't be detected in daily life. In other words, we break the rules."

"I heard that same expression, breaking the rules, from someone else just the other day."

His face relaxed a little.

"If there's anyone apart from us who breaks the rules, I think it's God. That is, if there is a God. Of course we do it on a much smaller scale."

Outside the thick hotel windows a train made its way quietly past. Its distant lights stood out vividly in the darkness.

"I've put myself right in the middle of those violations, of my own free will. If you're crazy, then so am I."

When I stood up from the sofa, he rose as well.

"Steer clear of Kaori's past, please. What I want to know about is the present. Boyfriends too, just stick to her current ones."

I could feel that my face was gradually losing its composure. The television, its sound turned down low, was reporting a dull story of rocks being placed on railway lines all over the country at the same time. I watched him leave and then went back inside.

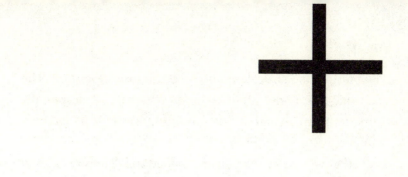

3 PAST

WHEN I LEFT my room and followed my father down to the cellar, my insides were churning violently. It felt as though something was dragging me. I was conscious of the backpack on my shoulders, and the knowledge that if I didn't pull this off I had no future echoed through my head. In a disordered state of mind I stalked him, thinking that if I hesitated it would be all over, if I faltered even for a second I'd find some convenient excuse, like waiting for a better opportunity.

If my plan to lock him in the underground room failed, I'd hit him with a metal pipe or whatever came to hand. I would do whatever it took to end his life. I was still only thirteen, but I was tall for my age and his body had shrunk. If it came to a hand-to-hand struggle, I knew I could overpower him. The fact that as a minor the law couldn't punish me, despite my superior strength and murderous intent, gave me a modicum of courage.

Father went down the stairs, opened the door and entered the cellar. I waited for the light to peek through the gap, waited for him to move away from the entrance. Then I cautiously opened the door. I had oiled it in advance so it would make as little noise as possible. In the last year Father had grown extremely deaf, so he probably wouldn't have heard it anyway. He walked slowly through the area used as a storeroom, past old furniture and timber. I watched from the shadow of an enormous wardrobe, its decoration peeling and faded. My breath disturbed the dust that clung to the woodwork like threads. Scratches on the drawers flickered in the corner of my eye like bare skin, as though they were trying to tell me something.

Even in my distracted state, I wondered why he ventured to that hidden basement room. In the past he'd hardly ever gone there, but in the last couple of years he'd started visiting almost every month. What was he doing there? Returning to the matter at hand, I followed him with my eyes. What he did there wasn't important. What mattered, I told myself, was destroying the life force that was driving his thoughts and actions. He shifted the cloth and lifted the boards leading to the lower level. My vision grew blurry, as though I'd been hit over the head with something. Before me was the opportunity to kill a person. I was face to face with murder. I dug my nails into my knees, trying to convince myself that it wasn't murder.

I was just confining him, and the decision to die would be entirely his own. All I was doing was blocking the path by which he would take Kaori and me to hell. He went down the stairs to the secret chamber. I edged closer, my heart beating painfully, taking care to muffle my footsteps.

The boards of the hatch had no soundproofing, so even if I closed it and covered it with furniture, if he kept pounding on it from underneath someone might hear. No one came here usually, but it wasn't completely beyond the bounds of possibility. I held my breath and strained to listen, but all I could hear was my own heartbeat. From the bottom of the stairs came the faint sound of the door opening and then closing. My hands were growing numb, but I forced them to move and took a few deep breaths.

Now I had to go down the stairs myself, take the case containing the death caps out of my bag, open the door for an instant, throw them in and slam it shut again. Then fasten the handle with the bar I'd brought with me to lock him inside. After that I'd replace the bar with the broken air conditioner, sliding it tightly under the lever to block the door. The unit was exactly the right height, as if it had been made for that purpose, and fit with curious precision in the gap between the handle and the stairs. Finally I'd race back up the steps, close the hatch, move some heavy furniture on top of it and it would all be over. All I had to do now was do it. It wasn't murder, I told myself over and over. I was just stopping his access to me and Kaori. For the first time in my life, there was something that I absolutely had to do. He was like a massive stone blocking my way, and if I didn't remove it my future would be ruined. I took the fungi from my backpack and crept quietly down the steps. My legs were shaking, but that couldn't be helped. My throat was dry and sore, and for some reason I knew I'd remember that pain. Deep cracks ran along the concrete wall beside the stairs, and I knew I'd remember how deep they were as well. I could dimly make out the door handle. Just as I was about to jerk it open, however, it opened by itself and my eyes were struck by a blinding light. Father was standing there, his back to the light. Heart racing painfully, I cried out and shoved him with both hands.

I don't know why I was able to push him then, why I was able to knock him back into the room. Two steps led down from the door, so the floor was slightly lower. Stunned, I wondered foolishly how long it had been since I touched him. Perhaps not since my earliest memory, when he had brushed me aside with his foot just after I'd learned to walk. Probably I'd been able to lay hands on him, to push him, because with the light behind him he was merely a shadow and I couldn't see him clearly. He lay sprawled on the floor, looking up at me standing in the doorway. I was frozen in place.

He was holding his foot in his hands as though he'd hurt it. I continued to stand there, with the two steps between us. The white bed in the center of the room seemed to bulge slightly. I could faintly see something that looked like a body, but I couldn't worry about that now. I knew I had to toss in the death caps and shut the door, but I felt like I was going to pass out. My brain couldn't communicate with my limbs, my arms had no strength, I couldn't even move my fingertips.

I just stood there, staring at him, unsure how to handle this new situation.

"So that's how it is," he said softly.

When I heard his voice, a sharp pain shot through my heart. His eyes fastened on the bag over my shoulders.

"So you're going to kill me. Then you did remember. I see."

He kept rubbing his foot, expressionless. His left ear, half of which was missing, stood out clearly.

"You remembered what I said about your education. Not just as a scary event, but as a definite plan that I was actually going to carry out. It looks like calling the girl to my room had an effect on you too."

I still couldn't move.

"You've really got what it takes to be a cancer. You've got the makings of a real monster, because you can think of something like this. You're not passive like a sheep. You can think of killing your own father."

Even now his face showed no emotion.

"Remember this. Happiness is a fortress."

My attention was drawn to the mound in the bed. The white light from the ceiling had grown slightly weaker. I realized that my mind was drifting, and forced myself to look straight ahead once more. Father was still there, of course.

"Naturally the main reason you've got what it takes to be a cancer is that you've got my blood in your veins. Some day you should ask your brothers what kind of life I've led up till now. I won't be able to show you hell, but it's all the same in the long run. Because you're going to kill me. Because you're going to murder another human being."

"No, you're wrong."

I wonder why I suddenly found my voice?

"It's not murder. I'm just blocking your . . ."

Father ignored my words as though they weren't worth listening to, kept on talking.

"Killing a person is crossing a critical line in this world. Why? Because that's our nature as living creatures. All creatures are fundamentally designed not to kill their own kind. Their instincts stop them. Try reading some biology. Cannibalism only occurs in extremely rare, unusual circumstances. Since prehistoric times all living things have operated on the principle that you don't kill your own species, instinctively—as humans would say, subconsciously. This has been the basic rule for all creatures since time immemorial. When someone overcomes that with human rationality or will and commits a murder, of course he will start to fall apart. I'm not talking about guilt. From that time forward he will suffer from the distortion of his nature as a living creature, unable to reconcile the instinctive rejection. On the intellectual level, the guilt associated with murder is the pain that comes from the stress of hiding a secret, from the loss of the belief that one is a good person. On a human level, though, as a living creature, it is simply the conscious, outward manifestation of the perversion of killing one of your own. Since long, long, ago, conventional wisdom and morality are simply the products of that perversion, codified and made universal. That's why it's stupid to preen oneself for having transcended morality. Wrapping yourself in rational justifications for murder is a fraud. It's just brainwashing, trying to persuade yourself.

"Of course, people sometimes kill others involuntarily, in the heat of the moment. What was originally an impulse to attack a different species, or a powerful sexual impulse, is transformed on the way to the surface as it passes through the layers which have been eroded by humans' reason and will and dark passions, and the aggression is diverted towards another human. These moments of madness burst forth unexpectedly, but they are short-lived. At the stable, long-dormant level that could be called the deepest root of the subconscious, a realm that is closer to animal than human, the sense of distortion this causes continues to fester for a long time as an unpleasant shadow. Animals are hard-wired to kill other species but not their own kind, even if they do attack them violently. When human consciousness stops fooling itself and looks at the situation straight on, it can't cope. You're definitely going to become warped. Just like me."

I couldn't help getting the feeling that Father was sitting in his chair in his study, the light behind him, his figure just a silhouette, and I was standing in front of him listening to his monologue. But of course that was impossible, crouched on the floor in this windowless room.

"Nothing will change. You will become a cancer. You will act as a negative force in the world. By killing me, you will take me inside you. That's what taking another person's life means. And in a sense, that's the most tempting part of murder. Absorbing another person, in exchange for warping your nature."

He paused. I still felt like I was in his study.

EVIL AND THE MASK

"You will suffer from pangs of guilt caused by awareness of that deformation. As a murderer, you won't be able to stand yourself. Someone who has killed another person is unable to accept any warmth or beauty with a pure heart. Whenever something good happens, at that instant you'll be confronted with the fact that you're a killer. When you feel joy in your life, you'll be troubled by the fact that you destroyed someone else's. Especially a weak spirit like yours, you won't be able to bear it. What's more, you've inherited my genes. The DNA of the man you killed, who you denied the chance of life, is embedded inside you. From now on, whenever you feel happy, I'm going to appear inside your head. The image of me, locked in this room, cursing you, starving, writhing in agony. Through my blood, which runs in your veins, as though my blood is boiling inside you, through all your brain cells which you inherited from me, through your whole body. Because you will have taken me inside you. I'm going to be acting inside you. Forever. You'll never be happy again."

I stood there dazed.

"From now on, you won't be able to look at the world's happiness calmly. Why are other people happy, you'll always wonder, when I'm in so much pain? And why will that happen to you? Is it my fault? No. It's just human nature. Because that's how humans have been since the very beginning, creatures with the potential for evil. Because even though they are fundamentally designed not to kill their own kind, they are also able to contemplate entering that forbidden territory, to enter it for real, to possess passions of all kinds. What you should resent is the way of the world, humans' imperfect and contradictory nature. It's this nature that gives rise to injustice. Happiness is a fortress. Because happiness is an enclosed space only a lucky few can enjoy, the lucky few who can turn a blind eye to people like you, people with pain and sorrow, who can turn a blind eye to poverty and hunger. You must resent all happiness. People who have killed cannot attain one hundred percent virtue, but they can attain one hundred percent evil. That is your life path. You have power and money. Destroy everything. By sublimating yourself to the fires of hell, to the mighty, evil energy that destroys all people and all joy, you can obtain a piece of an incredible pleasure. Pathetic individuals like serial killers or terrorist bombers will never obtain it. It's an even greater evil. Even greater."

The room went quiet. Though I had been watching my father as he stared at me blankly, I couldn't tell if the words I had just heard were really his. I grabbed the doorframe to keep my balance.

"But if I don't do it," I pleaded, "Kaori—"

"That's right."

Father stood up slowly.

"I will bring many men and they will defile the girl in front of you. If you don't lock me up, I absolutely will do it. Even if you run away or go to the police, nothing will change. You can't stop me. I couldn't even stop myself."

For the first time I realized that he was drunk again.

"If I live I will definitely do it. My mind may be going, but that is my sole remaining desire. I couldn't even stop it myself. More than taking you to hell, more than pleasure, my whole body is burning for the sight of that girl being completely corrupted, while I sway in my alcoholic haze."

He was putting his weight on his good leg.

"Listen. I sired you on purpose to raise you as a cancer. You have no intrinsic rights. You will be a cancer. Even in trying to avoid it, you will become one. That cannot be changed."

At that moment the case holding the death caps slipped from my hand. There was a loud noise and the rough fungi scattered from the container. Father looked at them impassively. Then he took a small vial from his breast pocket.

"I don't need those," he said. "I've got this drug which will kill me quickly. You won't triumph over your powerful father. Starve a revolting, whiskey-soaked old man. If I'm going to starve to death in this room, wide-eyed and suffering, cursing your name, I'll take this and die in agony. At that moment, I'll invade you. Invade the cancer who starved a poor old man to death."

"But if I don't . . ."

"That's right, I'll hurt you both by whatever means necessary. And if you do kill me, you'll definitely be damaged anyway."

"I won't be killing you," I shouted, but my voice came out as a whisper. "I'm just blocking your way. It'll be your own decision to commit suicide."

"I'm a corpse already. Since a long time ago."

I slammed the door with all my might as though something was propelling me forward, locking my father firmly in the room. He had turned into this weird creature, this stringy, incomprehensible old man who I couldn't understand even to the very end. I thought of him starving painfully to death, ugly, shriveled, insane. At that instant, when there was no turning back, I heard a harsh, metallic clang. Whether it was the sound of the door or inside my own head, I couldn't tell.

4

WHILE I FASTENED the door handle, while I closed the hatch at the top of the stairs, while I replaced the cloth and the furniture on top of it, not a sound came from inside the room.

Father, that gigantic, malevolent thing that had been suffocating Kaori and me, had transformed into this strange substance that clung to us like glue. As I weaved my way between the old junk and building materials I thought to myself that I was surprisingly calm. I had wiped my fingerprints off the case with the poisonous mushrooms beforehand, and had worn gloves whenever I handled it. One day, I thought, maybe I'd find out why my father had turned out like that, what had happened in his life. At the time, though, I still didn't have the leisure to consider it deeply.

I left the cellar and closed the door silently behind me. I listened carefully, checking that none of the servants were nearby. Holding my breath and tiptoeing along the corridor, I thought that I really was composed. I had planned to go to my father's room and make it look like intruders had been there, but somehow that didn't seem necessary. Though I had no grounds for it, I felt that his absence wouldn't become a problem any time soon. I crept past his room and opened the door to my own bedroom. Kaori was sitting on my bed, wearing white pajamas. She looked at me helplessly.

"What happened?"

"What?"

"You're white as a sheet."

I realized that my pulse was erratic, and that in fact it had been erratic for some time.

"And you're sweating buckets. What's wrong?"

I'd been so sure I was calm.

"Nothing."

"But . . ."

Kaori's figure, lit by the small bedside lamp, took my breath away. I was seized by a fierce desire. I moved closer, not understanding why such feelings should emerge now. When I asked if I could kiss her, she nodded quietly. I could see her pale skin at the opening of her white pajama top. Trying to conceal my trembling, I kissed her slowly.

"About your father, thanks. But I don't know how long I'll be safe."

"No."

My arms were still numb.

"It's fine. He's not going to do anything to you."

"But . . ."

"We talked. He promised. It looks like he's found himself a girlfriend, so he won't come near you again."

I was determined that she should never learn the truth.

"Really?"

"Yes. Kaori . . ."

I kissed her again, pushed her gently down on the bed. She felt that I was shaking and stroked my head, though she didn't know why. I undressed her, and then myself.

"Fumihiro?"

I felt the fear rising inside me again. I was terrified of my father. Just remembering my conversation with him was terrifying. Suddenly I cried out and embraced Kaori tightly, trying to control my shivering. She continued to stroke my hair. As I held her in my arms, I was filled with love. Her body was warm, and I had eyes only for her. I would do anything for her. To please her, to make her happy, I didn't care if I had to turn into the devil himself. I kissed her small mouth, touched her breasts, hugged her narrow shoulders. Her body grew hotter. She stuck her tongue in my mouth, wound her arms hard around my back. Then she seemed unsure what to do next, told me she wanted to stay like that forever. She sucked my nipples, thrust her tongue between my lips again. It moved softly inside my mouth, and I felt faint. I wanted her.

Then Kaori and I made love. She tensed for a moment, looked into my eyes and quietly opened her legs. Her sex was tight, and it was sore for both of us, but I really wanted to be inside her. In the unfamiliar warmth and pain I came quickly, but then I entered her again. The second time still hurt her, but presently she started to cry out in a small voice. At that moment I was in heaven. Kaori was everything to me, more precious than anything else in the world. I would do anything for her. Whimpering, she put her arms around my neck and wrapped her legs awkwardly around my waist, kissing me over and over. As long as I could stay together with her, I didn't care if I had to destroy the whole world. Perhaps we were mad—but can fourteen-year-olds be mad?

From then on we made love every night. Kaori's body was starting to blossom, her breasts growing larger. I don't belong to your father any more, she told me many times. Let's stay together forever, she said. As long as I'm with you everything will be all right. Every day she seemed to grow more beautiful. For the next three months, until Father's disappearance came to light, we were always at each other's side.

5 PRESENT

WHEN I WOKE I was blinded by the strong white light.

An apartment I'd just rented on the seventh floor of a condominium, a large room almost empty of furniture. The glare left pale green spots at the back of my eyes. Yesterday's clothes were strewn across the wooden floor. Bundles of DVDs, Shintani's taste in movies, were still piled up in their boxes.

I was hungry so I ate some instant noodles to fill myself quickly. It occurred to me that my new self would continue to get hungry as long as it was alive, whether I liked it or not. The idea filled me with a kind of despair. I finished half the noodles while watching TV, then got dressed and went out.

On the news they were making a fuss about a series of small explosions in a number of towns.

Outside it was sunny. I started to sweat, and wiped my face with my sleeve. A thin dog on a leash approached me, a boy and a woman in a hat walking alongside. The dog nuzzled me, its tongue hanging out. I crouched with a smile and patted its neck. I was smiling because that's what the animal wanted. The boy standing next to it tugged at my jeans. For some reason he wouldn't let go.

"Kai," the woman said. "Kai, stop it. I'm sorry."

She turned to me, to Shintani's obscenely handsome face. I looked at her with the same smile I'd directed at the mutt.

"Is this your boy?" I asked, though it would have been more natural to say something about the dog.

"Yes. Kai, that's enough. I'm really sorry."

"You don't look old enough to have a son."

As I stood up I looked into her eyes, reflecting that women with children often seemed to apologize. She was somewhat taken aback, and her eyes grew wary, but she didn't seem displeased. I'd only said it because until a moment ago she'd been walking like she was bored.

"Nice clothes. They really suit you. You look beautiful."

I knew that I was going off course, but I was waiting for some kind of shock or regret to appear inside me.

"What?"

"You don't look old enough to have a son. You really are beautiful. Especially your eyes."

The woman started to look a little nervous. I felt no change in me at all. Without another word I walked off across the hot asphalt. The sunlight was glinting off the windows of hundreds of apartment buildings.

I TOOK A cab to the Shinagawa Prince Hotel. When I opened the door to the room the detective was already there. My pulse gradually quickened, and I made a mental note of the fact. He bowed slightly. I sat down and he placed a photo on the table.

"This is Kaori Kuki now."

My eyes dimmed as though I'd been dealt a violent blow to the chest. Her large eyes, her thin lips, the narrow bridge of her nose. Softly drawn eyebrows, styled hair that fell to her shoulders. It was Kaori. As she was now, at twenty-seven. She was wearing a white pantsuit and carrying a brown handbag over her shoulder, looking at something off to the side with a melancholy expression. She was beautiful. I went to light a cigarette and found that my hands were shaking. The detective shifted quietly in his chair, acting as though he hadn't seen it.

"Ms. Kuki is living in an apartment in Koto Ward and working at a club called Je le Répète in Roppongi."

I noticed that he had spotted my reaction—he'd switched quickly from calling her 'Kaori' to 'Ms. Kuki'—but I didn't say anything.

"It's said to be a high-class club. Apparently their service is limited to serving drinks, nothing illegitimate about it. It seems to be a sound business at the high end of the market. We're still investigating Ms. Kuki's friendships, but this woman, Azusa Konishi, is going to try to get close to her."

He held out another photo.

"She had an interview at Je le Répète, and yesterday she heard that she's been hired. In the future she'll report to you as well."

The woman Konishi was incredible. Most people would probably have thought she was even prettier than Kaori, but for me Kaori was the epitome of beauty. The detective took a USB memory stick out of his bag.

"This is a recording we took of Ms. Kuki. It's less than a minute, from the time she comes out of a convenience store until she gets in a car."

I reached for it with nervous fingers.

"There's something else I've got to tell you," he continued.

I noticed that I'd left my cigarette smoldering in the ashtray.

"It looks like someone else is watching Ms. Kuki too."

"What?"

I thought that was probably the first word I'd uttered in this room today.

"We don't know who's doing it, but they seem to have employed someone to investigate her very thoroughly. The man they've hired is a real pro. Shall we find out who's behind him?"

My throat was dry and I felt uneasy. I realized that I'd been staring at him for some time.

"Yes, please. But Shozo Kuki is dead."

"I don't think the person who's following her has any link to her adoptive father, Shozo."

I continued to watch him, bewildered.

"Whether I did any work for the deceased Shozo Kuki is still something I want to keep confidential, but since this is connected to what you've asked me to do I'll tell you this much. This man isn't one of those hired by Kuki. I know it's a bit vague, but he smells different. I can't account for it, but he doesn't seem like the kind of investigator Kuki hired."

The room went quiet.

"What's your best guess?"

"I'm not sure. But my instinct tells me it's nothing good."

His tone had become more urgent.

"I see," I said. "Could you investigate that person too, please?"

"Yes, I will."

He shifted in his seat again, unconsciously scratching his knees. I thought he kept doing it for a bit too long, so I averted my eyes as I stood.

6 PAST

FATHER'S DISAPPEARANCE FIRST became a problem on the estate three months after Kaori and I started having sex. One of the companies in the Group tried to get in touch with him. When the servants told them that he wasn't here, they left a message asking him to contact them as soon as he returned. Of course, he didn't come back. They called again, and when they received the same reply they began to show signs of concern. The staff thought he was probably holed up with a woman somewhere, as had happened many times before, and his business associates assumed the same, but there was some important business to take care of, so they called the lawyer who managed Father's assets. He made a few educated guesses and phoned around, but everywhere he received the same answer, that my father hadn't been there. Suddenly, there was panic in the house.

I was aware of the fuss, but at first it didn't concern me. Even if he was dead, even if they found out that I was responsible, I didn't care as long as I could spend my days with Kaori. If I were unveiled as the killer, though, my idyll with her would obviously come to an end. If my handiwork were discovered, everyone would realize that a third party had locked Father in the room. Besotted and living in a dream world, it was only after the commotion started that I felt a sense of urgency.

My original plan had been to clear away the evidence two months after I was sure he was dead, either through starvation or suicide. With nothing blocking the door, everyone would think that he had entered the underground room of his own volition and committed suicide, by eating nothing at all, by eating the death caps out of hunger, or by drinking the poison he had brought with him. I couldn't imagine that he would have just waited for death, enduring the torments of hunger. The reason I hadn't removed my homemade barricade was that I was scared. I was absolutely terrified of going near what I had done. I pushed the fear to the back of my mind, thought only of my life with Kaori, of Kaori's body.

After Tanabe left, another servant called Yoshigaki, a woman in her thirties who had been there for quite a long time, took over as housekeeper. She rang my father's lawyer. As I eavesdropped, I couldn't help feeling uneasy. They were talking about contacting my father's other children, all many years older than me. Whenever he went away, the servants were under strict instructions not to seek his whereabouts. But the situation facing the Group company was serious— serious enough to warrant asking the police to search for him. In those circumstances, they were supposed to inform the other children and wait for directions.

That night I had to act. After the servants were asleep I had to go to the cellar, shift the broken air conditioner and remove the furniture from on top of the hatch. It wasn't much, but it took all my courage to make my body do what I wanted.

It was Sunday. Kaori came to my room as soon as she got home from volleyball practice. Mischievously she switched off the light at the door, then came over and kissed me. I touched her shoulders and arms. We had both turned fourteen.

"What's happened to your father?"

I couldn't see her face.

"Sounds like there's some problem at his company, but they can't get hold of him. Same as always." I did my best to speak nonchalantly.

"Hmm."

"But maybe it's my fault," I continued.

Her body trembled slightly.

"After I talked to him about you it must have been awkward for him to come home and look me in the face. He'll be with a woman somewhere. I hope he dies there."

Kaori seemed deep in thought, but in the darkness I couldn't read her expression.

• • •

THAT NIGHT SHE came to my room once more, but I told her that it would be better if we slept apart. I made up a story that Ms. Yoshigaki wanted to talk to me about my father's failure to return, but she hadn't come yet and might turn up at any minute. Kaori's face still looked full of questions, but it was the best I could do.

After she left I lay in bed, wide awake. Now I had to visit my father. I had to remove my device, right next to the room where his body lay. Sweat was streaming off me, but I couldn't get up. I was completely unprepared. Hours passed. However, I had no choice.

Compared to shutting him up in the first place, this wasn't such a big deal. That's what I told myself, but it was after 3 A.M. before I was able to leave the room. I went through the hallways, treading softly. I kept moving, though I couldn't believe that I was going down to the cellar again. When I reached Kaori's door I crept past on tiptoes, trying to control my breathing, one foot after the other. I went down the steps to the basement and cautiously opened the door. Thanks to the oil I'd put on the hinges, it moved quietly.

I made my way slowly between the old furniture and lumber. There was a musty smell, and the dust penetrated my lungs as though it had a will of its own. I felt like the junk was watching me solemnly in the stillness. The silence, as though the lifeless objects themselves were holding their breath, seemed to insist that I was an unwelcome intruder. I walked carefully, forcing my way through the narrow space, trying not to make a sound. Just as I put my hands on the silent, scornful furniture, wanting to get it over with quickly, I sensed a movement behind me. My body tensed and I stopped breathing. There was definitely a noise, a kind of creak. My heart raced uncontrollably, and what little strength I had deserted me completely. The dust was sticking to my perspiration. I didn't know what to do, but at the same time I couldn't just stand there. Still unable to make up my mind, I turned around slowly.

In front of me I could see an old bookcase, a wooden wheel whose use was unclear, and a tall pile of tightly wrapped rolls of material. I took one pace forward, then another. Just as I was thinking the place was deserted, I sensed someone on my right. There's no one there, I told myself. I was being too jumpy. I concentrated on making my feet move, not wanting to stay there for long. I reminded myself over and over that no one ever came there, that all I had to do was remove the obstruction. The only thing I could see was the entrance to the underground room with the furniture stacked above it. I grasped the silent object with both hands, even though I was still not ready for what I might find.

When I felt the cold, rough surface my pulse grew even faster. I endured it and gradually shoved the heavy obstacle aside. Moving without thinking, like a puppet, I opened the hatch and peered down the narrow flight of stairs. Light was seeping under the door to the hidden room. At first I imagined that someone was in there, but then I realized that Father must have died with the light still on. There was no sound from inside. I crept down the stairs, conscious of the beating of my heart. I could see something under the frame of the air conditioner that was holding the lever in place. Nauseous, I tried to look away but couldn't. It was blood.

My eyesight went dim and I put my hand on the wall to steady myself. The blood was leaking out from under the door. It had to be Father's. Perhaps he had taken the poison right beside the door on purpose, so that when he vomited it would flow outside. The moment of his actual death had occurred out of my sight. His blood, however, seemed to be showing it to me, forcing me to visualize it, as if he knew I'd come to unlock the door sometime and he wanted to twist his suffering and death into my heart through my eyes. His body was lying just on the other side of the door. This was the revolting creature who made up half of my being, whose perverse evil I had been unable to understand even at the very end. For the first time the words echoed in my head, *You killed a person*. The blood in front of me, more than enough to be fatal, forced me to confront the fact that I had killed a man, my own father. I made someone cough up that much blood, I thought, through my own intent and actions. A sulphurous smell came from behind the door, wormed its way inside me. I tried not to inhale. If I breathed out, though, I had to breathe in the same amount. I flopped down, feeling dizzy. But I kept moving. If I threw up here I'd be leaving evidence behind. His death would end up defeating me as well. With all my strength I dragged the frame away. At that instant, however, I heard a cry from inside and the door burst open.

Blinded by the light, I collapsed on the spot. But it was

just a hallucination. The door remained closed. No, perhaps Father had already slipped past me, as agile as an ill-favored monkey, and was scampering up the stairs, hunched over on spindly legs. I shook off the image and took hold of the air conditioner. It hit the door with a harsh metallic noise. I tried to run, but my lifeless legs stumbled and I ended up half crawling up the stairs with the appliance. I stuck my head out the top, managed to climb up and closed the hatch, barely aware of what I was doing.

Suddenly it went quiet. I felt like Yoshigaki, the lawyer I'd never met, my father and Kaori were in a circle, staring down at me. I stood up and shifted the broken air conditioner between the stored furniture. Then I sat down again, gazing blankly at the boards of the hatch. With the trapdoor exposed like this, probably no one would ever guess that it had been blocked. I imagined my father coming up the stairs. Climbing the steps, gnawing on a bunch of death caps, slowly lifting the hatch from below. I couldn't get the image out of my head. I moved on feeble legs, resting my hands against the ancient furniture. It's over, I said out loud, but I didn't believe it.

My vision still blurred, I opened the cellar door and went upstairs. I was too wound up to care about the fact that I was covered in dust. I went to my room and collapsed onto the bed. The voice inside my head repeating, *I killed my father*. The crimson of his blood flickered before my eyes. I was starving, my throat was burning, I kept pounding on the door, I pulled at it, but it wouldn't budge no matter what I did. I hit it, I stroked it as though asking for forgiveness. I pressed myself against it and shouted. When I came to my senses I was lying on my bed with my eyes open, staring at the unlit bulb on the ceiling. This was my room. I tried to get up, thinking that I'd slipped into a dream, but I had no strength in my body. The house was silent—everyone seemed to be fast asleep. When I noticed that the room was cold and I was thirsty again, suddenly my father was glaring down at me on the bed. I was falling. I knew that I was in bed, yet I was still falling. I woke up. My shoulders ached and I was soaked in sweat.

The following morning I couldn't get out of bed. The next thing I knew, my father was lying right beside me, bent with age, naked, throat parched, desperately trying to lick the sweat off my body. As he licked me, he was begging for more perspiration. I pinched my arms and legs fiercely to wake myself up so I wouldn't dream any more, but I didn't have the strength to lift myself out of bed. When the servant came to check on me, I told her I was taking the day off school. Kaori looked in and the woman whispered that I'd probably caught a cold.

In fact I did have a temperature that day. I felt like the blood that I'd seen had entered my eyes and was circulating throughout my body. And indeed, my father's genes, his blood, really did exist inside me. The realization that I'd killed a man struck me much more violently than I'd expected, shaking me to the core. I had nightmares, and when I woke I urgently demanded food and drink. Even though I was delirious with fever I stuffed them in my mouth and vomited immediately. It's revulsion as a living creature, my father had said. It's the feeling of your body rejecting the fact that you've murdered your own species, another human being. Maybe that revulsion was what was making me crave food, and then throw it up when I ate it. I grew thin, extremely thin, and the fever just wouldn't abate.

While I was sick in bed, changes were happening on the estate. Three and a half months after my father's disappearance his oldest son—my brother—turned up. He was middle-aged and had taken over the Kuki Group after Father retired. From time to time his face would appear in the media. With small eyes and a big nose, he bore an uncanny resemblance to my father. He stuck his head in my door for a second, muttered something about not wanting to catch a cold and left immediately. He showed no interest in me whatsoever.

My brother dealt with the business from the company and secretly asked the police to start a search. Even though Father had already retired, he was still chairman of the Kuki Group, and apparently his disappearance had to be kept from the affiliated companies. My brother made sure that it didn't leak to the media, just contacting my other siblings through back channels.

When he went back to Tokyo, my second brother and eldest sister came to take his place. My brother, who Father had called a cancer, didn't visit my room, but my sister barged in. I was still in bed, but she pestered me with rude questions about what my mother was like. She was more somber than I'd expected, but scruffy and loud. Like my brother, she looked horribly like my father. She had married the president of a realty firm, one of the companies in the Group, and my brother was running another subsidiary, a trading company.

My second sister and third brother didn't come to the estate. There was a rumor that daughter number two was the director of some religious organization, and son number three was overseas. No one seemed to know what he did for a living. While I'd been ill, the housekeeper Tanabe, who had been there since time immemorial, returned. I felt uneasy, but I had no resources to dwell on it.

Drifting in and out of my fever, I told myself what I'd known all along. That I'd decided to kill him, that I'd done it to remove a danger to Kaori and myself. He'd said he would never give up his plan of making my life hell and defiling Kaori, at any cost, as long as he was alive. He'd said he couldn't stop it. Since that was the case, what choice did I have? Faced with such a powerful madman, what else could I have done?

Even if I'd gone to the police and Kaori had been sent back to the orphanage, Father would have used any means possible to get her away again, because he was surrounded by people who were willing to break the law and take the penalty. Taking the blame was almost a business in itself. There were plenty of people, mainly foreigners trying to provide financial security for their families back home, who would commit crimes for cash. He'd persuade them by promising to hire top lawyers so they'd be out in a few years. The law and punishment meant nothing to my father. What sort of deterrent would work against that mad old man, his blood thickened by alcohol, who carried around poison for his own suicide? The only way to thwart his plans was to lock him up.

I thought I could live happily ever after. I cared about no one but Kaori, and apart from her everything was worthless.

The problem was what she would think of what I'd done. Should I tell her or not? I agonized over that question. It wasn't beyond the bounds of possibility that she would say something bizarre, like that was the role she was destined to play in life. Raised as an orphan, Kaori was diffident about happiness, and she seemed to be used to bottling up her feelings. Probably what made her like that was her family that abandoned her, and the society that had created that family. In spite of this, she was always trying to fit in, always adjusting herself to her surroundings.

During my nightmares I once saw myself from somewhere up above, groaning in my sleep. I wasn't floating, only my eyes were up there. The door was open and a man and a woman were observing me. After a while she disappeared, leaving only the man, tall, dark as a shadow, just staring at me. I merged with his gaze as though I was being absorbed. I was watching myself dreaming through his eyes. Sensing danger, I tried to get out of bed. That woke me up. The door was closed.

Two weeks passed and I left my sickbed. My body was weak but I couldn't stay lying down forever. I went to the bathroom to clean myself up. As I stood under the shower I told myself that I was washing everything away.

I was still apprehensive, however. I tried to shake it off by taking another shower, unsure what this disturbance meant. I was scared of finishing. As I dried myself off, I was terrified. My heart was pounding, fast and uncontrollable. Gripping the washbasin with both hands, I looked at the mirror in front of me.

There I saw my reflection, painfully thin with bulbous eyes. No doubt about it, traces of my father were visible in my face. Until now I'd thought I had my mother's eyes, her nose and lips. Only the overall shape of my face resembled his, and there were even times when I doubted whether I was his child. But the face looking back at me today, while it was mine, obviously shared his features, even his aura. Cursed, that was the word that sprang mysteriously to mind. I washed my face, but no matter how much I scrubbed, it didn't improve.

While I was laid up in bed, Kaori came and nursed me every day. I remembered that I had caught her stealing glances at my face. Maybe she'd seen him in me too. I tried to convince myself that I'd return to my old self as I regained weight, but I couldn't help feeling that once Father's image had revealed itself, like some hidden creature oozing to the surface, it would remain as though it was engraved there. And that's what happened.

I returned to school and my classmates welcomed me back. Laughing, they said, "You're really skinny," and "God, you look like a thug!" but I was unable to laugh with them. Kaori was watching me from a distance. Our eyes met and she smiled, but I could see the fear in her face.

As always, though, she was constantly at my side. We talked together, and in the evenings we'd go for walks, but I never touched her and she never touched me. I could see the horror in her eyes when she looked at me. Then I'd tell myself that I'd imagined it, but it was definitely there. I would stare at my face in the mirror, not knowing what to do.

One day when it was raining heavily Kaori's practice was cancelled and we walked home from school together. She was the same as ever, smiling and chattering about her club and her friends. Suddenly I couldn't stand it any longer, and took her hand. Then I moved my face close to hers and kissed her. She let me do it, but her expression was tense.

"I'm nervous because it's been such a long time," she said with a laugh, but gradually she spoke less and less.

When I told her that I'd like her to come to my room, she nodded. That night she slipped in softly. Sometime the rain had stopped and a bright moonlight was peeping through a gap in the curtains. She was wearing a pair of white cotton pajamas. I touched her soft skin, gently started to put my arms around her, but she was trembling faintly. Again she said she was nervous because it had been a while, but when I undid her buttons and embraced her I could feel the goosebumps on her back. Her body froze, even as she told me everything was fine. When I realized that she was simply trying to endure it, I stopped.

"Kaori . . ."

"No, it's not like that. I wonder what's wrong, it's odd."

She wrapped her arms around my neck, but her goosebumps became even more noticeable.

"Kaori?"

"No, it's not what you're thinking. I don't know what it is, but it's not that at all."

I tried to hide how upset I was, but I didn't succeed.

"Maybe, it's because I look like . . . ?" My voice shook. Her body was tense.

"No. You're not him."

"He didn't just look at you, did he?" I asked quietly.

She flinched slightly.

"Kaori?"

"It wasn't sex, but he touched me, licked me, I don't know how many times."

She started to weep. What she didn't say was that when I approached her with lust in my eyes, I was the spitting image of my father.

"So . . . us. It's all over?" I said, half to myself, my throat tight. "I get the feeling I'm gradually going to look more and more like him. I saw some photos the other day. It happened to all my brothers and sisters. I guess I'm no exception. Kaori, from now on are you going to look at me like you looked at him? Are you going to see him inside me? In this horrible face?"

Suddenly she kissed me and tried to throw me down on the bed.

"No," she repeated. "It's all right. You're completely different."

But it was obvious that she was gritting her teeth and forcing herself to do it—or rather, that she was flustered by the change in herself, by her own body's instinctive rejection of me.

"So that means that you can't love me anymore? This me who's starting to look like him?"

Tears were streaming down her face.

"It's okay. You don't have to. It just means I'm no good for you, right? I'm my father's son, after all. What . . . what a fucking mess."

After that I went quietly insane.

7

I TRIED TO keep away from Kaori but I couldn't. So I tried
to get close to her instead. I knew that I mustn't touch her,
but I couldn't help myself. If just once I could have sex with
her the way we used to, I thought, everything would go back
to the way it was. I went to her room and climbed into her
bed as gently as possible, but though she whispered that it
was all right, her body tensed, she closed her eyes tightly and
tears rolled down her cheeks. No matter how tenderly I held
her, her reaction made me feel like my father, who had vio-
lated her. For me, the situation was a form of hell.

In an old photo album I found some pictures of my brothers
and sisters. As they approached adolescence, every single one

of them started to resemble him. His blood ran strong in our veins. My third brother looked a bit different, but you could tell at a glance they were all my father's children. I told Kaori that we should spend some time apart. Things were a bit strange at the moment, I said, but it's only temporary. Time heals all wounds, I said. I couldn't help noticing, however, that the face I saw in the mirror was becoming more and more like his, as though I'd been cursed.

I stopped going to school. I spent most of my days in bed. I dreamed my father lay naked beside me, and I'd wake pummeling his scrawny body. Kaori came to my room and informed me that she was pregnant. I was in a panic, but she was even worse. She went in secret to a doctor, who told her that it was a false alarm. Despite that, she still insisted she was, and that this meant we could be together. She went back to the clinic and got the same result. I tried to hold her but her body went rigid with fright. Even as she told me she loved me, she was trying to get away. Then she just wept silently.

Kaori started complaining of headaches and skipping school, and in the end they took her to hospital. Seeing her condition, I told her once more that we're better off apart. We were about to finish junior high, and it was decided that when she started senior high she would leave the estate. The doctor who was treating her had advised a change of scene. That was the only thing that could save her.

There's not much to say about my high school life. I passed among the new students, with all their hopes and fears, like a dried-up insect. I sat vacant at my desk in a corner of the classroom, and the teachers often scolded me.

My classmates were kind enough to worry about me, but I asked them seriously why they had such stupid faces. And when the girl at the next desk spoke to me, I demanded if she liked sex. I think I went as far as saying that even though she looked so prim and proper, I bet she loved masturbating and fucking. I couldn't stay at school, so I started staying in bed again, just trying to get through one day at a time. From the moment I woke until I went to sleep at night, I just tried to survive without sinking into a deep depression, simply enduring one day after another. Everything seemed worthless and irritating. I played video games for hours, and when I got bored I threw them across the room and broke them. I read hundreds of comic books, then flung them aside. I listened to music, took sleeping pills, then repeated the cycle. The air was thick and heavy, pressing down on me. When one day finished, I knew that tomorrow I would have to face another one. My future was a daunting, unbroken succession of days as far as I could see. From time to time I'd get a letter from Kaori describing her life, but it was usually a week or so before I could open it, and when I finally did I could only manage a brief reply.

One day when I was seventeen or eighteen I went to see her. I showered for the first time in ages, changed my clothes and left the house. The unfamiliar sunshine was too bright, so I pulled my cap down tightly over my eyes. I thought that everyone I met was looking at me, did my best to control the fierce beating of my heart. I went to a hairdresser and asked for a trim, I didn't care what style. The hairdresser chattered away, but I couldn't get myself together enough to answer properly. The guy was kind, though, and eventually I stuttered out a few suitable remarks.

I left the salon, walking deliberately. For some reason I'd got into the habit of treading carefully. A woman in red was walking along the street perpendicular to mine on the other side of a high fence, moving smoothly past the black palings. I watched absently as the black overlaid the red, as the red was hidden by a series of black stripes, until finally we met at the corner. She was quite a bit older than me, but I thought she was beautiful, so I stopped. She passed by quickly, giving me a funny look. She didn't seem suspicious, but I guess I must have looked pretty strange. I took a deep breath and made my way cautiously forward once more.

Kaori's school was in Nakamura in Nagoya. I waited for her in a small park a short distance from the gate. She'd been set up in an apartment on her own, and she'd have to pass this way to get home. I remember vividly how beautiful she was then. She was walking with three boys and two girls, laughing at something one of them had said. She screwed up her eyes and pushed the girl beside her playfully on the arm. Her expression held no shadow of the troubles of a few years earlier. She was free of us. I stood dazed, looking at her loveliness and glow. She was beyond my reach. Once we had been able to be together and happy, but it was like she had entered my life as some kind of mistake, as a brief fantasy. The loss of this blissful hallucination, combined with the confusion of being a teenager, rooted me to the spot.

"Fumihiro!"

I had intended to spy on her in secret, but I'd forgotten to make my escape and she'd spotted me. I have no recollection of what happened to her friends. I simply looked at Kaori as she approached. She was gorgeous. Far too good for someone like me.

"I haven't seen you for ages," she said with a smile, seeming untroubled by my sinister ambush.

"Yeah. I was in the area."

"I'm glad."

She started walking. I realized that I was walking with her.

"How's school?" I think she asked.

If I swallow my pride and admit honestly the ugliness that passed through my mind, I was thinking about attacking her. About touching the most beautiful, most precious girl in the world once more. After that, I thought, I would kill myself. That would be the end of my miserable life. If I could hold Kaori in my arms one more time, I didn't give a damn what happened to everything else. I opened my mouth.

"It's just before exams, so there are no classes."

I had no idea what I was saying.

"Everyone at your school must be really brainy," she said.

"No, there are some weirdos too."

"Really?"

"Yeah. It's fun. How about yours?"

"I like it."

As I walked, I said the first things that came into my head.

"So you don't need to worry about me, or the old place, or anything."

She was silent.

"It can't be helped. Just forget all about my father. You'll be fine. You can make a fresh start. First love often doesn't work out. We're like brother and sister."

She started to speak. I didn't think I wanted to hear it. I also suspected that my previous speech had been a waste of breath.

"Can I ask you something?" she asked nervously.

"What?"

"Your father, has he come back?"

"No."

"I thought maybe you . . ."

It's odd, but it was the first time in months that I'd remembered that I'd killed him. I imagined telling her. *I killed him to protect you, so there's no reason for us to be apart. Even if you don't like me, even if I disgust you, you should be always by my side, because Father's death means we'll always be joined. Because you're everything to me. Because if you're not going to be mine, I could drag you down here with me. Into my world, where we're both stained by that dark secret.*

"I'm not brave enough for that," I said, laughing.

I still hardly knew what I was saying.

"This is hard to talk about, but I can tell you because you won't tell anyone else."

I lowered my voice.

"My father's mixed up with a whole bunch of people, yakuza and some really scary foreigners. So they're saying he might have been murdered by them."

The sunlight was dazzling.

"That's why they can't go public with it. You'd better forget about it. It sounds like my brothers are handling it on the quiet."

This was just like my clowning around to hide my depression before I met her. I thought she looked slightly relieved. Still acting casually, I told her I had to catch a train and made my farewells. My malice hadn't grown so bad that I could hurt Kaori. The sun was slowly sinking, shooting powerful beams between the apartment buildings. I could hear the sounds of insects, and a faint breeze brushed indifferently against my cheek. I thought that something important in my life had ended. People would probably tell me that I still had a lot to look forward to. Maybe some would even say that killing my father had been a form of self-defense, that I had no choice. But my youthful heart, which had experienced great joy and the torments of hell, couldn't untangle those events and order them neatly. They had settled inside me, and as I grew old they would warp me even more. As long as I lived, I would continue to harm everyone who was important to me. I felt, however, that I was unnaturally calm. My mind was completely detached from my body. I was aware of the movement of my feet as I walked, and I spoke out loud on purpose. I just said something, I thought to myself. I wondered how people around me would react if I raised my voice and shouted.

8 PRESENT

ON THE SCREEN Kaori was moving. The projector, the latest model, was showing images of the recording the detective had handed me. It had been taken at night, but was very clear. She was beautiful. She was looking down as she opened the door of a convenience store, holding her plastic bag of purchases and her purse in her left hand and putting the receipt away with her right. I smiled, thinking how like her it was to keep her receipts tidy.

I rewound I don't know how many times to see what she'd bought, freezing the frame and zooming in. In the white bag I could see a pack of Morinaga 100% apple juice. A small brown box might have been chocolate. A packet that looked like supplements, I couldn't tell what kind. Her black hair grew to her shoulders, and under a white half coat I could see a cream sweater and a dark skirt. She climbed into a blue Stepwagon, a courtesy car for the women at the club. The driver was a young man, and the other women in the vehicle were about the same age as Kaori. The vehicle backed up a bit and then turned out of the parking lot. At that moment her profile was visible through the window, head down. The car drove off and the recording ended.

I lit a cigarette and played it again. Kaori opened the door of the shop, put the receipt in her purse. My heart rate quickened. Above her sweater, the skin around her throat was pale. Since she was on her way home from work, she was still heavily made up. I watched it again, lit another cigarette, watched it once more. Without my noticing it, the piano tune flowing over the stereo had finished.

MY LIFE SINCE I separated from Kaori had passed uneventfully. I dropped out of high school, took the university entrance exam and went to a college in Tohoku. Perhaps I realized that I could never get on with my life unless I left the estate. Every day I continued to wound the people I met and to harm myself. When I dated girls, Kaori's shadow was simply overpowering. Towards my friends, too, I couldn't keep up the pretence for long. Everything was distorted—those past events, which I had made no effort to come to terms with, and my existence since then. I was trapped in my memories of the time I spent with Kaori. After that my life passed as a series of meaningless images. No matter how much I tried to like other women, I just couldn't do it. Twice I made half-hearted suicide attempts. On the third time, when I climbed to the roof of my condo, I realized that I wanted to see her one last time. I knew that Yoshigaki, one of the servants Kaori had been on fairly good terms with, kept in touch with her from time to time. I got her to email me a photo of Kaori at the women's university she was attending in Tokyo. She was lovely. I made up my mind to become a statistic, one of the thirty thousand suicides in Japan each year. But then I heard from Yoshigaki that Kaori was having trouble with her boy-friend, and my feelings became confused. It was actually a common enough problem—he was two-timing her. My heart was empty enough to be relieved that she had found a new lover. Then when I heard that she'd finally been dumped, I headed for Tokyo, my mind all mixed up.

I hired a private eye out of the phone book and got him to approach the guy who broke up with Kaori. He succeeded in getting friendly with him and found out what sort of person he was—one of those guys you find everywhere, who seduce women and then treat them like dirt. I met him several times, posing as the detective's friend. He was a coward at heart, but that made no difference to me. I set fire to his apartment. I can clearly remember how quiet it was when I lit the match. He wasn't killed, but suffered burns to the chest. When I heard that he'd quit university I left Tokyo. It wasn't revenge. I simply wanted to set him on fire. Air, that was the word that came to mind. I felt as little emotion as air. And maybe I thought I was dead already. I went back up on the roof of my building, but then realized I could jump any time I wanted, it didn't have to be then. After I graduated my eldest brother contacted me about finding a job. I ignored him and stayed in my apartment in Tohoku. Occasionally I'd pick up a hooker, get her to put on a white dress and have sex with her. Lust was depressing, but so was its release. Father had intended me to be a cancer, and I'd ended up this melancholy creature who couldn't make anyone happy.

Several years went by, and finally I started thinking about becoming a different person, not so much to start a new life as to make my old self disappear. To extinguish myself, to vanish, to become a bystander in life. The messages I received at infrequent intervals from Yoshigaki told me that Kaori's life wasn't going all that smoothly either. Idly I imagined myself as the air that hung around her.

Everyone plays the lead role in their own life. The world progresses through gathering all these leads, through the jumble of different ideas and values. But I planned to drop out of my own play, to expunge myself, to drift into the cracks between the actors who make the world go round. When stagecraft or dramatic tricks were required, I wanted to work in the background, quietly and unobtrusively. I wondered if there were others besides me who had disappeared while they were still alive. Somewhere there must be, I thought vaguely.

I went and bought a can of coffee from the vending machine out front. A group of children was playing in the park, their mothers watching. The intensity of their happiness was too much for me. The sun was just about to set behind the apartment buildings. A motorbike delivering evening papers stopped nearby, a truck loaded with boxes swept past, an elderly man out jogging ran by me.

I put my hand in the pocket of my jeans and sipped my coffee, wondering what would happen to me. I thought about that, unable to marshal my thoughts. How would a life like mine turn out? What meaning would my existence have in this world? But even if my new life was full of despair, I reflected quietly, my real life had ended when I leapt to my death several years ago. I made my way slowly back to my room.

On the screen Kaori was moving. Looking down, she was opening the door of the convenience store, holding her plastic bag and purse in her left hand and putting the receipt away with her right. I thought again how typical it was for her to store her receipt carefully. She was still moving. I was smiling.

PART 3

PRESENT

1 PRESENT

"THERE'S A MAN who often comes to Ms. Kaori's club. He might be a bit of a problem. A con man. It looks like he's after her bank account, which has about thirty million yen in it. The Kuki family gave it to her as her share of the inheritance after Shozo Kuki was declared missing, presumed dead, but it appears that she's just left it there, never even touched it."

The detective handed me a single photo. It showed a man in a suit with longish hair and narrow eyes.

"He calls himself Takayuki Yajima, but his real name is Masayuki Nishida. He's thirty-four, and of course he's single."

"You mean this is the guy who was checking up on Kaori?"

"No, that was someone else. I'm still not sure who. My

EVIL AND THE MASK

guess is that it's some kind of shadowy company, the kind that avoids publicity. I don't know why an outfit like that would be investigating Ms. Kaori, but if I look into her past I might find the reason."

"No, don't do that yet. For the time being I just want to wait and see what happens."

Sitting next to the detective was his assistant, Azusa Konishi, who had started working at Je le Répète and become Kaori's friend. She was studying me with interest.

"But what puzzles me more than why he's doing it is how he knew about Kaori's bank balance in the first place."

"Did you know that one of the clerks at the Kuki family's law firm was accused of embezzlement?"

"Yeah."

"The lawyer filed a complaint against him, the police issued an arrest warrant and he killed himself in Wakayama. But at university he was in the same year as Yajima, and apparently they were friends."

"You mean it's connected to the Kukis?"

"Yes. Fraudsters like Yajima gather information from a wide variety of sources. Most likely he heard that Ms. Kaori had a large sum of money in the bank from this ex-employee."

"Is it possible that other people could have the same information?"

"I don't think so. Con men usually keep their information pretty close to their chest, and it was leaked to him privately in the first place, by a friend."

I leaned back on the sofa and took another mouthful of lukewarm coffee. The hotel windows were covered with raindrops. The TV had been left on, and a reporter was running somewhere with a microphone in hand. There had been another series of explosions. I could tell that Konishi was eager to say something, but was holding back out of politeness. With her dyed brown curls, her shorts and the white, long-sleeved T-shirt that accentuated her breasts, she was one of those striking women you see all over the place.

"Ms. Kaori," she began, her voice lower than I expected. "My impression is that she's very good-natured. She's cheerful and considerate, so she's popular with customers, but I still get the feeling that she's putting it on. Of course it's a service industry, so everyone fakes it to some extent, but it seems to me that she always has to force herself to be cheerful. Even her thoughtfulness is kind of painful to watch. She's pretty but, how can I put it, it's like she's afraid of living."

She looked at me searchingly.

"It looks like she's got a bit of a soft spot for this guy Yajima. She still thinks of him as a customer, but I don't know how things will pan out. Even if she finds out he's a con man, she might end up feeling sorry for him. She's got that side to her. Some women let themselves be fooled, even knowing the guy is a cheat. With his previous victims, Yajima was quite capable of continuing to work on them even after he was exposed, telling them that he needed the money, this time he really meant it. I can't say for sure that would happen with Kaori, but he's a nuisance."

She straightened up.

"I think she brings out the worst in people. It's like the part of her that's afraid, the part of her that's insecure, can't help accepting other people's weaknesses. It worries me to see that."

The man turned to look at her and she fell silent.

"It's okay. Please say anything that's on your mind. It'll be useful."

The detective took up the conversation.

"As well as that, Yajima's into drugs. It sounds like he makes the women take them as well, whether they want to or not, sometimes even injecting them by force. When you see a beautiful woman and think, what on earth's she doing with a guy like that, nine times out of ten there are drugs involved. It goes without saying."

"He injects them?"

He looked at me strangely for a second.

"So I hear. I got that from a woman he mistreated before."

"I see."

I picked up the photo of the man calling himself Yajima and stared at it again. I didn't feel the least bit disturbed, and my heart rate didn't alter. I was aware of the stillness in the room and I thought I could hear faint noises somewhere in the distance. When I glanced at the clock, it was almost time for Azusa to go to work.

"What should we do?" the detective asked.

I stubbed out my cigarette.

"Look for any obvious patterns in this guy's behavior. His regular hangouts, days and times he goes there. And then after a week I want you to stop watching him. One thing I need to ask you, though. How far are you prepared to go?"

The man's expression didn't change.

"As far as it takes."

"Okay. But it would still definitely be better if you stopped watching him. Ms. Konishi, for the time being, if he comes to the club, please do your best to keep him away from her. Right, I'll be waiting for a report a week from today."

"Will do."

The rain was still beating against the hotel windows. I'd planned to walk part of the way home but decided against it.

2

RUNNING MY HAND along the wall, I climbed the stairs of the dingy tower block. Sand and dirt clung to the soles of my shoes and every step made a rough, gritty sound. The narrow landings were cluttered with cardboard boxes blocking the way. I couldn't tell what was inside them. When I opened the heavy, black door, I was hit by a blast of loud music. The bar was overflowing with people, more foreigners than Japanese.

It held a counter, too long for the room, and tables with crude chairs. One corner was closed off with a heavy green curtain. I passed a laughing, shouting group of Chinese, stepped over the outstretched legs of some Arabs engrossed in serious conversation. The club was white with cigarette smoke, perhaps because the ventilation system wasn't up to it. A dark-skinned woman began kissing a long-haired guy. A group of black men in the back were watching them and arguing about something. I sat at the bar and ordered a gin and tonic. A Japanese woman with tightly braided hair and wearing a tank top was looking at my black suit with raised eyebrows.

As I looked around my vision lost its focus. All the people standing in their dark clothes suddenly appeared as vertical lines, and beyond them I noticed a young woman dressed in green. She was asleep, face down on the table. My eyesight wavered again, and the tall black lines of the men and the green of the woman turned faintly red. I seemed to be on the verge of remembering something, but it wouldn't come. Then a black man moved in front of me and the vision ended abruptly. He tried to lift the woman, his thick, bare arms glistening with sweat under the powerful lights. Another Japanese girl who was with her spoke to him in English. The woman woke up and cried out, trying to get away. Her eyes were big, her short skirt hiked up. I realized that I'd been staring at her face for ages. The people around were laughing, and so was the man as he tried to soothe her.

Yajima was at the end of the counter. I finished my drink and stood up, pretending I was going to the toilet. He was really drunk, accusing the Arab behind the bar of something. The bartender didn't argue, just spread his arms and smiled. I approached and quietly took the seat next to him. He glanced at me briefly, lost the thread of what he was saying and fell silent. I ordered another gin and tonic and lit a cigarette.

"You're Takayuki Yajima, aren't you?"

Sluggishly, he turned his face towards me.

"I'd like a word with you."

"Who the fuck are you?"

People were shouting to make themselves heard over the music. Three slim young Japanese women who I hadn't noticed before were sitting at the table at the back with the group of blacks. Smiling ambivalently, they were lounging against the men, who kept giving them long kisses and touching their bodies with thick fingers as though they were toys.

"If you need a name, call me Sato. Suzuki would do just as well."

"What do you want?"

The music grew even more intense.

"It's about Kaori Kuki. If we work together there's way more than thirty million in it for us."

"How do you know about her?"

"From Moriyama, who worked in the Kukis' lawyer's office and killed himself. He and I were friends. Plus I've got a bone to pick with the Kukis. We can get hundreds of millions from her. You interested?"

"I'm listening."

The women with the black men all laughed at once.

"Before that, how far have you got?"

He drained what was left of his whiskey and asked for a beer. His eyes flicked towards me.

"It's a straight-forward con. If I can get her hooked, that thirty million will be a piece of cake."

"I see. That's good."

He smirked slightly. He was wearing a plain white shirt and a cream jacket.

"But is it safe? If you get caught with drugs on you it'll be all over."

"No problem. I've never been arrested, so I'll be treated as a first offender. First-time users don't go to prison, they get put on probation. They'd soon let me off, so I could pick up where I left off. I'm the sort of guy, if I get interrupted in the middle I get even more determined."

"Even though she's just an adopted daughter, she's still a Kuki. So what's your plan after that?"

"Plan?"

He laughed drunkenly.

"Who cares? It's the danger that makes it exciting."

His voice suddenly grew louder, but I was careful not to change my expression. From up close, his eyes were hollow, his cheeks sunken.

"I need cash. I've got debts coming out my ears. But more than that, that girl Kaori, she's a looker, eh?"

"Yeah."

I sniggered coarsely, and his voice went up another notch.

"That's right. And she's good-natured and naïve. Women like that really turn me on."

He laughed again.

"I'll keep feeding her drugs till she sinks right to the depths of lust and corruption. Do you know how attractive a bitch is when she's abandoned all goodness and kindness and morality, just begging for a fix? It's the most beautiful thing in the world."

His rough skin caught the light and seemed to glow with vitality.

"Clinging to you as she takes off her clothes, weeping hysterically, crying give me some please, give me a fix. Naked, pleading, desperate, I'll do anything, as many men as you like, do whatever you want to me. At that moment a woman shines from inside. It's the truth. I swear it."

The black men had started sliding their fingers between the women's legs. The girls were still smiling, but they were getting more and more embarrassed, tugging weakly at their skirts to try to prevent anyone from seeing what was happening. They lowered their voices but all the other customers were staring. The lights continued to spotlight them through the white cigarette haze. The men's hands grew even bolder, and their laughter drowned out the women's feeble resistance.

"OK, tell me about your plan," said Yajima, giving me a twisted grin. "I could use a bit of extra cash too."

"At the Kukis' estate there's a document, a single sheet."

Yajima pushed his face closer to mine.

"I want you to ask Kaori to get hold of that paper. If you can, I'll buy it for fifty million yen. How about it?"

"But are you reliable? How do I know I can trust you?"

"I'll pay you half up front. We make the transfer in a crowded bar. As soon as I get it, I give you the other half. I'm not after money. It doesn't interest me, and I've got a personal vendetta against the Kuki family."

"Is that so?"

Yajima lit a cigarette and raised his eyes lazily to the ceiling.

"What's the document?"

"It's better if you don't know. It's safer that way."

"I told you I don't care about safety, didn't I? Nothing can stop me."

He laughed.

"Fine. You don't have to tell me. Even our world has its rules. I like you, you're funny. You've got a dishonest face, same as me."

The black men vanished behind the heavy curtain at the rear, taking the blushing women with them. A drunk couple at a nearby table, perhaps inspired by them, draped their arms around each other's necks and started tongue-kissing.

"Can we meet here at the same time next week? This is big business. I'd like you to move slowly on Kaori."

"I get it. I'm a pro."

"Here's a token of my appreciation."

Under the counter I handed him a crumpled cigarette packet. A small plastic bag filled with white powder rustled inside.

"This is top quality stuff, completely different from what you get around here. It's really pure."

"You're pretty smooth, aren't you?"

Yajima opened the packet a crack, keeping it out of sight. After checking the contents, he put it in the inside pocket of his jacket.

"That's really wicked shit," I said, "so to start with you should only take about half a normal dose. It's bloody dangerous if you get it wrong. It'll be hard to get the job done if you're dead."

I laughed and so did he.

"Yeah, it's that good? Could you get me some more?"

"I will next week," I said as I got up to leave.

3

Drug Addiction Spreading
Man Found Dead on Shinjuku Street

Late last night the body of a man was discovered by a police patrol in a parked car on a street in Shinjuku.

The victim appeared to be in his mid-thirties, and based on the fact that syringes were found in his vehicle, the cause of death is believed to be a drug overdose. The police are trying to learn the man's identity and who supplied him with the narcotics. Since the beginning of this month there have been more than thirty drug-related deaths in the city, and the police are strengthening their countermeasures.

Drug Overdose Turns Into Murder Inquiry

Traces of cyanide have been detected in the powder believed to have been used by the man found dead in a car on the third of this month. Based on syringes found in the vehicle and scars on the victim's arms, the cause of death initially appeared to be a drug overdose, but police are now treating it as a possible murder or suicide.

They have reported that the man's identity is still unknown. Even the acquaintance from whom he borrowed the car claims not to have known his real name.

It was a minor incident, and articles appeared once or twice in a few newspapers, buried on the inside pages, but after that the information dried up. I thought that was the mark of a true con artist—even in death they couldn't figure out who he was. In front of me the detective was drinking his coffee. For some reason the surroundings seemed to stand out sharply, as if the air was crystal clear. I contemplated that unusual sight for a while.

"This man is definitely Takayuki Yajima," said the detective, "but I don't know yet if it was suicide or murder."

It was like he was reading from a script, and I grinned slightly. He continued.

"We can assume that it will be impossible for the police to track down the culprit. They don't know Yajima's true identity, and the best they'll be able to do is look for people who had a grudge against him. Then they'll try to find out his normal suppliers, and that will be as far as they can go."

"I think so too. But please keep watching Kaori."

My eyesight was still unnaturally sharp. I could clearly see the dust on the table, the seams of the sofa he was sitting on.

"This man's death is extremely fortunate for Ms. Kaori," he said, looking at me.

"It is, isn't it? Extremely fortunate."

I wondered why it was so quiet and glanced at the clock. It was already after two in the afternoon. The movements of the second hand were crisp and precise.

"Here are some photos and video of Ms. Kaori from last week, in a bar she went to with Azusa Konishi. She's managed to make friends with her quite quickly."

"Great. I'm really glad I hired you. The next thing that's bothering me is this firm that's been investigating her."

The detective bowed slightly and left the hotel room where we always met. After he left the room was still.

I TOOK TWO taxis and got out part-way, in a residential area. The plastic surgeon had an unwritten rule that I couldn't go straight there by car, because cars were conspicuous and people would notice that he had lots of visitors. Although it was a clinic, from the outside it looked like an ordinary house.

When I pressed the buzzer and gave my name, the door opened silently. A woman of about forty with no make-up ushered me in with a smile. She was the doctor's assistant, but wasn't wearing the usual white nurse's uniform, just an apron over her clothes.

The doctor stood up from a white sofa as I entered the room, giving me a neutral smile. Several plants were arranged in white pots and sunlight seeped through the blinds. The walls were stark white, not a speck or stain on their antiseptic surface. My room had been upstairs, and the operating theater was farther to the back.

"How are you feeling?" he asked.

"Not too bad."

The doctor pushed an ashtray towards me and I lit a cigarette. The clear glass of the ashtray reflected the light. It looked white, as if it was trying to hide something.

"I want you to keep taking the anti-inflammatories for a little while longer. Just to be on the safe side."

"Okay."

In his sweater and cotton trousers, he didn't look like a doctor. For some reason the stickiness of my rubber slippers was bothering me.

"It fits nicely. Your face. Though whether it's your face that's adjusting to you or you that's adjusting to your face, I don't know."

"It feels like there isn't any 'me' any more. Like there's no such thing as me."

"Are you still getting those flashbacks?"

"I've already ceased to exist."

He passed me some tea. The room was warm, and the clink of cup on saucer rang out in the quietness. The tea was as strong as ever.

"My wife found a dead baby."

"A baby?"

"Yes. In the toilets in a department store. A corpse."

He sipped his tea.

"Floating in the bowl with the umbilical cord still attached. Isn't that cruel?"

"Yeah."

"They called an ambulance and apparently there was a huge uproar."

He stared at the gray blinds.

"That baby should have enjoyed life. That's what my wife said. She said she wanted to wrap him in a towel. Babies come into the world screaming from the pain of being forced out of the womb and the fear of being outside. Being squeezed through that narrow channel. And after all that, to be dumped in a toilet, in cold water so he couldn't breathe, isn't that just dreadful? For that baby the world was nothing but an oppressive place."

The ceiling fan was spinning indecisively.

"Normally when they come out they're hurting, and their mother or a nurse wraps them in a towel, right? A soft, clean white towel. Of course the baby keeps crying out of fear, but it can feel that it's wrapped in something soft, can't it? Then eventually it gazes at things in wonder, someone makes it smile. But this baby, as soon as it was born, its suffering increased. Shuddering at the touch of the cold porcelain, the cold water, unable even to breathe. And then it died. At the last second he must have looked up at the ceiling. That's what I can't stop imagining, the look on his face at that moment. What did his life mean? He grew into flesh and blood in his mother's womb just to experience pain. For him this world existed only to hurt him. And he didn't know anything. My wife said that even if that baby was going to die almost immediately, she still wanted to cuddle him, to wrap him in a soft blanket for that brief time. She wanted to make him feel that the world contained soft, warm things, things that cared about him and held him gently."

The doctor was watching me.

"Why are you telling me this?"

"I don't know. Whenever I see you I just want to tell you stuff."

"Me too. I wonder why. I get this urge to talk to you too. Maybe it's because you're the only person who knows the boundaries of my face."

There was a knock at the door and when the doctor answered the woman who had let me in entered and gave me some pills in a paper bag. Then she left the room silently, smiling the whole time.

"A while ago you said your life was over. Now you seem to have a bit more of a spark."

"I do?"

"Yes. I could even say you're excited. Ever since you came in."

I looked at the clock, unsure how to reply. When I stood up, he did the same.

"This life is a gift. You may as well make the most of it."

"Don't worry. I've had plenty of happiness in the past."

With chapped fingers I fastened a coat button that I'd missed. The frayed threads were twisted tightly.

"For example," I went on, "even if this was some kind of fairy tale with a happy ending, real people's lives keep on going after the story finishes."

He turned towards me to show he was listening.

"As a story it ends happily, even if the characters die of something immediately afterwards. In the same way, I suppose you could present my life as a happy tale if you ended it in the right place."

"I'd rather talk about the future."

He opened the door, still smiling, and I felt the cold air rush in. He followed me quietly into the hallway.

"Your future. There are many kinds of fortune-tellers who claim to know people's futures, aren't there? People who communicate with spirits, people who use statistics based on your date of birth, and so on. But for me the most—what's the word?—interesting method would be predicting the outcome by looking at a person's character, heredity and environment, and the character and heredity of everyone around him. I'm interested in people who can plot these variables to find the line that indicates the direction a person is heading."

I walked down the corridor without answering. When we reached the entrance hall the doctor started talking again.

"I normally prescribe two months' worth of pills, but I've only given you one, because I'd like to see you again. There aren't many cases where I've altered someone's face to look like someone else. You interest me."

"Professionally?"

"As a person. If I can still call myself human, that is. Because I'm the same as you. This isn't my original face."

I looked at him. It was a soft, forgettable face with narrow eyes.

"I'll be back," I said.

"I know."

When I went outside the sun was already setting.

I WENT HOME and took a nap. For some reason I was exhausted. My hands and feet wouldn't move properly, as though they were refusing to do what I told them. As I was mulling over what the doctor had said, the doorbell rang. I ignored it, thinking they'd go away, but it went on ringing. I got out of bed, the noise hurting my ears, and walked across the hard floor. When I looked at the screen on the intercom, a man I didn't know was standing there.

4

HE WAS QUITE short, broad-shouldered and wearing a dark gray suit. His left leg jiggled as he stood there, giving him the air of an unpleasant insect. After staring at the screen for a moment, I lifted the receiver. His shadow stretched along the corridor. My heart started to beat faster. As soon as I picked up I wondered why I'd done so, why I hadn't just pretended to be out. But it was too late—he was reacting to the noise coming from the speaker. I inhaled, feeling faintly uneasy.

"Yes?"

"Ah. Were you asleep? It's been a long time. It's Aida."

The name didn't ring a bell.

"Yeah, well, I knew you'd be surprised. Hey, that's just how

I am. Would you believe me if I said I just happened to be in the neighborhood?"

My pulse quickened even more. I was certain I didn't know him, but his tone suggested ominously, powerfully, that he was someone I couldn't just turn away. After a brief hesitation I flung on a tracksuit and opened the door, which seemed to have grown heavier.

The man stared sideways at me through narrow eyes. His hair was short, going gray in places. Suppressing a rising sense of panic, I forced my face into a surprised expression.

"Long time, no see," he said. "Have you got a cold?"

"Yeah, I was asleep."

"With gel in your hair?"

He eyed me doubtfully.

"I had to meet someone, but I'd had enough so I came home."

"Yeah?"

Even though he was right in front of me, he kept stealing sidelong glances at me out of the corner of his eye. The soles of his shoes were paper-thin. Suddenly it struck me that he might be a cop.

"Don't you have better things to do than coming all this way?" I grumbled, trying to work out what was going on.

It was clear that he knew he was unwelcome. A grin crept across his swarthy face.

"Got a short fuse, haven't you? Well, I don't blame you. It must be at least eight years since we last met. I bet you thought it was over."

The cut of his suit was really old-fashioned.

"It's a bit public out here. Can I come in?"

"I've got a temperature. Can't we do this another time?"

For the past several days the news had been full of reports of an influenza outbreak.

"Me, I don't care if I catch it. It would give me a break from chasing crooks. Anyway, I think you're faking it. You've changed. Age, perhaps? Looks like you've gotten more cunning."

So he was a cop after all, I thought, struggling to control my breathing.

"But I'm surprised to see you living in a fancy building like this. When did you come back to Japan? I'd begun to suspect that you'd run away."

"I do what I want."

"You really have changed. That blunt way of talking."

I kept telling myself not to reveal my discomposure. He obviously knew Shintani, my face's original owner, whose past was littered with dead people. Maybe he was under suspicion over one of them. If this guy hadn't seen Shintani for eight years, he must have had a pretty good reason for coming to his condo. I tried to stay calm, thinking furiously.

"Can't I come in? It's cold."

"Some other time."

"You look terrible. Is it such a big shock, me turning up again? Or are you really sick?"

"I told you I was in bed, didn't I?"

"But you're not even coughing. Well, you can't help that, I guess. Nothing sounds more artificial than a forced cough."

He continued to stare at me, smirking. There was something really irritating about him.

"After eight years it's not surprising that you've changed. You look pretty haggard, like a completely different person. I guess you've been through the wringer too. It's odd for me to say this, but that case is never going to turn into a murder inquiry, not after all these years. Of course I knew Sae since she was little. I know her mom too. And you had a perfect alibi when it happened, but Yaeko was adamant that you were behind it. She got kind of strange—she's still saying it, and she's never stopped hating you. Her and me, we've known each other a long time, so I think it's the least I can do to work on the case whenever I can find the time, at least until the statute of limitations runs out. Hey, your neighbors will be watching. Won't you at least let me into the hallway?"

I hesitated, then gave up and let him in. He started to take off his shoes, but I stopped him with a gesture. Sae had been Shintani's girlfriend at university, who died in a traffic accident after they broke up. I figured that Yaeko was probably her mother.

"Why are you here?" I asked, looking him in the face.

"You really don't get it, do you? Because the statute's about to run out on what you did. The time limit is different for different crimes, and the years you spent overseas don't count. But then I felt the hand of fate, so strong it was spooky."

He held out a photograph.

"This man, his name's Takayuki Yajima. Do you know him? He's a drug user and a dealer and some kind of con man, a marriage swindler."

I felt a dull pain in my heart. I tried to look bored but I

couldn't speak. Inside my head I sorted through various reactions, but couldn't decide which was best.

"When we were looking into his activities before he died, we found that he'd been to a bar called d'Alfaro. If he didn't kill himself, maybe the person who gave him the poison went to the same bar. He had a lot of enemies. If one of them was there that day, maybe he's the culprit. It would also make it less likely that he committed suicide. A shitty bar like that doesn't have security cameras, but the sex shop next door has one at the entrance. They put it in so that they can check people's faces when there's trouble with customers. And sure enough, there was a picture of Yajima walking past. And then I saw a familiar face. Yours. I was flabbergasted. I felt like you'd come back into my clutches, and before the time expired. That's when I decided to pay you another visit."

My head was aching slightly. I was finding it hard to keep up with the pace of events.

"Am I under suspicion?" I said without thinking.

I could feel beads of sweat on my forehead, but couldn't do anything about them. He was staring at me intently.

"Why? Should you be?"

"No . . ."

He burst out laughing.

"Come on! Why would you kill Yajima? There's nothing tying you to him. There's absolutely no link between your life and his. No matter what I think of you, I'm not going to set you up for that. He was either tricked by some woman and murdered, or he topped himself. Anyway, his body was already falling apart. That's not what I'm talking about. I'm saying I felt the hand of destiny. It's a hunch I've had for a long time. And my hunches, they've been a friend to me my whole life, they're always right on the money. When I meet someone again out of the blue like that, something is definitely going to happen. I started to think that maybe you really had killed Sae after all. Sorry, but you know I'm stubborn. In fact I don't have that much time right now because of other cases, but I decided to have another look anyway."

He continued to watch me.

"Yaeko's health isn't very good."

"Huh?"

"Finally I get a reaction. That's right. She might not have much longer. That's another reason I'm here. Don't you think that everything fits together, like cogs? Hell, you look really bad. Okay, we'll leave it there for today. But before I leave, can I take a quick look at your room?"

"You really are obsessed with my room, aren't you?"

"Haven't I told you before? If you see a person's room you can pretty much understand them. Fyodor Dostoevsky said that. I'm putting all my cards on the table here, but I want to get a feel for what you're like now. After all, it's been eight years. My instincts about you aren't as sharp as they used to be. You seem really different from before, somehow. You even look different."

"Okay."

Casually he slipped off his shoes and opened the living room door.

"That's far enough. You can see from there, can't you?"

"Kind of a lonely room, isn't it?" he said, gazing around.

"None of your business."

"That reminds me. You liked movies, didn't you?"

The projector screen was still down, and the shelves were overflowing with DVDs, mostly French and Italian. Shintani's taste in movies.

"With a place like this, I bet you don't get many visitors. No girlfriend either. This is definitely a one-person room."

"I said, it's none of your business."

"People often die around you. Your family, Masao Yaeda at high school, then Takayuki Isoi, Mikio Suzuki."

"Give me a break. They got sick and died. Well, Yaeda was an accident."

"I know. But I always thought you were weird. It suddenly occurred to me that if I got mixed up with you I might drop dead too."

"Maybe you'll catch my flu and die. Apparently this year's virus is really dangerous for diabetics."

He laughed.

"I'll come back another day. Actually, I don't have much time, because I've got to follow up on those terrorist attacks. But shall I tell you my impression, seeing you after all these years? I get the feeling you're a bit more upset than I expected. I wonder why? But don't disappear overseas again."

He opened the door carelessly and left. The smell of his old-fashioned hair oil lingered behind him.

5

I SAT ON my bed and lit a cigarette. Then a second, and a third. Breathing quietly, I considered my situation. As I stared at the gently dissolving trail of smoke, I felt sharp, stabbing pains in my head.

Shintani's girlfriend at university, Sae Suzuki, had died in a traffic accident. Her mother, Yaeko, and that detective, Aida, had always harbored suspicions against him. From my conversation with Aida, I gathered that these suspicions were solely his and the mother's, not shared by the police force as a whole. Yajima's death was also tricky. Aida had claimed that there was no connection between Yajima and Shintani, but was that what he really thought? I had to be careful. I wondered how I'd gotten into this mess. But it goes without saying that taking on another person's identity involves a degree of risk. I drank a glass of stale water that had been left on the table since I don't know when, and finally stubbed out my cigarette.

After transferring the picture of Aida from the intercom camera to my computer, I lifted the receiver of my phone. Then I stopped and grabbed my cell phone instead. I'd bought it from a professional part-timer in Tokyo, so there was no tie to me or Shintani. The bills were paid through his bank account, so I'd bought that as well.

The phone rang three times and the private investigator answered in a quiet voice. I could hear a buzzing sound.

"Something awkward has come up. I want to move next week's meeting forward."

It sounded like he was in a bar somewhere.

"Okay. What's happened?"

"I'll tell you then. But put everything on hold until we meet, please. There's a cop sniffing around."

"Okay."

"Maybe we should avoid the usual hotel. Do you know somewhere safe?"

"I think so. I'll get back to you. Is this cell phone all right?"

"Yes. Let's meet the day after tomorrow. Maybe it's best if we lay low tomorrow, as a precaution."

"Okay. I've got some new information too."

I hung up and sat on the bed. Looking back on my exchange with Aida, I thought about how uneven my pulse had been, how perturbed I was. Even now my heart was still thumping, like a persistent echo. I got up, irritated by my body's reaction. I was hungry, and that annoyed me too. I thought about going out, but changed my mind because Aida might still be there. I could hear low voices whispering right beside my ear. I ignored them and started walking, but something felt wrong with the floor. It seemed to be sticking to the soles of my feet, as if it had a mind of its own. The second hand on the clock moved sharply, jerkily. I felt the glass was urging me to pick it up and drink more of that stale liquid. I fired up my computer and forced down the rest of the water.

The video playing on the computer came up on the projector. I watched it again, leaning back on the sofa, trying to forget my unpleasant meeting with the cop. The screen changed from black to orange, and then Kaori appeared, wearing a thin white sweater, resting her elbows on a table in a café. Her beer glass was half empty, and her dinner was salad, spring rolls and a small pizza. She was beautiful, so beautiful that I forgot all about Shintani's life and the shock of Aida's visit.

Suddenly I was surprised by Kaori's laugh. It was still the same high-pitched laugh it had always been. After an absence of ten years or more I was hearing her again. I moved to the chair by the table. Kaori clapped her hands lightly.

"I mean, really! Isn't that incredible?"

That was Azusa Konishi's voice.

"Yeah, yeah, it's amazing."

"So I said, 'That's incredible.' And he looked all smug."

Kaori giggled again. I didn't know what they were talking about, but I smiled too. I took a mouthful of whiskey from a glass that was sitting on the table, and its warmth spread slowly through my body.

"It was awful. It was all I could do not to laugh."

"I'm amazed you managed it," said Kaori.

Her cheeks were slightly flushed. I could see the curve of her breasts beneath her sweater. She picked up her beer mug with slender fingers and took a small sip. Her throat moved as she swallowed. Her eyes were moist with alcohol.

"Lots of guys are like that, aren't they?" Konishi said. "Hey, have you got a boyfriend?"

"No, I don't."

"Anyone you like?"

"Well, that customer, Yajima, he's pretty nice."

Bad taste, I thought.

"But a smarmy customer like that, he can suddenly stop coming, you know."

"Yeah, maybe. He's still just a customer, though."

"I don't know why you don't have a man. You're so pretty!"

"What? You're much prettier, Azumi! You became the top girl at work straight away, didn't you?"

Konishi had applied for the job using the name Azumi.

"I really wanted to be inconspicuous," said Konishi.

"But you're so outgoing!"

"Maybe."

Another giggle. A waiter approached politely and asked if they'd like another drink.

"Um, a gin and lime."

"Beer for me," said Kaori.

"More beer?"

"Well, okay, gin and lime."

"Kaori, can't you think for yourself?"

"All right then, gin and tonic."

Azusa Konishi laughed loudly. The waiter brushed the camera with his arm and the image tilted. Maybe it was hidden in a lighter or something. The picture shook and then the screen went dark. I watched the recording again, then switched it to continuous play. I watched Kaori's white sweater, listened to Kaori's laughter. I watched it over and over with a smile on my face.

Outside it started to rain. In the distance I could hear the sounds of car horns, and the lights in the surrounding apartments went out one by one.

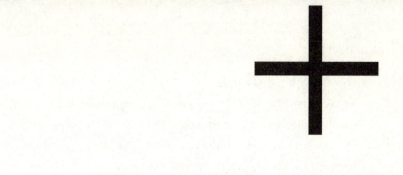

6

AFTER I FINISHED talking, the detective lowered his eyes.

We were in a room on the top floor of a run-down business hotel, but the interior was austere and clean. By parking in the basement of the vast shopping mall next door and walking through the Staff Only corridor, we'd managed to reach the hotel's underground car-park, so even if someone was following our car, from outside it would look like we'd gone into the mall. The detective had taken the stairs, avoiding both the reception area and the elevator. He had a connection in the hotel, so he knew there were no security cameras in the stairwell.

"It's my fault," he said, bowing deeply. "I'm very sorry."

I shook my head slowly.

"No, it's just one of those things. That cop, Aida, is kind of obsessed. Trading places with someone can never be entirely straightforward. When you do something unexpected and out of the ordinary, you've got to accept the risks."

"It was definitely treated as an accident pure and simple. Shintani was never questioned, even informally, and Sae Suzuki's family didn't bring a civil case against him either."

"Probably," I began, and then drank some coffee.

The cup had a red pattern, like deep gashes. I thought idly that my meetings with the detective always seemed to involve coffee.

"Aida had probably forgotten all about it until he saw me on the security camera. He spotted me, got a surprise and got in touch with Sae's mother, Yaeko, for the first time in ages. Then he heard that she was seriously ill. That's probably how it happened, I think. And he just felt that the coincidence must mean something. It's a real pain. So is the thing with Yajima. The Yajima problem will be fine though, won't it?"

He looked down, as though he was thinking. "I don't think they'll ever be able to catch the person who gave him the adulterated drugs. Whoever it was, they'd have handed them over under the table or something so that no one could see."

"Yeah. Under the table, and I bet he had special clear tape on his fingertips so he didn't leave any prints. Whoever he was." I no longer had any fingerprints, in case something like this happened, but I spoke deliberately and took another gulp of coffee.

The corners of his mouth relaxed as he debated how to

respond. "Then there's no problem. Even if someone saw them talking in the bar, that doesn't prove he gave him the poison. And they can't even be certain that the handover took place there. There'd have been hundreds of opportunities. He could have got the drugs a week earlier. A month, even. Since he was a regular user, he probably had a fair stash. The most obvious theories are that he added the poison to the drugs himself to kill himself or that a woman or someone who had ready access to his apartment mixed them."

"If they did track down the guy who was talking to Yajima," I said, "and asked him what the meeting was about, he could just say that he'd been interested in buying some drugs but had changed his mind."

"Sounds good to me. If he admits to something, they're more likely to believe him. It's like he's got no reason to hide the fact that he met him."

He stood and opened the refrigerator. Then he started speaking again, still with his back to me.

"But on the other hand, if they found out that this man really did have some kind of connection to Yajima, he'd be in big trouble."

He still didn't turn around.

"A murder inquiry starts by considering the victim and his associates. That cop might make the connection between Yajima and Ms. Kaori, but as long as he believes that this Shintani guy really is Shintani, he can't tie him to Yajima's death, because he has no motive, no reason to kill him. Obviously there is no link between him and Ms. Kaori either. However, if he works out that this man is not in fact who he appears to be, and if he discovers that he did actually have a motive to kill Yajima and is connected to Ms. Kaori, then the situation becomes very grave. When one lie unravels, the whole story falls apart. The truth comes spilling out."

"So I need to completely immerse myself in my role as Koichi Shintani."

The room was too warm. The black table in front of me was damp.

"I'll have another look at his background. If by some chance he did have something to do with Sae Suzuki's accident, we're in a much more difficult position."

"Please do. For the time being, Ms. Konishi's reports on Kaori will be enough."

"About that . . ."

The detective returned to the couch with two cans of coffee.

"The organization that was investigating Ms. Kaori, it was a company after all. A corporation in the munitions industry."

"Munitions? Why?"

My throat was dry. I poured the coffee into my cup.

"After the war the Japanese government banned all arms exports. This company deals with overseas arms manufacturers and acts as a broker for weapons imports and exports in other countries. It's a legitimate company, but it's hard to find out much about it. The man who was following Ms. Kaori often visits the building where the company's got their office. It's in Roppongi."

He handed me a photo of a building.

"The company register?"

"I've got hold of a list of the directors. We're still investigating."

I glanced at the paper he gave me. I didn't recognize any of the names.

"I don't understand this at all."

"Shall I look into Ms. Kaori's past?"

He was studying me.

"Yes, please. Start with her work history rather than her friendships."

"Okay."

His suit was slightly worn. I knew it helped him blend into his surroundings, but he was quite good-looking and it seemed a waste that he didn't wear something a little more stylish.

"I'm making trouble for you," I said. "One problem after another."

He smiled slightly.

"And you're paying us accordingly. Anyway, we don't like doing a half-assed job."

"Thank you. I'm worried about Aida, so we won't meet as often. Call my cell phone and put any recordings from Konishi in the post. Just to be on the safe side. Email leaves a trail."

"Understood. We'll use a different sender's name every time, so please check all your mail."

I realized that even though his clothes and belongings were scruffy, they were all cleaner than they appeared. His carelessly tousled hair was always messy in the same way and the wrinkles in his suit were always in the same places. I saw that his unremarkable black bag was perfectly polished. Such excessive cleanliness struck me as kind of lonely. I finished my coffee and used the room phone to call a cab.

WE DROVE FOR a while and I got out when I saw Ueno Park. Konishi called and told me that she'd mailed a photo of Kaori and her. She said jokingly that usually she was cool towards people she was checking up on, but that she'd come to like Kaori, perhaps because they were about the same age, and it was quite difficult.

"And another thing," she continued in a low voice. "I can't work out what she wants from life. It feels like she doesn't really have any big dreams. She said when she was younger she wanted to be a nurse, but . . ."

I thought about that. She'd probably have made a good nurse.

"Thank you. Please keep going."

I hung up and looked around me. I couldn't exactly remember why I'd gotten out in such a crowded place. From a vending machine I bought a coffee and drank it as I walked. An elderly couple was out for a stroll, a mother pushing a baby buggy. A child holding a balloon was smiling proudly. A gang of guys, probably university students, was joking around in loud voices. A beautiful woman was walking along, ignoring her surroundings, eyes fixed on her cell phone. A group of kids with schoolbags. An old man chatting cheerfully on his phone. Surprisingly, he was holding the latest model.

Happiness is a fortress.

That's what my father had said before I locked him up, before I killed him. A young couple, junior high school students, came walking towards me. The boy was striding earnestly and the girl was pretty. When she teased him about something he blushed and got angry. Maybe she didn't know how seriously teenage boys take themselves, how important they think they are. I grinned.

Father hadn't been begging for his life. He didn't blame me, saying I was murdering him to preserve my self-contained life with Kaori. He knew exactly what would happen to me after I killed him. But I had no desire to destroy this happy scene around me now. Having said that, faced with this mass of other people's happiness, I didn't feel like giving them my blessing either. I was just walking. Wondering if in this huge park there were any other murderers. And if there were, did it bother them?

When I looked back at the high school couple they were holding hands. I watched them expressionlessly. I started having impure thoughts, and left the park and hailed a taxi. Maybe my sudden arousal was their fault? Probably not, I decided. It made no difference if I kept on walking or went home to bed alone. It made no difference if I threw the can of coffee I was holding at someone or if I didn't. It didn't matter if I was horny or if I wasn't. Nothing mattered.

I WENT INTO d'Alfaro, where I'd met Yajima. I didn't have any particular reason for choosing that place, but if Aida learned that I hadn't been back there since Yajima's death he might get suspicious. I sat at the battered counter and ordered a gin and tonic. As before, the bar was noisy and full of foreigners.

A small hole had been punched in the wall, and I felt like it was watching me. It seemed to be imploring me to peer though it, so I turned away and looked at a woman approaching my seat. Something stirred inside me. I watched her casually. She glanced at me briefly and then sat down next to me. There was a half-finished cocktail of some kind on the bar in front of her. I figured she must have been sitting there before I arrived and had just got up to go to the toilet.

"Excuse me," I said, looking at her face.

Her eyes were large, with dark rings underneath, and her full lips were curled up slightly.

"I've got a hundred thousand yen here. Let's get a room."

"Huh?" She stared at me, the smile frozen on her face. She was wearing a short denim skirt and a black, long-sleeved T-shirt that showed the lines of her body.

"Are you some kind of freak?" she asked.

"Are you on your own?"

"Yes, but . . . What the hell?"

"So I'm saying I've got a hundred thousand yen, let's find a hotel. If that's not enough, let's make it two hundred."

After gazing at me for a bit longer, she burst out laughing.

"Seriously? Wow! That's the first time anyone's said anything like that to me. What are you up to? Are you crazy?"

"No?"

"Hold on a sec. Let me get this straight."

Still laughing, she finished her drink and ordered another in a loud voice. She was probably only a bit younger than I was. Suddenly I realized that I'd seen her in here before.

"Hey, the other day you were passed out at that table over there, and a black guy was trying to put his arms around you."

She looked me in the face.

"Yeah, that's right. That was a close call. I was sound asleep. He almost dragged me to that back room. I don't like foreigners. They're big."

"Big?"

"Their dicks. And they're bent."

She was watching me seriously.

"Really bent! Like they're alive. As bent as Kuwata's curve ball."

"Kuwata?"

"Used to play for the Giants. You must know him."

I nodded.

"Me, I'm a Hanshin Tigers fan," she continued. "My ex-ex-boyfriend was a Tigers fan and I ended up becoming one too. Now if you were a Hanshin fan as well, I wouldn't mind getting a room."

"You don't go off with a stranger for a stupid reason like that!"

"Hey, you invited me, remember?"

She laughed again. The people at the table behind us laughed too, but obviously not at the same thing.

"So you come to bars like this, hunt out girls who look like they might let you into their pants and start hitting on them? Do you do this often?"

"Not regularly. And I don't just talk to girls who look like they might let me into their pants. It's because you're kind of pretty."

"Nice of you to say so. Though I don't like that 'kind of' so much. But it was quite a good comeback. And the timing is perfect. I need money desperately right now. I need it but I'm flat broke, so I've been sulking and spending money on drinks. Seriously, I thought they'd kill me."

The bar's air conditioning was still bad and the room was thick with cigarette smoke. At a table in the distance a woman was crying hysterically and a man was laughing as he comforted her.

"Kill you?"

"For real. I really thought they would. And even if they didn't, I'd definitely have to work as a pro to pay it off, because I didn't borrow it from a regular bank. I'd rather have sex with you than a whole bunch of other guys."

She pushed her face close to mine.

"But you're weird. You're pretty good-looking, so if you'd chatted me up in the normal way you might have got it for nothing."

"That's okay. Let's go."

She continued to stare at my remodeled face, at Shintani's face.

WHEN WE GOT to the hotel room she started kissing my ears and neck, saying that she couldn't possibly ask for two hundred thousand, that my first offer of one hundred would do. I wanted to ask her to put on a white dress, but I missed my chance so I kept my mouth shut. When she asked my name I told her it was Shintani. For some reason she chuckled slightly and said it was funny. I pushed her onto the bed, taking off her clothes. I could smell alcohol on her breath. I put my tongue in her mouth, and accepted her tongue into mine.

While we were having sex, she kept looking at the big mirror next to the bed. She lowered her hips like a crawling dog, with me lying on top of her. As her cries grew louder, she whispered to me to push her head down.

"What?"

"It's okay, do it."

I forced her head down and she began to shriek, still watching the mirror.

"It feels like I'm being raped. I love it. You can be rougher if you like."

I pushed her head into the bed and gripped her neck.

"Yeah, like that. Hey," she said breathlessly, raising her voice. "Don't you get the feeling that all the people in the world are inside that mirror?"

She continued to stare at the glass as she gyrated her hips.

"Everyone's watching. Watching me now, being fucked like this by a guy I hardly know who gave me money. There'll be some men who are turned on, some women who are disgusted. So I want to show more of myself."

She started shouting, a smile on her face.

"While they're watching me . . . I reach a place no one can understand . . . I want to come over and over. With everyone watching me, and, and, I wish they'd all just die. Yeah, they can all die. All fucking die!"

She changed position and wound her arms tightly around my neck. For some reason her expression was full of sorrow.

IT WAS ONE o'clock in the morning. I realized that I must have fallen asleep for a while, so I got up and took a bottle of mineral water from the hotel room fridge. She was sitting up in bed, her breasts exposed, lazily reaching for the remote. The lighting had a bluish tinge and the room was quiet. When she turned on the TV, a photo of a missing boy appeared on the screen. She lit one of my cigarettes, blew out a plume of smoke. I missed my mouth and a trickle of water ran down my neck. The picture changed, and the Prime Minster was surrounded by reporters.

"Do you know about this?" she asked. "It's funny."

"What is?"

"This terrorist group."

The PM frowned in response to a question.

"There's this group doing strange things recently, isn't there? Like simultaneous explosions in different places. The ones calling themselves JL? They're on the news all the time. The media are condemning them, calling them 'The Invisible Terrorists,' but that's just spurring them on. It looks like there have already been copycats as well."

On the TV the interview was still going on.

"And now they've made a threat. 'We're going to assassinate all the politicians, starting with the baldest. If you want to stop us, the Prime Minister has to hold a press conference and do a perfect impression of the singer Hiromi Go.' Wouldn't that be hysterical?"

She laughed out loud.

"Really? That's crazy."

"Yeah. It'd be a riot."

She laughed again.

"I wonder if he'll do it?"

"I bet he won't. But it would be amazing if he did."

My cell phone rang and I reached for my jacket, still lying where I'd dropped it. I looked at the screen. The only people who knew this number were the detective and Azusa Konishi, but I didn't recognize the caller. When I pressed the button, I could hear a crowd of people, and for a few seconds there was just the sound of someone breathing on the other end.

"Fumihiro Kuki?"

A man's voice, someone I didn't know.

"Sorry?"

"Ha, good reaction. Well, talk to you later."

He hung up.

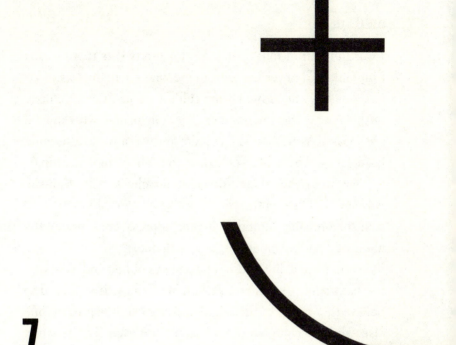

7

I REALIZED THAT I was still just standing there, so I sat on the bed. Out of the corner of my eye I could see my damp glass. I took a deep breath and reached for it. My heart was racing.

I picked up my cell phone again, hesitated for a second and then punched in the detective's number on the room phone instead. He answered in a low voice just before it switched to the recorded message. The music I could hear in the background stopped abruptly in mid-tune.

"Shintani here. Sorry to call so late."

"No problem. I was still up."

At that point it occurred to me that I'd never told him that

I was Fumihiro Kuki. Even if he was pretty sure that I wasn't Shintani, he'd never heard from me who I actually was.

"Someone called me on my cell phone just now. He obviously knew it was my number. The only people who know it are you and Azusa Konishi. Is there any way anyone else could have got hold of it, like you losing your phone or something?"

"Not from me, that's for sure. I'll check with Konishi. Anyway, I didn't enter your number under Shintani. And Konishi probably stored it in her address book under the name of a bar or something. I have no idea."

Without speaking, the woman got out of bed and went into the bathroom. I sat there, racking my brains. It was hard to believe that either of them had passed my number to anyone else. There was no benefit for them, and even if there were, they weren't stupid enough to do something that would be discovered straight away. I tried to relax.

"Well, please get in touch with Konishi right away, just in case. And I'll check if the number could have leaked at my end. I bought the phone from a job-hopping part-timer in town, so the contract isn't in my name. I bought his bank account as well. He has no idea who I am, of course."

"I'll contact Konishi. Have you got the man's number?"

"It wasn't blocked, so I still have it."

"Maybe he wants you to call him back?"

"Maybe."

I hung up and lay back on the bed. I couldn't work out how he knew my number, but more than that, how did he know I was Fumihiro Kuki? Even the plastic surgeon didn't know that, and nor did the former gang member I'd used to buy my current identity. He was a broker whose name I'd found in my father's secret papers, but we never did business face to face and I didn't tell him who I was.

I picked up my phone again and looked at the unknown man's number, still showing on the screen. My finger touched the button, but then I stopped. If I called him back I had the feeling that I'd be playing into his hands. The woman came out of the shower, naked, and looked at me. I left the cell phone alone.

"It suddenly seemed like you were in trouble."

"Yeah, thanks."

She put on a robe. It was white.

"You were talking like it didn't matter if I heard or not. Does that mean you're not going to see me again?"

"That's not it. I was so shocked that whether you heard was the least of my worries."

On the TV a man was weeping next to the rubble of a stone house. The flames visible under the debris glimmered red, stubbornly refusing to go out. *It was a fighter plane*, he mumbled between sobs. *A fighter plane did this. It was flying low, I could see the pilot.*

"Are you some kind of criminal?"

"Well, I'm no saint, that's for sure."

She stared at me.

"You were talking in your sleep."

"Was I?"

The strong blue light left her face in shadow.

"You were apologizing for something. Crying."

My pulse quickened.

"What was I saying?"

"I didn't really understand it, but you said something about handing over drugs. I'm sorry, you said, over and over, like a kid."

Suddenly I saw Yajima's face. But why should I be bothered about killing him?

"Is d'Alfaro the name of that bar? Then you were like, gonna die soon, gonna die soon, sorry."

I looked at her blankly. She had no reason to lie. Her face moved deeper into the shadow.

"If I really had murdered someone . . . You've got guts. If I thought you knew too much I might kill you too, right?"

"I don't think so. You won't kill me. And I wouldn't care if you did."

She sat on the bed, her robe still open, lost in thought. I decided to leave, so I took out my wallet and went to give her the hundred thousand yen. She watched me lazily.

"Are you going home? Oh, right. Look, I do need money, but . . ."

"Just think of it as a present if you like."

"I can't see it that way."

On the TV a building of some kind was sitting in the crosshairs of a gun. Probably it was file footage. The building crumbled in a white cloud.

"But that's fine. It's where I am at the moment. Hey, do you want to see me again?"

"Even if I'm a dangerous person to know?"

"I don't care. But a hundred thousand is too expensive for someone like me."

She laughed.

"No, money doesn't mean much to me," I said.

"Me, even if I no longer needed money, it would make no difference in the long run, because I'm always losing things. It's always been like that. Everything that's important to me, I lose them one after another. I wonder what will happen to me?"

A skinny old woman in a veil was glaring at the TV camera. A child with no arms and wearing a Yankees cap was laughing in response to some question.

"Hey, can I be your girlfriend? I wouldn't mind if I was your second or third pick to begin with."

"No, I'm not the person you think I am."

"Not interested?"

"I've had my face completely reconstructed."

The building continued to burn. As I stared vacantly at the orange flames, I wondered why I'd told her that so easily.

"Are you on the run or something?"

"No, not exactly."

She was still watching me. Her gaze seemed to penetrate right to the unstable core of my being, and I was lost for words. She thought for a moment.

"For someone who's had plastic surgery, you don't seem very attached to that face."

"I'm not really invested in it."

She approached softly.

"Hey, do you want to do it again? You don't have to pay."

In the distance I heard a police siren. When I put my arms around her, her back felt much frailer than it had before.

8

Aichi Prefecture Assemblyman Dies of Poison at Party

Mr. XX, a member of the Aichi Prefectural Assembly, collapsed suddenly about 8 P.M. yesterday at a party in Nagoya. He was taken to a hospital by ambulance, but was pronounced dead soon after arrival. As soon as he tasted his beer after the opening toast, he was seen to collapse. The deadly poison aconitine was detected in his body. There had been suspicions that he had been receiving illegal contributions, and the authorities had just begun a thorough investigation.

• • •

"THIS NEWS JUST in. Mr. YY, a member of the House of Representatives, has died at a hospital in Tokyo. He was visiting the Tokyo Independent Vocational Center when he collapsed suddenly while eating lunch. He was taken to hospital and received treatment, but passed away a short time ago. Traces of aconitine poison were found in his system. It appears to be similar to the substance that was used in the murder of a Prefectural Assembly member in Aichi Prefecture. The metropolitan police have opened an investigation, including whether there is any connection to JL, who had issued threats."

While I was looking at the newspaper, the TV announcer hurriedly read out a piece of paper he'd been handed. I turned up the volume a little. The commentator sitting next to the newsreader started to speak, leaning forward and drawing his eyebrows together.

"I think it may be premature to assume that this crime is the work of JL. Until now they have caused damage to property, but have not targeted people. I think a thorough investigation is required."

THE DOOR OF the hotel room opened and the detective came in. He glanced at the TV for a second and then sat down on the sofa opposite me. Cold air from outside seemed to emanate from his suit. He looked rather tired.

"I'm very sorry," he said, lowering his head. "Konishi lost her cell phone for a few minutes without realizing it. At around lunchtime that day she called you about Ms. Kaori. She was in a café, and after the call she went to the toilet, paid her bill and left. Of course she thought she had her phone with her the whole time. Immediately afterwards, however, the waitress came running after her with a phone, asking if it was hers. Another customer had picked it up from under her table, so she knew she'd dropped it, but thought it had only been missing for a few seconds. Even when I talked to her, at first she denied it and only remembered later. It seemed like such an insignificant event."

My mind whirled.

"If that's what happened," he continued, "it means that someone must have stolen the cell phone while she was in the café. Then the thief gave it to the waitress so that Konishi would think that she'd just dropped it, not that it had been lifted. She hadn't stored your number under your name—it was listed as a bar. But she had called you just before, and she probably mentioned Kaori's name several times. Someone must have been nearby, listening to the conversation. If they stole it after that and looked at the call history, they could easily find out the number of the person she was talking to."

"In other words . . ."

"Someone has been tailing me or Konishi. And whoever it is knows that we are investigating Ms. Kaori."

At that moment the TV newsroom grew hectic. There was a babble of voices from off camera and someone handed the announcer a sheet of paper.

"Apparently the group calling itself JL have just claimed responsibility for the murders," he said.

"Is it really JL?" the commentator demanded. "It could be a copycat."

"They've confirmed that it's genuine. When JL claim responsibility, they normally use a code word in the letter, one that hasn't been released to the public. It matches. The communiqué was faxed a short while ago to 'News Run.' I'll read it out."

He took a breath.

"This is JL. Okay, we said the Prime Minister had to do an impression, right? No good standing on his dignity, he's got to do it. By the way, we might start going after people now. If the PM doesn't do an impression at a press conference, we'll start targeting ordinary citizens next. No, we're just kidding. Most likely the next people will be other politicians—in order of baldness. But if he still doesn't do it, civilians really might get caught up in it. We hate happy people, so we might start with the ones who look happiest. Happiness is a fortress. Get it? You don't? Oh, well."

I stared at the screen with a sense of dread as the announcer started to read the proclamation again. Happiness is a fortress. My father's face appeared before me. What did it mean? I felt a headache coming on. The detective was speaking.

"I always wonder if it's a good idea to read the statement out like that. Isn't that what they want? Well, I suppose that news of groups like JL will make the ratings skyrocket, and during the recession the media . . . Mr. Shintani?"

He was looking closely at my face. Just as I was deciding how to respond, my cell phone rang. Somehow it sounded louder than usual. When I looked at the display it was the man who had called me Fumihiro. I glanced at the detective, suddenly nervous.

"It's the same guy. The one who called me before."

He took a black ballpoint from his bag.

"We can record him with this."

I held it close to the phone and pressed the Talk button. From the other end I could hear the bustle of a crowd of people.

"Fumihiro Kuki?"

It was the same voice.

"I thought maybe you'd call me back, but I also knew you were very patient."

"Um, I don't know what you're talking about."

The room seemed to be gradually getting colder.

"A long line of cancers."

"Huh?"

"You're not exactly living up to the tradition, are you? Just a stalker!"

"Who is this?"

He laughed.

"Okay, so that's how you want to play it. Let's meet up."

He raised his voice slightly.

"Tomorrow at six o'clock. Nishiguchi Park in Ikebukuro."

"And if I refuse?"

"Then something bad will happen to Kaori. See you."

The phone went dead.

By now the room was freezing. I wondered what the hell this was all about. How did he know me? I cringed at that word "cancer." I was sure I'd never heard the voice on the phone before, and I had no idea who he was or what he wanted.

The detective was studying me. I realized that I still hadn't told him I was Fumihiro. My heart was thudding erratically.

"Can I borrow this pen for a while?"

"You click the top to record, and if you take off the cap there's a plug so you can connect it to a computer to play it back."

"I'll work on this guy for a bit. I'd like you to stick with my—Shintani's—past."

I stood up. He opened his mouth to speak, but didn't say anything as I left the room.

9

I HAD A dream.

I was sitting on a high-backed chair in a room so big I couldn't see the walls. Directly in front of me six empty chairs, solidly built and slightly larger than mine, were arranged in a line. They made me feel the difference in our relative power and status.

I'd been waiting for a long time for someone to come. For someone to come and sit in those chairs. For some reason I knew that this place was where my whole life would be judged. It was freezing but I didn't feel the cold.

I kept on waiting for the beings who would summarize my life in this vast and icy place, empty except for the chairs. No matter how long I waited, however, no one appeared. I was completely abandoned. Solemnly, calmly, the air around me grew colder.

When I woke I was sweating. My body was soaked with individual beads of perspiration, each clamoring urgently for attention. I remembered Kaori in a white dress searching my room for porn. I remembered thinking about all sorts of things—my future with her, building a house by the sea and living there, not passing on my melancholy to our children, what I should do when we quarreled. On the screen Kaori was chatting with Azusa Konishi in a bar. The recording was set on continuous play. I stood up, still watching the video, feeling like I'd come a long way.

NISHIGUCHI PARK IN Ikebukuro was busy. I walked past a group of homeless men drinking and looked around. Hidden at the bottom of my bag was the bottle containing the poison I'd given to Yajima. Maybe that was why I had so little energy. A mixture of powders, with potassium cyanide as the main ingredient. My body grew heavier, but my vision cleared. Among the crowd in the park, however, I couldn't tell who the caller was. I took out my cell phone and dialed his number.

Far away, a man sitting on a chain that formed part of the fence started hunting in his pocket. A black daypack was slung over his shoulder. He was wearing acid-washed designer jeans, a loose gray knit cap, a sleeveless white down jacket and a long-sleeved T-shirt of the same color, covered in English writing. I ended the call and walked towards him.

He was still young, with narrow eyes and a thin nose, an oddly clean-cut face. He was staring at his phone, which had stopped ringing abruptly. I stood beside him, conscious of the drugs in my bag.

He turned slowly to face me. His neatly trimmed eyebrows suddenly drew together as though I'd taken him by surprise.

"What do you want?" he demanded.

The rain had just stopped, and the ground was still unpleasantly damp.

"What do you mean? You told me to come here."

He glared at me for a second.

"What?"

"You called me here, didn't you?" I repeated. "What the hell is this?"

"You? But the voice is the same. How come?"

I looked at him blankly. "What are you talking about?"

"Aren't you Kuki, Fumihiro Kuki?"

I thought for a moment, trying to make sense of the situation.

Looking up at me, he went on. "Who the hell are you? Why are you checking up on Kaori Kuki?"

I realized that he was genuinely puzzled. He knew about Fumihiro, the person I used to be, but maybe he didn't know about my plastic surgery or that I'd bought Shintani's persona. I hesitated, thinking furiously. I couldn't understand how he knew about Fumihiro, how he knew about Kaori, how he knew my number. I'd have to worm it out of him.

"You summoned me here. What's your game? And how did you get my number? That's what I'd like to know."

He continued to stare at me.

"I don't get you," I went on. "I don't know what you're up to, but we're getting out of here."

"I'll decide where we go," he said, standing up at last.

WE WALKED PAST a police box, turned left at a convenience store and went into a different park. It was dirty, full of homeless people's light blue tarpaulin shelters. I thought we were heading to a coffee shop or something, but he sat on a bench, took a bottle of mineral water from his backpack and started to drink. It was a brand I hadn't seen before. I perched on the same bench, leaving a space between us. When I lit a cigarette he frowned rudely, then turned his gaze to my bag.

"I'm warning you," he said. "Don't do anything stupid."

"Stupid?"

"Why are you carrying that so carefully?"

He was still looking at my pack.

"Why, are you chicken?"

"Just so you know, even though you can only see one of me, I'm not the only one watching you."

I stared straight at him. There was no way I was going to look around, let him call the play. I thought back to what I'd seen on the way here. Apart from the homeless guys, there had been a number of people, male and female, laughing in a friendly fashion in front of the convenience store on the other side of the fence. There were also two cars parked on the street directly behind me.

"Would you like to see what I've got in here?" I taunted.

A dusty, gritty wind started to blow. He began to speak, then fell silent and looked away.

"Okay," I said, "there's lots of things I want to ask you, but first, tell me what you're after. You must have had some reason for phoning me. What was it?"

He stayed quiet, head bowed.

"I asked you what it was. If you're not going to answer, I'm leaving."

"Before I tell you," he said after a long pause, "who are you?"

I noticed for the first time that his skin was abnormally pale. He had a white wristband on his left arm and two hoop earrings. I chose my words carefully.

"You called me here, and you're asking me who I am? The first thing you said on the phone, you called me Fumihiro Kuki. Then you said that if I didn't come you'd hurt Kaori. In other words, you tried to threaten this Fumihiro by bringing up the name of this Kaori woman. And then someone different turns up. Am I close? So what are you after? Money? You've worked out that I've been checking up on Kaori. If you tell me what you know, I'm happy to pay you, if that's what you want. Who is Fumihiro? Kaori's brother?"

He didn't move, just kept looking at the ground. His expression didn't change, but he seemed to be thinking.

"What do you want? Money?"

"Yeah," he spat. "Money."

"What's your name?"

"That's not important."

"Okay then, we're done talking. I don't talk to people I

don't know. You can't use Kaori to intimidate me. If you need money, try someone else."

I stood up.

"I told you I wasn't the only one watching you," he said.

"So they're going to attack me? In a public place like this? You're dumber than I thought."

"My name is Ito."

I looked at him, shocked. My heart started to beat faster.

"And your first name?"

"Last name's enough."

An idea struck me.

"Okay . . . are you from a family of cancers?"

He looked me full in the face.

"I get it," I continued. "So that's how it is. And maybe you're JL, is that right? In that case . . ."

"How do you know that? What is this?"

He leapt to his feet, mouth open. I sat down again and tried to gather my thoughts. This place was starting to get to me. I lit a cigarette to calm my nerves.

"If you are," I went on, "then I see how you know about Kaori and Fumihiro. I lied before. I know Fumihiro Kuki too. I'm a . . . Let's just say I know him."

"You know him? Where is he?"

"He's dead."

"Dead?"

"Suicide. There was this woman he was obsessed with. I was intrigued, so I thought I'd check her out."

He sank onto the bench again.

"So he's dead?"

"Yeah."

"Idiot," he shouted.

I was taken aback by his sudden outburst, but I kept a poker face.

"That's so lame. If he was going to die he could at least have blown up his house first. Loser."

His face had turned slightly red. I watched him, continuing to pick my words carefully.

"So I know some stuff about the Kuki family. That's if Fumihiro was telling the truth. I know the story of the cancer line too, that branch of the clan. This one guy was a soldier, and when he got married he took his wife's surname, Ito. He was killed when that cult took over the nuclear power plant, but according to Fumihiro he might already have had a son. It's a common name, but seeing how you know so much about the Kukis, it all fits."

"And what makes you think I'm in JL?"

"When I heard the line 'Happiness is a fortress' in the statement claiming responsibility for the attacks, I remembered hearing Fumihiro say it. It's not exactly a popular expression. I did some research on it later and found that even though it's peculiar, JL sometimes use it in their communiqués. That's when I thought that maybe someone connected to the Kukis is in JL. And if I'm right, it's not hard to guess that they're from that separate cancer line. When I thought about what you were probably after, it was easy to put two and two together. The press is always trying to work out who funds JL. In other words, you knew Fumihiro was rich and you were using Kaori to try and blackmail him. And with a bit of luck you thought you could get him to join you. Am I right? Fumihiro was a cancer too. He can't have had much of a life. What's more, for the pranks you're pulling, you've got to the stage where you need funds. You need a backer. Isn't that how it is?"

The rain started again fitfully. We sat side by side on the bench, a bit apart, looking straight ahead. Two homeless guys were arguing over the water fountain. In their hands they were both holding battered teakettles.

"If I tell you what I know, will you really give me money?"

"That depends what you say. Tell me about Kaori as well."

He took a deep breath and turned to face me.

"You're nuts. I still don't exactly get why you were checking up on Kaori, but it's, I don't know, creepy. Going to the trouble of hiring a PI to investigate her, even looking into the family background. But just for that reason maybe there's still a chance. Perhaps we can talk about that. Just a bit, though."

"Still a chance?"

"We'll discuss it later."

The homeless men were still quarreling. Ito took a swig from his bottle.

"Like you say, I'm what the Kukis call a cancer. From that side of the family. You know that much already, so there's no point hiding it. Like you said, my father was a leader of the Rahmla cult, that bunch of morons who committed suicide. But that's not important."

The rain grew heavier.

"So it's true that I'm in JL. For various reasons, we need money just now. Really urgently. I've had my eye on the Kukis, the main line of the family who we've hated for years. Ever since I was little I've often gone to peek at their mansion. Not out of envy. Out of hatred."

He fiddled with his wristband.

"There were two kids there, about the same age. They looked happy. Fumihiro and the one you've been watching, Kaori. They seemed close. Sometimes one of the housemaids who knew my circumstances, what's her name, she would slip me a bit of money or some sweets. I asked her. She told me that Kaori was adopted and that Fumihiro was Shozo Kuki's son, not his grandson. That rang a bell. The old man was following the custom of the cancers. That got me interested. From time to time I'd go to spy on Fumihiro, but then my situation changed and I couldn't leave the house for a while. The next time I saw him he was in high school. It was amazing. He was like a different person."

I got a sinking feeling in the pit of my stomach, but was careful not to let it show.

"He'd shrunk, and he looked like an invalid. Really ugly. Did you notice that too? He was the spitting image of the old man. Something bad has happened to him, I thought. Actually, maybe I should have talked to him then. Both of us being cancers, maybe we'd have found we had something in common."

He was still looking at the ground, unmoving.

"I joined JL. We were strapped for cash, and by chance I saw Kaori on the street. A weird coincidence, it was almost scary. I figured I might be able to get some money out of her, because I thought she still had ties to the Kukis. But someone was tailing her. A private eye. I knew him. He used to work for Shozo Kuki. A long time ago he was asking questions about me, I don't know why. That got me thinking. Since Shozo had disappeared and was probably dead, maybe this time it had been Fumihiro who hired him. Another detective, a woman, was secretly filming Kaori in a bar. Not doing anything special, just her daily routine. I thought there must be romance in there somewhere. Apparently Fumihiro had gone missing, but I thought he might be stalking her on the sly. And I thought that could work out well for us. If I could team up with him, money wouldn't be a problem anymore. Since I figured his life was probably pretty twisted, I thought we might get on. One of our gang is light-fingered, so I got him to tail the woman detective, and he saw her calling someone who was probably her client. The easiest person to tail is someone who's tailing someone else. She was saying something about photos and recordings of Kaori. He stole her cell phone for a few minutes and looked at her call history for the time she made that call. I was willing to bet that number would be Fumihiro's."

He sighed and started playing with his water bottle.

"But I was too hasty. I made up my mind too quickly, even though my hunches are usually right. But it's okay, this interesting guy turned up. I've decided to let you join us. You're crazy, aren't you? I can smell it."

"Join you? No way."

He laughed.

"But you seem really interested."

His cell phone rang and he looked at the screen. It seemed to be an email, and he frowned slightly. Though I was nervous about my surroundings, I couldn't show it by looking around. I could see two men who hadn't been there before, in front of the office block on the other side of the fence, but they soon disappeared behind the building.

"And we're not exactly peace-loving. We don't care what we do to Kaori. Don't worry, I'm not trying to threaten you. You look like a prickly bastard, and I guess threats wouldn't work anyway. If money isn't an issue for you, just a donation from time to time would be fine. You can afford to hire Shozo Kuki's private eye, and looking at your clothes, you'd probably hardly even notice it. If you helped us we'd show you some good stuff."

"What are you up to, exactly?"

He stood up, still holding his phone, and stowed the water bottle in his pack.

"We're attacking all accepted values. Authority, class differences, shared perceptions. We don't care what happens to the social structure—revolutions are for suckers. Our target is people's collective consciousness. It's like throwing a cream pie in their face."

By now it was raining quite heavily.

"Come see me again, and I'll give you some specific examples. You're not the type to tell the cops. You're not a loser. You hate people, don't you? And you don't give a damn about society. I can see it in your face. I've got a gift for spotting kindred spirits. But I'll tell you one thing. If we move right away from ethics and morality and common sense, a completely different world will emerge. Sort of as a bonus. Okay, see you."

And he walked off, getting soaked by the rain. Maybe it was

just a coincidence, but while I wasn't looking the people outside the convenience store had gone, and so had the cars behind me. Ito was already a long way off and I didn't have the energy to follow him. The homeless guys' battle over the drinking fountain was growing louder. The bottle of cyanide in my bag suddenly felt heavy again.

I WENT INTO a run-down bar with blue lighting and asked for whiskey. Parking myself on a stool with uneven legs, I rested my elbows on the counter. I'm not sure why but I got drunk quickly. Faint jazz was playing on the sound system. I couldn't make out a melody.

I wondered what Shintani thought of his own life when he was alive, before I took his identity, turning the question over idly in my head. Had he really killed Sae Suzuki? If he had, I'd end up being hunted by the police for something I hadn't done. I had a vision of Aida's slit-like eyes and remembered that he was involved in the Yajima investigation too. As my PI had said, if the police found out that I really did have a connection to Yajima, I'd be in trouble. If Aida worked out that I was Fumihiro and that I was keeping an eye on Kaori, he'd immediately draw a line from me to Yajima, with Kaori right in the middle. So together with Sae's death, Aida might end up hounding me either way, if stopped being Shintani or if I stayed as I was.

I had murdered my father, who had fully intended to make me experience hell, and taken another person's face and identity. You could say that everything had become weirdly distorted because I'd broken the rules so many times. I hadn't expected to meet someone from the cancer line like that. Ito had said that he'd sometimes come to spy on the estate. He'd seen me when Kaori and I were living in peace, and also when, as he put it, "Something bad had happened to me." I thought about what kind of life he must have led. Before my father had died at my hands he had talked about "an even greater evil." Certainly I was surprised that Ito was a member of JL, but given his background, perhaps it wasn't so odd after all. For one thing, his father was a leader of Rahmla. And he'd asked me to team up. I wasn't sure what to do about him. Plus I was watching over Kaori, and I didn't know what I was going to do there either. I had no idea why I was doing all this stuff when I was trying not to exist. Nor did I understand why I'd ended up crying in my sleep for murdering Yajima, as that woman had told me.

The plastic surgeon claimed that fate was driven by the combination of people's character, heredity and environment, and those of the people around them. I didn't know where those threads would lead, or how much they knew, but I thought that over time they must lead somewhere. What would happen in the future? What would I do? What would happen to me? I was raised by my father to be a cancer, so Kaori and I should have been doomed from the start. We'd dodged that, but I'd paid a price for it. However, in the perverted life caused by my violations of society's rules, I'd committed more violations, so presumably in the future I'd grow even more perverted. Did I break the rules deliberately? Was that my tendency?

As my vision blurred with drunkenness, I phoned the

woman I'd picked up in the d'Alfaro. After six rings she answered in a quiet voice. The background was raucous, and I figured she was in a bar somewhere.

"Um, it's me. I mean, we met the other day . . ."

"Ah."

The noise died away.

"Look, I was wondering if we could meet now? Of course I'll pay you."

"That's okay . . . hey."

She must have moved somewhere because there was no sound at all.

"The other day you didn't tell me your number, but now I can see it clear as day."

"Ah." I snickered. I figured that letting her see my number was just an aberration, not deliberate. "Yeah, I guess I slipped up."

"Are you drunk? Where are you?"

"Ikebukuro, but I'll come to you. You in a bar?"

"Yeah, but I'm just leaving. I'm in Shibuya."

"Okay, in front of the station. Thirty minutes."

I hung up and tried to stand. I was definitely a bit drunk. I paid my bill and as I headed through the low doorway my cell phone rang again. I thought she was calling me back to tell me that something had come up, but it was the detective.

"I've found out who it is, the person investigating Ms. Kaori."

"What?"

"I couldn't tell by looking at the company's list of board members, but the principal shareholder is Mikihiko Kuki."

My older brother, the second son.

"He doesn't have a good reputation. Not at all."

I realized that I'd half expected this, but my pulse still started to beat faster. So it was the Kukis after all, I thought. Everyone dancing in the shadows around Kaori was connected to the Kuki family.

"Can you find out more about this Mikihiko?"

"Yes."

"Tell me if you need any extra expenses. I don't care how much it costs."

"Understood. And about the missing cell phone—I think he was following me because he recognized me from somewhere. He found out about Azusa Konishi as well."

"No, that was someone else."

"Someone else?"

"Yes. I'll take care of that, so you please concentrate on Mikihiko. I want you to find out all about him."

"Got it."

I ended the call and left the bar. My head was killing me.

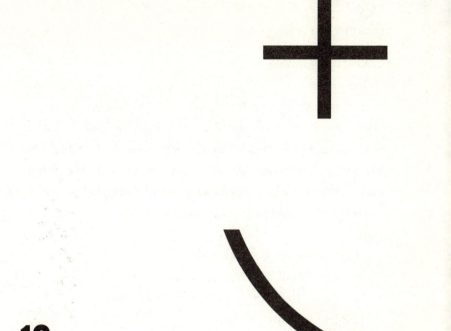

10

THE FUZZY GREEN light gradually resolved itself into trees, and a narrow street of damp terra-cotta bricks stretched lazily into the distance. Curled up in the darkness, she was tinged with that green and russet glow. The gentle tones shone only on the spot where she was sitting, casting deeper shadows in the gloom behind her. It took me a moment or two to work out that she was watching a movie on TV. Kyoko Yoshioka, that was her name.

A slender foreign woman appeared on the screen. She stared out at us expressionlessly, not with a Mona Lisa smile encompassing everything, but with a blank face that rejected all meaning.

"Oh, you're awake."

"Yeah."

The woman on the television was still looking at me. I didn't know what to make of her. I felt a shiver of fear, and then realized that the picture had changed back to the wet street scene some time ago. Or perhaps she had never been there in the first place. My head was still thick with sleep.

"Hey, you should put some clothes on," I said. "Aren't you cold?"

"I like not wearing any clothes."

The pale skin of her back seemed to float in the darkness.

"This movie, it's nice to look at but it's very slow."

I chuckled. "Yeah, maybe."

She scratched her neck lightly as if she were thinking.

"I tend to watch stuff like this using my own frame of reference," she said. "Anything outside that I don't like."

"Mm."

"But someone told me I'd never broaden my horizons like that, that it was a waste, that I'd miss out on the small details. It would be nice if I could expand my horizons a little bit at a time, though."

"But just realizing that is pretty impressive."

"This man told me, in an institution I was in a long time ago. He was nice. He showed me lots of stuff. Books and movies and music."

"Well, it's a little surprising."

She was smiling. I could still feel the alcohol in my system from the night before and my temples ached.

"So you watch this kind of stuff?" she asked.

"Yeah, recently. A little bit at a time."

Lately I'd been working my way through Shintani's movies.

"And those books?"

She pointed at the bookcase.

"Yeah, those are new too, so I've only read a few of them."

They were mostly foreign classics.

"Until now," I continued, "I've been completely wrapped up inside my head. We use words to think, don't we? The people who wrote those, they're thinking about nothing but words. While everyone else is doing all sorts of different things, those writers are just thinking about life, about words. When I read their words, I don't know how to explain it, I thought I wanted to expand my own thoughts. I've been too narrow-minded."

"Hmm. Have you read anything that really inspired you?"

"I've only just started. But before I get enlightened, I feel like the world is rapidly becoming more complicated. I don't know if I can catch up."

For some reason her face softened.

"But books like that must be difficult."

"They sure are. And they're pretty old. But I think they're still relevant to today's society."

The movie ended and the credits began to roll.

"I am cold after all," she said, and came back to bed. "But hey, you realize that you let me see where you live?"

"Yeah, I did, didn't I?"

"I thought you were hiding something, but . . . are you all right? Don't you think you've been careless?"

Certainly I'd been getting lax lately.

"I bet you've always been really careful, haven't you? You've got to keep on being careful."

"Maybe it's because I'm getting tired. Bad, eh?"

The room was slowly cooling down. When I thought about it, the only people who'd been in this apartment were the cop, Aida, and her. My exposed skin felt dry. Suddenly I remembered the dream I'd been having. I was outside, somewhere with no sign of people. No towns, no buildings, no evidence of humans at all, dark and barren as far as the eye could see. It had been cold there too, cold enough for me to start worrying about what would happen if the temperature dropped any further. Gray clouds hung low in the sky, so dense I could feel their weight. As I stood in that desolate place, I thought it could have been anywhere.

"It's because you're different. I tell you stuff."

"If you like me, why don't you let me be your girlfriend?"

"I told you, I changed my face. I'm actually ugly."

"That doesn't matter, does it? After all, it was your choice."

"And because I killed someone."

She looked at me blankly. "Hang on. You spring that on me out of the blue like that?"

"What?"

I was watching her face, wondering what I was saying. My pulse, however, didn't waver.

"Is that your ego talking? Does it turn you on?"

I noticed that she'd snuggled a little closer to me in the bed.

"I wonder. I don't know."

I stared at the ceiling, puzzling over why I was so calm.

"When I was I kid, I thought I'd do whatever it took to protect the most important thing in the world to me."

I breathed in slowly.

"I was still just a child, but even then I knew that doing so would ruin my life. But I did it anyway, because that thing meant everything to me. Even if I weighed everything else in my life against it, I was dazzled. And in fact I did become twisted. I could never be at peace. It was obvious that would happen, but at the time I couldn't think of any alternative."

"Was this to do with someone called Kaori?"

"What? I did it again?"

"Yes, you were talking in your sleep again. This time it was just her name."

I turned on the heater. She moved even closer to me.

"After I changed my face, it was a weird feeling. I felt like I was already dead. I thought I'd become one of the thirty thousand people who kill themselves every year in this country, that I was a living corpse. I felt so detached, from myself and from my life so far. Everything seemed so clear. Looking back, perhaps I enjoyed it. Losing all my hopes and desires, just being an observer, it gave me a strange sense of relief. But then I went and did the same thing all over again."

I could feel her eyes on me.

"It turns out I'm still alive after all. I get hungry, I sweat, I still like feeling a woman's touch, like this. My bodily functions and desires, they were distasteful, but I can't help them. They make me aware of my own life. It feels like life is forcing itself on me, lifting me up. But I ruined the lives of people who were just like me. Whenever I feel life stirring inside me,

I remember that I killed others who felt the same stirrings. This contradiction, I think it's twisting me even more. It doesn't matter what kind of people I harmed, it makes no difference. You said I was talking in my sleep. That's one of the consequences. That brief feeling I had of being an observer faded rapidly, and what I did festers inside me. Every day I grow wearier and wearier. Like you said, I have nightmares and I get careless. The human mind is weak—they often say that the conscious is the slave of the subconscious. So in the long run I'm slowly growing distorted from the inside out, from my subconscious. Maybe I'm rejecting myself as someone who's killed another human being, I don't know. But at the same time I think this feeling is important. If you watch the news, you see people who are killed wantonly, people who kill wantonly, don't you? War is the same. Somehow I get the feeling that this sense of distortion is important for us. It's something fundamental about this world."

I could feel the warmth of her body next to mine.

"But what puzzles me is why you aren't running away as fast as you can."

She looked at me in surprise. "Why would I do that?"

"Isn't it obvious?"

"My life hasn't been so sheltered that I'll suddenly get scared by a story like that." Casually she took hold of my fingers.

"In costume dramas and cartoons," I continued slowly, "when the bad guy gets killed everybody cheers. In real life it seems like it's not that easy. I don't know why, but Japan seems to be full of stories and games and stuff where people get killed and no one seems upset, even though they teach that killing people is wrong. But in real life . . ."

"But even if life is hard, you mustn't die," she said quietly. "I don't know all the details about what happened, but you've got to get over it."

"Get over it?"

"That's right. Because here and now you're alive."

She put her arms gently around me.

"Did you know this?" she went on. "Every year far more people kill themselves in Japan than die through war or terrorism in Iraq. We go on and on about other countries, but I think Japanese society is pretty cruel too."

She took a deep breath.

"Let's sleep like this today. From a distance we'll look like a contented couple."

"You're weird, you know that?"

"It's just that I don't like the world very much."

When I woke the next morning, Mikihiko Kuki's secretary was standing outside my apartment.

PART 4

PRESENT

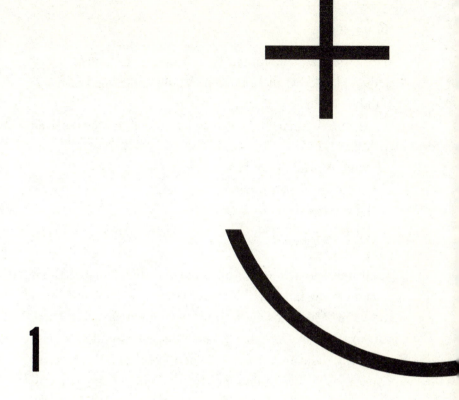

1

WHEN THE DOORBELL rang, I was still in bed and Kyoko was sitting at the table watching TV. The news was reporting on Diet members who'd secretly taken to wearing wigs after JL threatened to assassinate politicians in order of baldness. One guest, a young politician, was calling it pitiful. Another, a self-declared liberal, said that the PM should do the imitation of Hiromi Go, a comment that infuriated the third guest, a member of the conservative party. The directors of a chemical plant where three employees had died of overwork had all suffered food poisoning at a nightclub, and it was suspected that JL was behind it. I ignored the bell but it just kept on ringing, echoing through the apartment. Kyoko, who was laughing at the news, gradually turned to look at me. I climbed out of bed and looked at the intercom. A tall middle-aged man was standing there.

"Koichi Shintani?" he asked as soon as I lifted the receiver.

"What is it?"

"Mikihiko Kuki would like to meet you."

I could feel Kyoko's eyes on my back.

"I don't know him."

"Please get ready," he said, completely ignoring me. "The car is waiting."

He fell silent. I was a bit unnerved, but I realized that more than anything that I was just weary. The moment I heard the name Mikihiko, my fatigue grew much stronger. I was sure that no matter what I said, this guy would just keep repeating the same message. When I replaced the receiver Kyoko was still watching me. In the light seeping through the curtains her skin looked white.

"I'm going out for while."

"Is everything okay?"

"Maybe."

I started to get changed.

"What should I do?"

"If you've got things to do you can go home, but you can stay here if you like."

"But if I stay here, you know I'm going to go snooping around, at your computer and stuff."

"That's okay. Anyway, I don't think you will."

"You should be more careful."

When I opened the front door the man gestured for me

to walk ahead of him. I could feel his looming presence. I remembered stories of jailers accompanying prisoners like this, walking behind so they could keep an eye on them.

WE GOT INTO a black car, expensive but tasteless, and drove slowly along the dark road. The streetlights were just coming on. There was a matte cigarette case in the car but I lit one of my own instead. I saw that the smoke bothered him and he opened the window, so I made up my mind to keep smoking until we arrived.

"Why does this guy Kuki want to see me?"

The man didn't reply. No response at all, not even a shrug.

"What's he like? Just give me your impression."

"Mr. Shintani," he said, still facing ahead and gripping the steering wheel.

I noticed that he had a dark red scar on his neck.

"It's not my job to answer your questions. Mikihiko Kuki told me to bring you to him, and that's all I'm doing. I wasn't told to be polite. Just to deliver you."

He didn't overtake any other cars, nor give way to them.

"Obviously we are in close proximity at the moment, but that doesn't mean we have to establish any kind of relationship. Is that understood?"

What a hard-ass. I just kept blowing smoke at him without saying anything.

WE GOT OUT of the car in front of the Lille Durant Hotel and took the elevator to the top floor. He swiped a card key through a scanner to open the automatic glass doors. "At the back, on the right," he said from behind me, and when we reached the room he stretched out an arm and rang the bell. An indistinct voice came from inside. My heart rate, which had been gradually increasing as we came closer, grew even more ragged. The voice sounded exactly like my father's.

The man opened the door and we entered. I saw a carpet, garish under the dim lighting, a white table with white chairs. The rough, vulgar chandelier was unlit and some potted plants, struggling to grow in the restricted space, glowed pale orange under the indirect lighting. On the wall opposite was a painting, too big for the room, of a lake that looked like a pit. Behind the low table was a black sofa, and sitting on it was a man in a black tracksuit. I thought it was Father. My body went rigid, as though it had tensed of its own accord. He was tall, much bigger than Father, but if my father were fifty years old the similarity would have been remarkable. With a large nose and eyes that slanted down at the corners, he should have been ugly, but somehow his face had a kind of dignified balance. Even from a distance I could tell that his clothes were made of expensive fabric.

"That will do," he said quietly.

"But—" protested the driver.

"It's fine. Go home."

The man who had brought me here bowed low and silently left the room.

For some reason the picture of the lake had really grabbed my attention. The man gazed expressionlessly at me, not saying a word, as I stood in the doorway. The orange lights threw random shadows around the room. I moved slowly towards him, doing my best to stay calm. The closer I got, the more he looked like my father. I stood before the sofa with the table between us, staring at him. My pulse just wouldn't settle. I felt I was reliving all those memories of being summoned to Father's study. A bottle of whiskey and a glass with spiral patterns etched in it cast long shadows on the table.

"What can I do for you?" I asked.

My throat was incredibly dry. His dark form seemed like the wreckage of something huge and soft.

"You brought me here, remember? If we've got no business then I'm leaving."

"It's so depressing."

He watched me lazily, leaning back in the couch. He was big-boned but, cloaked in languor, he showed no energy at all.

"Koichi Shintani, eh?"

The corners of his mouth turned up slightly.

"You've done well. Nice to meet you, Fumihiro."

Suddenly I felt like I was suffocating. He didn't take his eyes off me.

"I don't know what you're talking about," I said.

"That won't work. Tricks like that, they never work with me."

Even though I'd half expected this, the strength in my legs deserted me. Confronted with his bland gaze I had no idea what to do.

"Have a seat. Something to drink?"

"I'm fine."

"Relax. You must be thirsty."

Slowly he stood and took a beer from the fridge. When he moved, his blurred shadow danced on the wall behind him.

"Everyone who meets me seems to get nervous. It's not me they're afraid of. It's the hell inside me. Especially now. It's really depressing."

I sat on the couch and looked directly at him. He wasn't drunk, but he reminded me of Father when he was intoxicated. His skin was dark, as though the dullness was oozing out from inside, and I couldn't read the emotion in his clouded eyes. I sank deep into the sofa, feeling uncomfortable. It was like the couch was alive, holding me in place with its strange, soft springiness.

In the quiet of the room I was aware of a faint ringing in my ears. He continued to sip his whiskey without speaking. I opened my beer. He reacted slightly to the sound of the cap coming off, turned his dead eyes on me as though he was surprised. But he still just kept drinking in silence. I lit a cigarette, unpleasantly aware of the sofa subsiding beneath me. Finally he opened his mouth again.

"I'm in the war business."

His voice was extremely low.

"You're going to work for me."

"Why?"

"No special reason."

He sighed. His muddy eyes were pointed in my direction, but he seemed to be looking right through me.

"Do you know the story of Nayirah?"

"Not really."

He set his glass on the table. His speech was very slow.

"In 1990, when Saddam Hussein of Iraq invaded neighboring Kuwait, the USA called a simple young woman from Kuwait to testify at the Congressional Human Rights Caucus."

His face betrayed no emotion, only his thick lips moving.

"She spoke of how cruelly the Iraqi soldiers were acting in Kuwait. She spoke of how they had ripped new-born babies from their incubators in the hospital and left them to die. America—no, the whole world—shook with rage. A UN force led by the US started aerial bombing to drive the Iraqi army out of Kuwait. The Gulf War."

Slumped on the sofa, he droned on in his low voice.

"But afterwards it came to light that it had all been a lie. Nayirah was really the daughter of Kuwait's ambassador to the US, and her whole story had been scripted by a PR firm. It turned into a huge scandal, reported all over the news, though it was only discovered after the war was over."

He sighed again as though he was bored, and slowly reached for the whiskey bottle.

"There are two main ways of making money."

I couldn't tell where the conversation was heading.

"One is to develop an attractive product or service and to exchange it for the money in people's wallets. The other is to squeeze money from the government, money they've taken by force in the form of taxes. That way is usually more profitable. Now I'm going to give you a brief lecture about how wars are started."

Somehow I couldn't get the giant painting of the lake behind him out of my head. His monologue looked like it was never going to end.

"Imagine a small country in Africa, with copper and

EVIL AND THE MASK

diamond mines. The big powers want the mining rights, but the king refuses, so the big powers scrape together the forces opposed to the king and secretly encourage them to form a rebel army. Then they start a propaganda campaign in their own countries, about how the king is oppressing his people, how he's resisting freedom and democracy. They might send soldiers in to assist the rebels, or they might send in private companies to do it instead. Lots of modern wars have been privatized. Companies that supply weapons, companies that provide tents and food for the soldiers, companies that provide the rebels with military training and strategic guidance. These private companies are usually set up by ex-officers, so naturally they have ties to politicians and defense officials. They get their financing both from the rebels and from taxes in rich countries in the name of international cooperation.

"Of course the rebels in a small African country don't have any funds, so how do they come up with that kind of money? How can they get their hands on such high-powered weaponry? They do it by borrowing money from the multinational mining corporations, in return for promising them the digging rights after they overthrow the monarch. With those funds they buy more weapons from private western companies and depose the king. War is big business. Any war has business interests involved in it somewhere—if you look deep enough, you'll always find someone making a profit.

"Even after the fighting's over there are plenty of business opportunities. Multinational construction firms get the contract to repair buildings and other stuff that's been destroyed in the war. Naturally that's also paid for out of rich countries' taxes, under the guise of friendship. It's a conspiracy by the politicians, the bureaucrats and the corporations to grab their own country's taxes and the small country's resources.

"I'll tell you another thing. After the war, western non-profits go into the country to help the exhausted populace, right? But it's hard to offer aid in places that are still unstable, and they have no choice but to use guards from private companies to take care of security. Even if their motives are pure, they still generate concessions. No matter which way they turn, they can't avoid them. Wars are fought in order to create concessions. Throughout human history, killing people in conflict has always stimulated the economy. And for generations the Kuki family has been intimately involved in the war business."

The whole time he had spoken in a soft monotone, with a distinct lack of enthusiasm. The level of whiskey in the bottle gradually grew lower.

"So what's your point?" I asked.

His expression didn't alter. "I'm talking about the Kuki family. About us."

"Nothing to do with me."

The room felt too quiet. The sound as he swallowed seemed really loud.

"I told you that's not going to work. You're Fumihiro. I know it, because we're Kukis. And you're desperate to hear my story."

"I'm not interested."

"Just listen. How many times do I have to tell you? It's not going to work."

His blood-shot eyes were staring straight at me.

"The Kuki family began as merchants. They started a money-changing business around the time of the Meiji Restoration in 1867. In the turmoil of that period, we curried favor with the new government and made big profits."

He took a long, slow breath.

"But we really started to prosper around the First World War. By then we already held the rights to most of the mines, and we were mass-producing warships and guns and selling them all over the world. We raked in huge profits and set up a wide range of companies, which became the emerging Kuki Group. At the time the whole of Japan was booming with special procurements for the war. But while the economy was thriving through sales of instruments for killing people and transport ships to carry those instruments, the Japanese people still believed that their nation was founded on peace and harmony. And then World War Two started. Our father, Shozo Kuki, served in that war."

"Huh?"

I reacted without thinking. Mikihiko smiled faintly.

"During the Sino-Japanese War, the Kuki Group fanned the flames of war and cozied up to some of the military authorities to get the concessions in Manchuria. But why did their son have to go and serve? The son of a corporation that was still making enormous profits from World War Two? Because Shozo Kuki wasn't from the main branch of the family. You can guess. He was raised as a cancer."

"A cancer?"

My heart started to beat faster.

"That's right. When the family patriarch at the time, Yosuke Kuki, was sixty years old, he sired our father for his own amusement, to be a cancer on the world. The father of the man who was leader of the Rahmla cult, a high-ranking officer who committed as many atrocities as he could, was our father's twin brother. To prolong the entertainment, the old man decided to send the cancer twins off to war."

With a bored expression he lifted the whiskey glass to his thick lips. The buildings I could see through the window were already largely in darkness.

"And then they both went insane."

2

IN THE DARK, quiet room the rumble of the air conditioner rang in my ears like a low murmur. Outside the window most of the lights in the surrounding buildings had gone out, and a half-moon shone strongly between the tower blocks. Mikihiko kept on drinking, sunk deep in the sofa. The alcohol had not soaked to his core, however—rather than making him drunk, it had simply softened his gloomy exterior. Without thinking, I lit another cigarette. My heart continued to beat rapidly, ignoring my best efforts to slow it.

"It's going to be a long night," he said, rolling his tongue around his mouth. "Today I'm going to tell you the complete history of the Kukis."

I still couldn't read his face.

"What did Shozo Kuki do in the war?"

"So you're interested, are you, Koichi Shintani?" He smirked. "What did Father do in the war? I did some research and it gradually became clear. From his infancy, he was exposed to violence. Out of malice, he wasn't fed properly and was horribly thin. He was constantly beaten. Because of that, he became all twisted inside and learned to act violently towards other people. His father, that is Yosuke Kuki, used to thrash him repeatedly for no reason and without showing any emotion. You know that Father was missing part of one ear. His twin brother, who was raised in exactly the same way, twice got into trouble for assaulting women and had a juvenile record, but not Father. My guess is he just harbored that violence inside him. But then he was sent off to war."

The painting of the lake behind him started to get on my nerves again.

"He was posted on the front lines in the Philippines, places like Leyte and Luzon where the Japanese army had been completely destroyed. He was commanding a surviving platoon as a second lieutenant in the 356th Division. You probably know that most of the Japanese soldiers who died in World War Two died of disease and starvation. They weren't killed by the US army, but just wandered around in the tropical jungle until they died, waiting for supplies that never arrived because the central government was incompetent. Father's platoon was the same. There's almost no evidence that the 356th took part in battle. They were starving. They couldn't prevent their basic human instincts from coming out, terrifying though those urges were. It's not difficult to imagine what happened to Father, raised as he was, when he was put in that situation.

"In the area where his men were roaming there was a small village that was destroyed by fire. That got me interested, so I tracked down one of his men and asked him what had happened. This old man had a fine son and grandson. He had locked up his violent past inside him and lived in agony, unknown to anyone. He told me his story. We did everything, he told me. They set fire to the village to destroy the evidence of their ferocity, but it's not easy for me to condemn them. Do you think it was possible for them to act like civilized human beings in those circumstances, carrying the burden of certain death, suffering terrible hunger for days on end, never knowing when they might be killed? With Father, who was accustomed to violence since his earliest childhood, the platoon trudged through the jungle, resigned, just putting one foot after the other, watching their friends die one by one of hunger or malaria, walking the boundary between life and death, covered in sores, convinced that their lives were over. And there in front of them was a peaceful village.

"This village had a little bit of food, the people were weak and there were plenty of women—young women with beautiful bronze skin exposed to the tropical sky. With soft lips, gorgeous, fleshy legs peeping out from their skirts, smooth bodies. That's probably when Father's violence was released, with an ominous, overpowering noise, as though all the darkness of the world was concentrated there. They burned the villagers' bodies, leaving nothing but bones. They must have been trying to destroy the evidence, the evidence of the lust and madness that burst forth from inside them, that they had forced themselves on the fleeing women until they were all corpses. Father and his men killed the men of the village and ate all the food. Then they herded the women to the center and raped them all at once. Day after day after day they ravished their victims. They lost themselves in the madness. Apparently some of the men kept on assaulting the women, not even realizing that they were dead. Not out of some elaborate perversity—it was simply a time of chaos, when humans revealed their true viciousness. The soldiers were no longer in full possession of their reason. They were already convinced of their own impending cruel death. Their dark lives were squirming, their reason was probably almost lost to insanity, and in its place their black unconscious minds were whispering to them. Whispering, 'If this is the end, why not?'"

His face still betrayed no feeling.

"In nineteen forty-five we were defeated. Father answered the Americans' call to surrender, became a prisoner and was returned to Japan. Apart from him and a few of his subordinates, the Three Hundred Sixty-fifth Division had almost entirely perished. The survivors were no doubt appalled by the cruel fact that they were still alive. Many of his comrades committed suicide. Father probably surrendered less out of a desire to keep on living than because of the thought that he still had unfinished business here. On his return, at first the other members of the Kuki family could hardly recognize him. That's how much he had changed.

"Japan had been occupied by the Americans and was ruled by MacArthur's GHQ. The Americans dissolved all the conglomerates, because they figured that the close ties between some of these industrial giants and the military had been the cause of Japan's aggression. The Kuki Group was one of the corporations that was broken up. Some of their shares were also confiscated. Amidst the confusion the head of the family, our grandfather Yosuke Kuki, died of stress, and his eldest son, who was much older than Father, and his son were killed in a car crash. They said it was caused by faulty maintenance, but I suspect that Father was behind it. The direct line had died out and Father, from the branch that was supposed to be cancers, became head of the Kuki clan. His twin brother, who was also a cancer, died during the war, completely insane. They say that he was killed by his subordinates, who could no longer bear to witness his vicious acts, but that's not definite.

"The Kuki family had lost some of its earlier power, but times were changing. Under the nineteen fifty-one Treaty of San Francisco, Japan became independent again and financial combines started to revive. The Americans wanted to use Japan as a defensive bulwark against Communism, against the Soviet Union, who were a threat at the time. To do that they judged that they needed a powerful economy, so they allowed the big corporations to reform. The Kukis started to mobilize their companies once more, as the Kuki Group. Then our older brother was born, I was born . . . and you were born."

He stood up. Maybe he was tired. He moved to the window and opened the curtains wide. The neighborhood was almost entirely in darkness. I heard him take a seat at the table behind me, but I was too drained to turn around.

"Most of the companies of which I'm the major shareholder deal with war in one form or another, from brokering arms deals overseas to rebuilding after the wars are over. I can't tell you what I'm up to yet, but I'll tell you one thing. To start with, I'm putting all of my efforts into abolishing the article in the constitution that says that Japan can't export weapons. If we can repeal that we'll be able to sell locally produced weapons to other countries, then whenever a war breaks out we can reap vast profits. The arms business is a gold mine, because weapons are consumables. The longer the war drags on—in other words, the more people are killed—the more money we make. Japan's superior technology will take the world by storm. Imagine we develop a fighter plane. We can include the maintenance in the contract, the whole works. It's a gravy train with no end. Obviously it's not the money I'm interested in. What I'm looking at, as an end in itself, is hundreds of thousands of people dying in those economic currents."

"What's that got to do with Kaori? You're sniffing around her, aren't you? Why?"

Behind me I could hear him breathing. He continued in the same tone.

"So you noticed that. Well, I'd expect that from someone who hired that PI Sakakibara. You're sharp."

He got to his feet again.

"But the two things are separate. I've got a personal interest in Kaori. Well, I guess I've got a personal interest in all my schemes. Would you believe me if I said I'm doing it to get revenge for Father?"

"No."

He slumped deeply onto the couch in front of me again. In his hand was a fresh bottle of whiskey.

"I'm the one who set Yajima onto Kaori."

"You?"

"That's right. Takayuki Yajima, the guy you murdered."

Without my noticing it the air conditioning had gone off and the room was even quieter. My forehead was covered with perspiration. He sat slouched on the sofa like some giant, limp worm.

"I was surprised when the man I put on her came back dead. It's your handiwork, that's not hard to figure out. But why did I get him to target her? To get my hands on her. Here's what I asked him to do—get her addicted and then deliver her to me."

"Why?" My voice shook violently.

"Because I'm depressed. Father adopted her to show you hell. The Kuki family's sacrificial lamb, as it were. As his son, I plan to destroy the girl that Father wanted to destroy but couldn't. It's an interesting echo, isn't it? If I get her addicted, I can possess her forever, body and soul. I'm thinking about hiring another guy to get close to her."

"Stop it."

He laughed.

"Fallen for her, have you? Don't lie."

My field of vision narrowed. My headache grew fiercer and shadows stretched before my eyes.

"What?"

"I said don't lie."

All I could see was his thick lips moving.

"You want to hurt the girl, don't you? You want to totally destroy her. You're a Kuki. I know all about that. You want revenge on the woman who ruined your life. No, strictly speaking it's not revenge, because you fell for her of your own accord, ruined your life of your own accord. Here's a more accurate way of putting it. Unconsciously, you want to create the maximum evil. That means completely destroying the one thing that is the most valuable in the world to you. In other words, Kaori. To do that, you placed her on a pedestal above all else, just so you could harm her one day. You don't love her. You fell for her so you could hurt her. You offered up your own life so you could hurt her. You made her the number one thing in your life so you could hurt her. So at some time you will hurt her for real. You long for the time when that overwhelming urge to destroy her will explode, and for the overwhelming despair that will follow. Your whole life is directed towards that instant. You long with your whole being for that explosion of darkness that will blaze forth in a way it never does in ordinary people's lives, with lust and sorrow and despair all heaped up together. At that moment you will shake with an overpowering pleasure. With the pleasure of thoroughly insulting this world and your own life."

"You're wrong."

"Maybe you really did like her at first, when you were kids. But now you've changed. I think that you killed Father. I'm pretty certain about that. I understand you. Because we're Kukis! It's obvious, isn't it? Now you've lost everything. What's left for you to ask for from life? Just to pray for Kaori's happiness from afar? I don't think so! Now your sole purpose in life is that moment of destruction. You're carrying the curse of the Kukis, the burden of their wars and their atrocities."

"Stop talking bullshit!"

His eyes bulged.

"Or what? You'll kill me? Like you killed Father and Yajima? Just try it!"

Suddenly he started to shout, still staring at me with eyes wide. He lifted his head and thrust it forward to expose his neck. His breathing grew harsh.

"Everything's boring! I'm bored! Really, really bored. If death were right here in front of me, I'd love to see it. Ha, try and kill me, quick!"

I couldn't tear my eyes away from his. For a second his face was filled with exaltation, like he was glowing from inside. He kept staring at me, but little by little his eyes lost their intensity, until he was gazing at me listlessly again. He began languidly sipping his whiskey once more. I didn't know what to make of the change that had come over him, and my brain wasn't working at all.

"I'll put someone else onto Kaori, whether you like it or not."

"Stop it."

"I'll send in guys one after the other. I guess that won't bother you, because you'll just kill them all. Learn their habits and kill them, isn't that what you do? Either that, or you approach Kaori yourself."

His slack lips twisted as he studied me, indifferent to his excitement of a minute earlier.

"Get her hooked and bring her to me. If you do that, I won't send anyone else in the meantime. At least you can have a taste of her before I finish her off. That wouldn't be bad, would it? If you refuse, I'll start the same thing all over again. Maybe I'll use my subordinates to bring her to me by force."

"Why?"

"I told you. Because I'm depressed. I'll call you again to get your progress reports. You're smart, you won't do anything stupid like calling the cops. Basically, they can only act after a crime has been committed. You know most women who are killed by their stalkers ask for police protection before they are murdered? Next time I'll tell you more. Maybe even about why you're attracted to Kaori."

3

WHEN I MADE my way through the lobby and left the hotel, the guy who had driven me there was already gone. I figured that Mikihiko Kuki was probably going to sleep all by himself in that gloomy room. I hailed a cab and we drove across the dry asphalt, past the sparse lights from the office blocks, the lights from the apartment buildings, the headlamps of innumerable cars. I watched them flash by without really seeing them, pondering my father's missing ear. Various thoughts flitted through my mind—how his alcohol consumption had increased as he grew older, the fact that when I closed the door to that underground room he had been carrying poison to kill himself. I wondered if his hunger in the basement had reminded him of the hunger he'd experienced as a child or during the war.

When I checked my cell phone I had an email from Kyoko, saying that I shouldn't come home because a shady-looking guy was hanging around outside. I was pretty sure it would be Aida, so I sent a reply saying that I didn't care and I was on my way. After thinking for a minute, I rang the private eye. He answered straight away. There was an indistinct buzzing in the background, but a few moments later it abruptly went quiet. I didn't want the taxi driver to overhear our conversation so I made him stop the car, got out and leaned against the trunk.

"I met Mikihiko Kuki," I said.

"Just now?" His tone grew tense.

"Yes. It was a big surprise. Apparently he was behind Yajima's targeting Kaori."

"Then that means . . ."

"He wants to get his hands on her. To get her addicted so he owns her. He must be totally insane, to do something like that even though he's not particularly interested in her. I still don't know what he's really up to, though. By the way, about my phone, they did get it from Konishi after all."

"Sorry about that."

"Can't be helped. The thief was in JL."

"JL?"

"One of their members is related to the Kukis, the grandson of Shozo Kuki's twin brother. His father was the head of Rahmla who killed himself. It looks like he's trying to use Kaori to get money out of me. The ones who've latched onto Kaori, they're all Kukis."

He didn't reply.

"It's one crazy family. They really are. It would have been better if they'd never adopted her in the first place. It's because she got mixed up with such an insane mob that she's had such a hard time. That's what the Kukis are like—stubborn, malevolent, vindictive. Maybe it's Shozo Kuki's curse. No, it goes back further than that."

I realized that my speech was growing more rapid. I took a deep breath to calm myself for what I had to say next.

"Would it be possible for me to meet with Kaori?"

My voice cracked and faltered. Despite my best efforts my heart was still racing, disturbed by my audacity.

"Also, could you study Mikihiko Kuki's habits? What bars he frequents, anything."

This was the same thing I'd asked him to do for Yajima.

"Will do."

"Thanks. But aren't you going to ask why?"

There was a pause, as though he was thinking. Cars sped past as I leaned against the taxi.

"In our job," he said, "we never question a client's request. I think I've said this before, but in our line of work we see things you don't normally see, and we make the impossible possible. Our job is to do the client's dirty work, things outside the scope of day-to-day-life."

"But why do you put yourself in that position? Sorry, it's none of my business."

I didn't know why I was talking like this.

"No, I don't mind answering. I think I'm taking revenge on the world."

"Revenge?"

"I want to change everything about the world, change what is assumed to be the normal course of events. I can't say for sure if that's a kind of revenge or not, but at any rate, I feel like I'm fighting against the tide that's always pushing people in one direction. By breaking the rules."

"Don't you think people make their own choices in life?"

"They do, but in many cases their choices are limited— unless they break the rules."

I stared at the lights of the apartment buildings in front of me, conscious of the hard metal of the taxi against my hips.

"But maybe those transgressions are part of the tide," I said. "Sorry, we've gone off topic. What have you found out about Shintani's past?"

"Well, I don't see anything suspicious. It's true that after they split up, Sae Suzuki had some serious emotional problems, and some people said that might have caused the accident."

I tried to remember if any of Shintani's favorite movies dealt with a theme like that.

"The mother, Yaeko, seems to think so. That's probably why she hates Shintani. She didn't even let him go to the funeral."

"Really? Not even the funeral?"

The stream of cars had gradually diminished. I closed my cell phone. When I started to get back into the taxi I realized that someone was sitting in a black car that had been parked behind me the whole time. If he was tailing me, I thought, he was making his presence very obvious. Pretending to be checking my email, I used my phone to record the car on video. I climbed back into the cab, checked the picture and sent it to the detective. When we took off again, the other car followed right behind, as though it wanted to be seen. The detective sent me a reply saying that the car belonged to the investigator hired by Mikihiko Kuki.

I watched it in the side mirror, reflecting that as soon as Mikihiko stuck his oar in, this guy showed up—even though there was no point tailing me, since he obviously already knew where I lived. I decided to ignore it, and didn't turn around again.

WHEN WE REACHED my apartment, Aida was standing out front. I paid my fare and got out, feeling wearier than ever. He was on the phone, but hung up as soon as he saw me. In his hand was a half-finished cigarette. The car that had been following me drove straight past, perhaps because Aida was there. I headed for the entrance but he held up an arm to bar my way.

"It's good manners to say hello, even if you're not going to roll out the red carpet."

"I've got nothing to say to you."

I tried to move past him but he grabbed my shoulder. In the distance the black car disappeared reluctantly around the corner, as though delivering a warning.

"What's the big deal?" he said. "I won't be able to see you again for a while."

I stopped and looked at him. He was still wearing the same worn-out shoes.

"No matter how much I look at Sae Suzuki's death, you're

still in the clear. The more I look at it, the more it looks like it was her own fault. Unfortunately. And luckily for you, at precisely the time of the accident you were in a university tutorial presenting a report for your professor. The whole class saw you. Your alibi is rock solid. Yaeko's theory that you hired someone to do it just doesn't seem realistic."

"In that case you can give it up, can't you?"

"Yeah, I guess. But while I was reviewing the case I realized again just how much I hate you."

He was staring at Shintani's face.

"You never stop and think about things, do you? Never brood, never fret over small stuff. You just skate smoothly through life. I don't know if you were really interested in movies or not, but the other members of the film society said that you were just putting on an act."

I had no idea if what he was saying was true, but it seemed funny that I'd been watching the movies that Shintani was supposed to like, and had been moved by them.

"It's not just that I feel sorry for Yaeko. When I heard that a week after Sae's death you went out drinking with your friends, laughing hard enough to wet yourself, I couldn't forgive you. Sure, maybe you're not responsible. But right up till the day she died she was thinking only of you. That's what your life's been like since then too. For some reason people die all around you while you carry on blithely. It's a bizarre existence. As if they're carrying the burden for you. Personally, I despise people like you. But look at you now."

His eyes darkened.

"It's like you're a different person. Like you're always

thinking deeply about things. You even look quite different—
maybe it's your new haircut. You're not working at the moment,
are you? But still living in a place like this, going out all the
time. What are you up to?"

"None of your business."

"That's true, it's none of my business. And I'm pretty busy.
There's this guy we've got our eye on. He slipped up. We
think he might be JL."

"What?" I asked without thinking.

"Curious, are you? People like you generally don't seem
interested in groups like that. Well, it looks like this JL guy is
somewhere in Setagaya here in Tokyo. While I'm here I might
as well ask, have you seen this guy anywhere?"

He showed me a picture, a grainy photo, probably taken
from a security camera on the street. The man was wearing a
cap and a down jacket, and seemed to be in a hurry. Narrow
eyes, a protruding jaw. I didn't recognize him.

"Never seen him before."

"I didn't think so. I've been after this JL from the start. Me,
I think it's fate. What do you reckon? Don't you think they're
likely to have some connection to Rahmla, that cult who took
over that power plant and killed themselves? One man who
joined the occupation was tied to one of those big financial
outfits. That really got me interested. Still, JL may turn out
to be just a bunch of stupid tricksters, so I guess I shouldn't
get my hopes up."

I looked at the ground so I wouldn't have to face him. My
heart was beating painfully and my temples throbbed.

"Both your case and the JL case were stalled for a long

time, but JL finally began to move. That's why I won't be able to see you for a while."

He looked at me.

"In fact, maybe we'll never meet again. And since this could be the last time I've got to say this. Please pay a visit to Sae's grave."

"What's that got to do with you?"

"Maybe nothing. But I'm thinking that the way you are now, you might just do it. I get the feeling that I might run into you in front of her headstone on the anniversary of her death. I don't know what's happened to you. Well, see you."

And he walked off. I went inside, watching his broad, retreating back out of the corner of my eye. When I crossed the tiny foyer and turned the corner, a man in a black coat was standing in front of the elevators. He was about fifty, with short hair and slightly hunched shoulders. He looked a bit like the guy driving the car—but I thought he'd gone. I ignored him and went to push the button, but suddenly he grabbed my wrist.

He was staring right at me. I looked straight ahead, tried again for the button, with his hand still gripping my arm, but he tensed his muscles and I couldn't move. The lobby was chilly.

"You must be Mikihiko's dick," I said, but he didn't crack a smile.

"A message."

The hand holding my wrist was lukewarm.

"In the next two or three days, contact Kaori Kuki."

I still didn't look at him, but I couldn't move my arm.

"If you don't, his orders are that we do it ourselves. That'd be a pain in the ass. Get it? So do what he says. Get the girl hooked and then take her to him."

The elevator beside us opened and a woman with dyed brown hair came out, but he still didn't let go, seeming completely indifferent to her presence.

"You get in touch with her first and show us that you can do it. Before we take over."

He took a bag from his jacket pocket.

"This stuff is top grade. Don't waste it. If you want you can use a bit for yourself."

He stuffed the packet into my pocket, turned and walked away.

I OPENED THE front door, went to the bathroom and flushed the powder in the bag down the toilet. When I went into the living room, Kyoko was watching a movie in the dark again. On the screen a couple was arguing bitterly in the middle of a street. The woman was crying and advancing on the man. Kyoko welcomed me home in a soft voice. I tried to answer her, but my words wouldn't come out clearly.

"You look exhausted," she said.

"Yeah."

I tossed my coat aside and collapsed on the couch.

"Some letters came for you. I put them on that box."

"Thanks."

I sipped a glass of stale water that was sitting nearby.

"You get a lot of mail, don't you? Watch shops, clothes shops, hotels. But the addresses are all in the same handwriting."

"Did you open them?"

"No. Though I was really tempted."

I laughed.

"Things might turn a bit dangerous," I said. "It would be better if you didn't see me for a while."

She looked at me open-mouthed. "Really?"

"Really."

"That's a bummer. I've got nowhere to go."

On the TV the woman, still shouting, knifed the man at an intersection. His blood formed a pool in the middle of the road. Strangely, the guy who'd been stabbed was watching the scene from the window of an apartment a long way off.

"What about your own place?"

"Well, I've got one, but . . ."

I stood up shakily.

"How much do you owe?"

"It's okay."

"No, you can tell me."

"About eight hundred thousand."

I opened the white closet and took a million yen from the briefcase inside.

"Here, take this."

"Huh? No, I couldn't."

"Go on, take it."

"Why are you giving me this?"

She looked at me. And it was actually a bit weird for me to be handing her so much cash.

"It wasn't my money in the first place, and I don't need it. I was planning to give it all away in the end anyway."

"But still . . ."

She lowered her eyes.

"Plus I had sex with you," I said.

"You pay this much for sex?"

"Sex is much more valuable than you think."

I knew that what I was saying was kind of funny.

"All right then. I'll pay you back one day."

"That's okay."

"I insist. I'll pay it back."

On the screen the guy watching himself being stabbed had turned into an old man. Walking with a cane, he made his way slowly towards the intersection where his double had been attacked by the woman all those years ago, but just before he reached it he thrust a knife into his own stomach, as if he'd been possessed by something. As the withered trees lining the road looked on silently, the elderly man in the coat crouched down on the cobbled crossing. He looked resigned. Red blood stained the surface of the street again, like some kind of symbol.

"Anyway, it would be best if we didn't see each other for a while."

"Are you in that much shit?"

"Yeah, well, just in case."

The TV suddenly went dark. Or maybe it had been off for some time.

"I don't know how to say this, but are you all right?"

"I don't know." I grinned briefly. "When I think about my personality, my life so far, my future, somehow I get the feeling there's only one destination for me."

"Destination?"

Suddenly I remembered the bottle of cyanide. There was still some left.

"Yeah. In the end I think that getting tangled up in things, that's what life is all about. Even if you think you're following your own wishes and desires, those wishes and desires are formed by your entanglements. See what I mean?"

"Maybe."

"I guess I've only worked that out since I got my face changed."

She moved closer, took the cigarette from between my fingers and took a puff.

"Hey, you want to . . . ?"

"You don't have to."

"No, it's not that. I want to."

She started undoing her buttons.

"But that too," I said. "Maybe your DNA and character and environment are just reacting to my randomly altered appearance. You're getting tangled up."

She went to stop my mouth with her lips, like they do in the movies, but missed and bumped against my chin. She burst out laughing.

4

IN THE DARKNESS we walked through the narrow streets and up a gentle slope, ignoring the bright lights of a convenience store. Ryosuke Ito was wearing the same gray knit cap, a white, sleeveless down jacket with a hood, and ripped designer jeans. He walked in front of me, looked back once and then started climbing a rusty staircase outside an apartment block. Two communal washing machines stood in a row. The building was damp from yesterday's rain. Overall it seemed old, but the intercom looked incongruously new.

The guy who answered the door turned around and retreated back inside without even looking at us. He was still young, in his early twenties. The room was small, with a blue carpet and a simple loft. Apart from a low table and a TV, there was absolutely no furniture.

"That's Sato. His real name isn't important."

Despite this introduction, the guy just looked at me without responding. He was wearing blue-framed glasses and a blue hoodie, and his brown hair was styled with gel.

"Just the two of you?" I asked.

"Of course not," said Ito, sitting on the floor. "We're just one cell. Most of us aren't in Tokyo."

When I lit a cigarette the guy calling himself Sato opened his mouth for the first time to tell me I couldn't. I ignored him and kept smoking. Maybe he was used to it, because he passed a flattened can to Ito to use as an ashtray.

The TV was showing a report about photos of election candidates being replaced with pictures of a porn actress in eighteen places up and down the country. Their electoral offices were furious.

"How did it go?" Sato asked, pulling the cord hanging from the fan.

Ito opened his bottle of mineral water.

"I forget her name but apparently the posters are done well, so they look just like the real thing. She's smiling and saying 'Full penetration!' out of the corner of her mouth."

"Ah, that's pretty funny. It's borderline, though. Well, I guess it's okay."

"Yeah. I'll email them, then. And I heard they found a heap of dead pigeons in a park."

"That's no good."

The news program continued. There was a follow-up

story on a third politician, who had been found dead in a love hotel. The prime minister appeared, surrounded by reporters, and the announcer read that the police had further increased the number of detectives on the case. There was a big fire at the office of a car manufacturer that had laid off lots of contract workers. A foul smell had caused a disturbance on the subway. On their blog, JL had written that they were fighting back against the corrupt government. They had covered the house of a TV commentator who had publicly declared himself a friend to young people with vivid graffiti. There'd been numerous arsons targeting rich people's mansions. Two popular TV personalities had recently gotten married live on TV, and the husband had received threatening letters, which stated in childlike printing that they weren't going to kill him but that in the next five years they would definitely cut his balls off. Photos of a famous newscaster taking part in a bondage game at an S&M parlor were released. While the culprits were still unknown, enough palytoxin to kill several thousand people had been stolen from three different medical universities.

"You guys are pathetic."

Sato laughed briefly.

"Of course we are. Because we're just messing around."

"It's a waste of time and effort," I said.

He laughed again.

"You're right."

He turned back to the TV. A reporter was walking towards a university where the poison was stolen, a stern expression on his face.

"If it's just a joke," I went on, "then it's not too serious. But if you use it to start killing people it gets complicated."

"Yeah, well, that wasn't us," interrupted Ito. "Sure, whoever did it was a member, but we only heard about it after. It certainly wasn't approved beforehand. It's still a bit too soon. The police and Public Security taking us seriously at this early stage, that's a nuisance."

"Don't you guys have a leader or anything?"

"We don't need one. We're not even a proper group."

Laughing, Sato picked up the story.

"Recently there've been lots of copycat crimes, but if any of them take our fancy we issue a statement saying that it was us, attaching a code that's only known to us and the press. Of course the copycat puts out a statement of their own, but then everyone assumes that that's just to confuse the cops, or that they're a JL associate of some kind. Sometimes even the copycats themselves get the wrong end of the stick and think that we're accepting them as members. We send our communiqués directly to the media. That's something we learned from Al Qaida."

"Then . . ."

"Yeah, there are still real members. I guess you could say that anyone who knows that code, they're real members. By the way, killing those politicians, that was done by JL. Apparently they called for volunteers. We're only loosely affiliated—we don't all get together to discuss our plans. Our only rule is to keep the code secret. Because if newcomers muscle in, that's a pain."

"Okay, what things have you two actually planned?"

"I don't have to tell you. But me and Ito, we still haven't got mixed up in any killings, because we're not ready for it."

He laughed.

"We plan to do it eventually. What I mean is, it's best to leave the killing to others for now. To the extremists. Actually, JL's gotten lots of publicity since the murders started. Hey, Ito, is this guy okay? He's got no intention of joining us, has he?"

"He's fine. He's here, isn't he? That shows he's interested. And we need cash."

"That's true, we need cash. That's our biggest problem right now."

Sato stood up.

"Okay, so now you've got to convince him. I don't mind teaming up with him. He's kind of annoying, but he looks smart."

Glancing at the clock, Sato picked up his backpack.

"Where are you off to?"

"You don't need to know. See you."

He left the room. Ito started flicking through the TV channels with the remote.

"Where did he take off to in such a hurry?" I asked.

"We also have an unspoken rule not to pry into each other's business. Probably a part-time job. A while ago I spotted him from a distance handing out packets of tissues advertising a bar."

He drank some more water. The two rings in his ear glinted white under the lights.

"Before you get the wrong idea, we're not really social reformers. We're not even trying to change our own lives."

He began turning the band on his left wrist with his right hand.

"We're just having fun. We've only got one thing in common. We want to drag everything down as far as we can. We want to pull down all human achievements, all human successes, all authority. For example, this is a really small thing, but you know how a few years ago dozens of websites sprang up where you could download vast quantities of music, movies or whatever for free as compressed files? At the time, everyone was talking about how easy and fast the download software was, right? And they were getting millions of hits? The guy who did that is one of us, back before JL was formed.

"Apparently maintaining those sites was really expensive, but he got so much money from the ads for porn sites he linked to that he even made a small profit. He kept them updated from a PC registered to someone who was already dead, using a provider in Southeast Asia, and he had the money he got from ads remitted to a bank account in Shanghai. Someone he knew there paid homeless people to withdraw the cash, then his friend would wire it back to the guy's own bank account in Japan, so it was almost impossible to trace it back to him. That money was what got JL started.

"What he did was a felony, infringement of copyright. If everyone can get their hands on whatever they want for nothing, the people who provide the culture will lose their source of income and the culture will decline. But that's exactly what he wanted. He wanted everything to go down the tubes. Doesn't the word 'professional' make your flesh crawl? Traditional culture, underground culture, he wanted it all to collapse, everything to be done by amateurs. Enjoying things that non-professionals had created themselves in their spare time, enjoying them for free on the net, that would be cool. You see?

"Deep down, people who deliberately distribute other people's music and stuff feel contempt for professionals. And it's not just culture—these days lots of people are contemptuous of everything. Without realizing it, they're searching for things to despise. What we're doing is actualizing millions of people's subconscious desires. Wouldn't you piss yourself laughing seeing the Prime Minister doing an over-the-top imitation of Hiromi Go in the middle of a serious press conference? After a whole series of depressing stories about politicians getting killed and stuff, it would be a kind of comic relief. I bet lots of people couldn't help laughing if they saw that on TV. But of course that's not the only thing."

His eyes were mere slits.

"Next, people who've been successful in various other fields will become victims, one after another. And then gradually that feeling of contempt will extend to the people doing the laughing as well. Down with authority—it's definitely a sexy catchphrase. But from now on people are going to find JL harder and harder to understand. Finally we're planning a series of terrorist attacks against ordinary citizens. Whenever anything happens, society demands to know the reason. That's why we've issued statements for each incident. But we're doing that only to set the stage for the unpredictable events that are still to come.

"In future our communiqués will get weirder and weirder. Like, 'Such-and-such building was renovated, so we blew up several houses in the neighborhood.' 'The final episode of our favorite TV show was so exciting that we scattered poison around Shibuya in downtown Tokyo.' 'Today's Wednesday, so we left explosives in the subway.' No one will be able to make heads or tails of them. Then maybe we'll get the one percent to do some impressions again. While society is facing senseless violence, the people at the top will be earnestly doing imitations. Wouldn't that be really funny? I'd kill myself laughing. But it wouldn't even matter if they didn't do it. The people who've achieved things in society would be the first to go, but at the same time hundreds of ordinary people would also be dying every day in terrorist attacks. Authority, class difference, logic, meaning, common sense, they'll all fall to pieces. The country will be thrown into chaos by incomprehensible violence. By then I bet there'll be thousands of copycats."

"You guys will get caught and it will all be over."

"Haven't you been listening?"

Ito looked at me.

"Didn't I tell you we're not an organized group? By the time people can no longer understand where we're heading, we'll have grown even bigger. Let's assume that I'm arrested in the middle of it, for example. The other members or new members will take over. Since we're just a loose-knit collective and don't know each other, we can't be wiped out like Rahmla were. Maybe by then there won't be a single original member of JL left, but there'll be one part of us that will survive. Contempt. Contempt for the world, for love, for everything of value, and then contempt for contempt itself."

A motorbike raced past outside. Its muffled roar seemed to

be asserting something outrageous, though its exact message was unclear.

"It'll never work. You'll never be able to do it."

"Do what?"

"It's like Sato said before. You're even hesitant about killing corrupt politicians."

Ito was sitting on the carpet, his knees bent and his back against the wall. I realized that I'd taken up an identical pose beside him.

"We can."

He was staring at the opposite wall, like he was talking to himself. I imagined Father's blood oozing out from the surface.

"You really don't want to do that."

"Why?"

He grinned suddenly.

"Think about it. It's an old question. Why shouldn't we do it? Why shouldn't we kill people? Why shouldn't we blow the world to smithereens?"

I looked at his wristband. I didn't know why I was trying to stop him, but I went on.

"Those questions defy all logic, so no matter what I say you can turn it back on me. So I'll turn it around on you. Why is it all right to do those things?"

"Why? Because I want to."

"Okay, why is it acceptable to do whatever you want?"

"Hey, that's not a fair question."

"But it's the same as yours. Try turning them around. There's no difference." I took a deep breath. "I'm not really trying to save you or anything. You can go ahead and kill people, do what you like. I'm only telling you this because you asked. The reason you shouldn't do it is because maybe you'll keep on living, and someone who kills another person, afterwards they can't accept beauty or warmth with a pure heart. The instant you feel any kind of human beauty, the instant you feel any human warmth, the knowledge that you've killed a person will start squirming inside you, because those things—beauty and warmth—they can't exist without human life. Beauty is created by humans. Even natural beauty, we can only feel it because we are alive. Warmth is the same.

"And another thing—living things are fundamentally designed not to kill their own kind. I've read dozens of books on biology, and cannibalism is a really rare phenomenon. All animals know instinctively that they shouldn't kill other members of the same species. Maybe it's imprinted in our DNA. Of course there are people who say they don't care, people who snigger while they're on trial for murder. But people like that are weak. They can't cope with the shock of knowing that they've murdered another human being, a living creature just like them, that they've taken a life just like their own, so they bottle up their true feelings in the deepest recesses of their mind. Because our subconscious automatically tries to find some sort of mental equilibrium. Imagine strangling a monkey, for example. Even that's disturbing, isn't it? Killers who say they aren't bothered by it are just too weak to cope with the shock, and shut it up inside themselves. They're just brainwashing themselves. As proof, look at those pathetic people who do stuff like going around killing at random. Real monsters don't do those things. They lurk behind the scenes, calmly dispensing evil from positions of power. When people face up to the impact of killing, without locking it up deep inside them, they are bound to malfunction."

I recalled Father staring at me in that basement room.

"No matter what they gain from killing someone, it won't balance out that malfunction. So aren't you better off not killing anyone in the first place?"

Ito was looking at me with amusement.

"In that case, couldn't you just use a weapon to minimize that feeling? Then that malfunction wouldn't happen."

He was fiddling with the lid of his bottle as he talked.

"Have you heard the story about the US and World War Two?" he asked. "After the war was over, they studied how many of the guns of the soldiers in the front lines had been fired. It was about twenty percent. Around eighty percent of the soldiers at the front had never actually pulled the trigger. That's a sign that they really didn't want to shoot at the enemy, kill them, without a damn good reason. So the US army changed their training methods. They replaced the old bullseye target with a cutout of a human figure, complete with a photo of a face, to get the soldiers used to killing people. The result was that in Vietnam the firing rate increased dramatically. So we can change human nature any way we want."

"But that story has a sequel, doesn't it?" I said.

Ito's expression didn't change.

"Sure, I've heard that story," I went on. "And sure, the firing rate went up. But the flip side was that lots of soldiers came home with serious psychological problems. The army concluded that guns were no good. Even though the soldiers had been watching Westerns since they were kids, in which people kill each other all the time, the real thing took its toll. So they decided to develop hi-tech weapons, virtual, remote-controlled weapons, so that it didn't feel like you were killing a real person at all. That was the Gulf War. There was a terrible imbalance between the people being killed and the people doing the killing, between the Iraqis who were dying spurting blood in pain and suffering and hatred and the soldiers of the multinational force, who managed to completely avoid the feeling that they were killing people. That caused a different kind of spiritual decay.

"And then there was Iraq, which became a land war, an old-fashioned shoot-out with rifles. As a result, the rate of psychological disorders among returning soldiers was abnormally high. I can't help feeling sorry for them. The perverted history of modern warfare is all about trying to maintain the emotional balance of the soldiers who kill. That's been the constant refrain. But it's simply the difference between keeping the shock of killing bottled up in the subconscious and using weapons to numb the soldiers' sensibilities. If you think that'll work, you're just stupid. In fact, maybe the real purpose of war is simply to replicate itself, to create more wars."

Ito had stayed stony-faced throughout my monologue. He continued to stare fixedly at the wall in front of him, as though something was written there.

"You'll never understand," he said quietly. "Listen. Imagine there's this guy who's thinking about killing himself after murdering someone. Imagine he doesn't care when he dies—or rather, he wants to die but plans to kill someone else first. He wouldn't give a shit about beauty or malfunction or any of that. Ethics and morality are irrelevant to him. Because for us there is no god. We don't believe in an afterlife either. Look, the only reason I'm doing this crap now is because of the bloodbath that'll come at the end, that feast of contempt for life. Now it's all just a preview. Thousands of people dying for no reason, hundreds per day. It'll be a world of contempt for everything, where life is absolutely worth nothing. I can't wait. I've been yearning for that from the depths of my soul, ever since I was a kid."

He turned towards me. Again, the noise of a motorbike engine shook the apartment.

"Let's say," he continued, opening his eyes slightly and playing with his wristband again. "Let's say there's a guy like this. Brought up in violence from as far back as he can remember, brought up as though that was completely normal. Constantly beaten, beaten without love, without any feeling at all, as though even kicking him was a bother, indifferent kicking, because he was in the way . . . Shunned by people from warm, bright, caring homes just because he hadn't taken a bath for days. Nothing but pain; no food, only fear and hatred. Unable to sleep properly because of recurring memories of violence. Slashed his wrists many times but couldn't die . . .

"Can you tell someone like that to be kind to others? Can you tell him to think about how other people are suffering, that there are people in the world worse off than you, think of the starving children in Africa? Can you say that to a man who had those feelings beaten out of him from the day he was born? To a man who has lost the ability to cherish those things? To a man who suffers because he can't feel anything for other people, no matter how hard he tries? You can tell him not to interfere with other people's happiness? To a man who already wants to die, you can tell him to die alone, thinking only of others, like some kind of saint? To a man who's tried to protect himself by telling himself that the years of abuse he received weren't such a big deal, you can tell him that violence towards others is bad? To a man who was raised by an insane, drug-addicted woman whose adored husband died in a mass suicide as part of an evil cult, and whose only thought was to ruin her son's personality in order to pass on the malevolence of his father? To a man whose mother somehow blamed him for her husband's death, who was filled with crazy ideas she inherited from her husband and with hatred of her son? To a man who was raised by a monster who grew tired of him and only continued the violence out of habit? To a man who was so hungry that he used to eat his own hair? To a man whose birth wasn't even registered?"

His shoulders heaved as he gasped for air, and his frightened eyes stared directly into mine. Father's blood was still seeping from the wall opposite. Suddenly I remembered the doctor's tale of the baby who died in the toilet. I had a vision of my booze-soaked father, and it felt like his blood and alcohol were running off me, mixed with my own perspiration. I could hardly breathe. Ito fell silent. I felt like I had to say something.

"If that's how it is, my advice is just to keep on living. Sure, malfunctions and beauty don't mean anything to a man who's already made up his mind to die. But still, I'd advise you to live."

"Obviously. If you advise a murderer to live and he follows that advice, then the idea that malfunctions and beauty don't matter to someone who's determined to die, that no longer applies. So I'm listening. Why should he live?"

I couldn't answer, because the question was directed at me.

"Why should he live? With such a background and such an emotional vacuum inside him towards other people, why? You know what I mean. Enough with the sermon already. Anyway, will you fund us? JL needs money now." He put the empty bottle on the carpet. He looked exhausted.

"But you're still not ready to do it, are you?"

"I am."

"No, you're not. You're still putting it off. You can't join in the killing, you've stopped at pretend terrorism. That proves it. You satisfy the impulses inside you by stopping just short of exploding. You give yourself various reasons to make yourself feel better, but you steer clear of actually blowing things up. Besides, isn't JL in big trouble right now? I bet that's the real reason you need money."

He glared at me.

"What do you mean?"

"They're close to catching one of you, aren't they? One of the early members. If they arrest him, the whole group could be in trouble."

"What have you heard?"

"There's a guy on the run, isn't there, a guy with a protruding jaw? If they catch him, JL will be in deep shit. You said it yourself, when you were talking about killing politicians too early. There's a risk you could get wiped out before you get really big."

"How much do you know? What do you mean?"

"You're smart. You need escape money for when JL is eliminated. Yeah? That's what it's really for, isn't it?"

"That's beside the point. Just give me the money, and let me worry about what it's for. You've got money to burn, haven't you? You're rich, you don't need it. Besides, what's the matter with you? Acting like your shit don't stink, when we both know you're just a crazy mother. You and me, I think we're similar. Right? Because you could have ignored me but you didn't. I'm not saying you have to give it to me right now. Next time we meet would be fine, but could you get some money together for us?"

"How much?"

"Five million yen."

"You've got to be kidding!"

"It's much less than I wanted at first. Also, could you look after this for me?"

He put his backpack on the low table.

"What is it?"

"A bomb. It's just for a few days."

At the bottom of the squashed bag I could make out the shape of a square object.

"I don't have anywhere to store it any more. Coin lockers have security cameras. It's not for long."

"Why do I have to look after it?"

"We told you a lot about JL, so you should take some of the risk as well. It's not wired, so it's safe, but don't drop it. This took longer than I thought. I've got some other business to take care of. Let's get out of here."

"Where are you going?"

"Not telling. Don't be nosy."

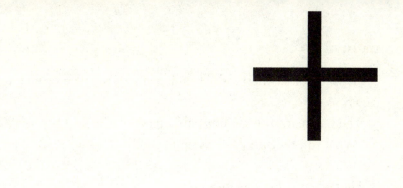

5

THE DETECTIVE WAS waiting for me in our usual hotel
room. He seemed to have lost a little weight, but his eyes
were as piercing as ever. As soon as I entered he rose from
the brown sofa and poured me a cup of instant coffee. His
fingers were long and slender, and remarkably smooth for
his age. Once again I reflected that we always drank coffee
at our meetings. He produced two well-worn files and put a
plastic case full of unlabelled CDs on the table.

"Here is the material on Mikihiko Kuki," he said.

"You got it this quickly?"

"No . . ."

He was watching me intently. I'd never seen him so serious.

"If you look at these, you'll understand what type of man he is."

The file nearest to me was particularly old.

"What you do with it, that's up to you."

"What's . . . ?"

He looked at his silver watch.

"It's almost time."

"Huh? Ah, so it is."

I stood.

"Does Konishi . . . ?"

"Yeah, no problem. It's on my way, I'll give you a lift."

JE LE RÉPÈTE was in the basement of a white, five-storey building in Roppongi's entertainment district. The detective spotted Mikihiko's PI's car tailing us, but I told him several times to ignore it. When we arrived at the bar I straightened my tie and waited until his vehicle disappeared from view, while Mikihiko's guy watched from his car. What had given me the push to visit Kaori was Mikihiko telling me that if I approached her he'd leave her alone, but whether I was playing for time just to hide my real motives, I wasn't sure. There were many things I still didn't know—not so much about what I wanted, but what I was going to do about the whole situation. Still, there I was, dressed in a suit, standing in front of Je le Répète's stylish neon sign. Meeting Kaori felt unreal, like some kind of bad joke, but I also couldn't imagine running away, going back to my own room. I made my way into the hushed building, feeling like something was dragging me forward, like something soft was pushing me from behind.

The dim staircase seemed to go on forever. At the bottom my eyes were assaulted by a brilliant light. A young man with a smooth smile opened the door—he must have seen me from inside. The bar was larger than I expected, filled with soft jazz and lit by rows of chandeliers, which showed vases of flowers, their stalks extended like arms, shiny sofas, red carpets and lots of mirrors around the walls.

"Hello," he said, the smile still fixed on his face. "Are you on your own?"

"Yeah."

"Are you wanting anyone in particular?"

"Um, Azumi."

"Fine. This way, please."

He guided me to a black leather couch beside a glass table. When I took out a cigarette he put down the menu, dropped to one knee and lit it for me. There weren't that many customers, perhaps because it was still early. From time to time I heard laughter.

Azusa Konishi was wearing a red dress, and her elaborately styled hair reflected the light from the chandeliers behind her. Staying in character, she sat beside me with a smile.

"You came," she said, as though we were friends.

The waiter bowed low and moved away.

"Are you sure it's okay?" I asked.

"Yes. She's free at the moment. I'm really sorry about that business with the phone."

"Don't worry about it. So . . ."

"Okay. I'll call her. Ah, what would you like to drink? Gin and tonic?"

She put ice in a glass and started to fix me a drink. With her pert breasts and beautifully made-up face, she looked every inch a hostess. She called the waiter over with a gesture. Thanking me and feigning a smile, she told him to invite Kaori to join us.

The tip of my cigarette glowed feebly, like a chink of light in a thick fog. I stretched out my hand slowly to pick it up, but my vision was dim and although my fingers managed to find the ashtray, they couldn't grasp properly. I heard voices, I saw the light reflecting off a corner of the table. Then the fog cleared, my view grew broader and I could see part of my glass, damp with drops of water. I heard a high-pitched voice, and when I turned towards it I could make out a white arm. A white arm extending from a white dress, elegantly curved at the elbow. It was lovely. My head felt like it weighed a ton, and as I looked up, the noise of the bar returned abruptly. And there was Kaori. Azusa was talking, but I couldn't hear a word she was saying. A white dress, black hair down to her shoulders, two bright eyes, a small nose, thin lips glossy with lipstick.

"Nice to meet you," she said.

Her voice, clear and light, exactly as it sounded through the projector. Suddenly I could hear again. Azusa was speaking, watching me with a smile on her face.

"This is Mr. Shintani, an old friend. He asked if I had any friends who could join us. He's very generous."

She continued to watch me closely.

"Thank you," said Kaori. "I haven't been very popular this month."

She was talking to me. Talking to me face to face. Her voice was high and pure, just as it had been back then. Her large, dark eyes shone in the light. I realized I was staring, but couldn't tear my eyes away. She held out her business card. On it was printed a single name in block letters—KAORI.

"Um, excuse me. Are you disappointed . . . ?"

I had to say something.

"No," I gasped. "Just the opposite . . . You're extremely beautiful."

"Liar." She laughed.

Kaori was listening to me, answering me. I could hardly breathe.

"If you're a friend of Azumi's, you won't look twice at me. That reminds me, the boss here is really rude."

She grinned mischievously. That smile pierced me to the heart.

"At the job interview he told me that I wasn't up to their usual standards, but that they needed someone like me as well. A second-stringer. Isn't that a terrible thing to say? Being told I'm not that good-looking, but they need someone plain?"

Azusa laughed.

"Are you still going on about that, Kaori?"

"No," I said. "You really are pretty."

And truly, she was so beautiful it took my breath away. No matter what anyone else said, Kaori was gorgeous.

"Very pretty," I repeated.

The waiter approached. Azusa had another customer, so she had to leave us. We had arranged this in advance. I asked the waiter not to disturb Kaori and me and he nodded pleasantly.

"Do you mind?" Kaori asked. "If it's just me?"

"Of course not. I don't often come to places like this, so I get nervous when I'm around lots of girls."

She looked at me, mystified. My forgotten cigarette had almost burned itself out in the ashtray. I stubbed it out, and Kaori immediately replaced the ashtray with a clean one.

"Eh?" I said. "That was still fine."

"It's a house rule. This too."

She wiped the condensation off the outside of my glass with a white cloth.

"But," she began, looking away hesitantly for a moment and then facing me again. "Um, have we met before or something, like, a long time ago?"

My heart beat faster. She pushed her face closer to mine. I couldn't tell if this was a spontaneous gesture or a practiced technique.

"This is uncanny," she said. "I don't know."

The jazz coming from the speakers seemed to have grown louder. Breathing unsteadily, I groped for my cigarette but couldn't find it. The room felt overheated. The ends of Kaori's black hair seemed to tremble in a faint draught. I lowered my eyes and took my driver's license out of my wallet.

"See, my name's Shintani, like I said. Look, the characters for 'new' and for 'valley,' first name Koichi. Have we really met somewhere? It might not look like it, but it's quite an unusual name."

She stared at the photo.

"Maybe it is. But mine's even rarer."

I knew I was supposed to ask her what it was, but I couldn't bring myself to hear that name. I tried to change the subject.

"Have you got any hobbies or anything?"

"Hobbies? Umm."

She glanced to one side, as though she was giving the matter some serious thought.

"Not really, but I like reading. Thoughtful stuff."

"Thoughtful?"

She nodded noncommittally.

"Oh, I don't mean really difficult books. I like books that make me laugh too."

A group of high-powered executives in expensive suits walked in.

"There's got to be some thought behind it. Of course it should be interesting as well, but if you only read shallow books, you're likely to absorb some of the ugly attitudes behind them."

"I see what you mean, I think."

"Apart from that, I collect hair-ties."

"Hair-ties?"

"Yes. Rubber bands to hold my hair when I'm removing my make-up. I've got about fifty at home."

I laughed. "Really? Why do you do that?"

"I don't know. Is it odd?"

The bar was slowly filling up. The music changed from jazz to classical piano, then back to jazz again. Several young women in sexy dresses were circulating through the room. I dropped my gaze, unable to look squarely at Kaori's breasts and shoulders in her white dress.

"You're nice, Kaori."

She shook her head.

"No, I'm not. For example, sometimes I get really annoyed. Look, see that important-looking guy over there?"

When I followed the direction of her eyes I saw a portly man in a bow tie.

"That's my boss. He's really strict—he comes around saying things like, 'You forgot to light that customer's cigarette twice.' So Azumi, she came up with a plan."

She smiled at the memory.

"Since he's really busy, he often takes a nap in one of the back rooms, and he keeps a toothbrush in there. She got the janitor to use it to clean the toilet, and then put it back."

I laughed again.

"That's mean."

"Yes. We're horrible. But please don't tell anyone."

I wondered what the hell Konishi was doing when she was supposed to be working on a case, but I found myself laughing too. Time was slipping by. Even though I knew it was an illusion, I felt like it was flowing backwards, winding back the years.

"You definitely don't seem like someone you'd find in a place like this."

"Really?"

She rested her slim arms on the table.

"The first time I was invited here by a friend. Before that I was working for a company, but it went bankrupt in mysterious circumstances."

She raised her eyes as though she were thinking.

"Several bad things happened around then, and I realized that I should have some money."

I reached for my drink. The sweat on my palm mingled with the droplets on the surface of the glass.

"At least if you've got money you can get a room somewhere and live by yourself, even if you've got no friends and nothing you can rely on. Don't you agree?"

"I guess."

"I didn't think I'd ever be lucky, so I decided to at least save some money. Just recently, a bit at a time."

She smiled faintly. It was exactly the same as her smile from all those years ago. I remembered her room, without a single doll or stuffed toy.

"You've got to be happy,' I said, and then choked up.

"What? You think so? Thank you."

The place was getting crowded. The piped music was still jumping from one style to another. My body felt limp but I managed to stand.

"I'll come again," I said. "Would you be able to go out somewhere with me, or meet me somewhere or something like that?"

"Really? I'd like that."

She smiled openly. I couldn't get my words out properly.

"But, are you sure? You don't know what kind of guy I am."

"I'm sure. Usually we only go out with regular customers, but you're a friend of Azumi's."

Her white dress was still painful to look at.

6

I WENT HOME and lay on my bed. I got an email from Kaori, saying that she'd enjoyed meeting me, that she wished I could have stayed longer, and that she hoped I'd come again. At the end she asked me playfully not to tell the manager about the toothbrush story.

I read and reread her message, which seemed to have fewer emoticons than a typical email from someone in her line of work. I was strongly tempted to watch her recording again, but I resisted. I waited for about thirty minutes, drinking whiskey, and then sent her a reply. The next thing I knew I was waking up on the floor. I had no idea how long I'd been asleep. Whiskey glass in hand, I moved to the couch and stared blankly at the wall. Its smooth, flat surface seemed to reject everything. I was covered in sweat. I'd had that dream about the chairs again. The one where there were six empty chairs in front of me, and I was waiting for something or someone that would judge my whole life. The phone rang, and I answered without thinking. It was Ito.

"Are you drunk?" he asked.

His voice echoed inside my head.

"Well, never mind. You told me the cops had identified a member of JL. Where did you hear that?"

"It doesn't matter who I heard it from."

I really didn't care. I had no interest in the subject at all.

"You were right. We're in deep shit. Actually there's someone else who's under suspicion, and I was more worried about him. I had no idea they'd spotted this other guy, the one you were telling me about, with the protruding jaw."

Ito's breathing was a little uneven, as though he was on the move.

"He's close to me. If he gets caught I'll be in real trouble. He's the one that stole the cell phone from that woman detective you hired."

"So what?"

"You're pretty slow, aren't you?" His voice rose. "That means he knows about you too. Even though you haven't done anything yet, if he gets arrested the cops might start investigating you as well, in connection to JL. And he knows about Kaori."

"What?"

"When I said I was going to use Kaori to get money out of Fumihiro, either by threatening him or by forming an alliance with him, he was against it. He said she must have money of her own, because she was Kuki's daughter, so we should just take it directly from her instead of going to all that trouble. I disagreed, because I don't like getting women involved on principle. But right now he's probably desperate. He needs money to escape. And I can't get hold of him, and I don't know why."

He couldn't hide the tension in his voice. I felt sweat trickling down my neck.

"Okay. Thanks for letting me know."

He was quiet for a second.

"Don't get me wrong. I'm only telling you this because if you're pissed at me I'll have no chance of getting money out of you. Plus I'm the one who got her mixed up in this. It's got nothing to do with her."

"Thanks. Bye."

I hung up and immediately called Azusa Konishi. She answered after seven rings.

"What are you doing now?" I asked her.

"We finished early, so Kaori and I went to a restaurant. I'm on my way home. How did things go with her today?"

It sounded like she was in a car.

"I'll tell you about that later, but could you get hold of her straight away, please? There might be this bad guy hanging around her apartment. It's just a possibility, but could you put her up at your place or somewhere, just in case? Just till I know it's safe."

"Sure. But why?"

"A member of JL is on the run, and apparently he's looking

for money. He knows a lot about her, that she's a Kuki and that she might be rich. I just want to play it safe."

"Understood."

"If there are any problems, give me a call, even in the middle of the night. And would you let me know as soon as you meet up with her?"

"Will do."

I hung up, prowled around my room for a bit, and looked at the clock. It was still midnight. I wanted to do something, but realized that at the moment there wasn't much I could do to help Kaori. I couldn't just stay home, though, so I went down in the elevator, bought a can of coffee I didn't really want from a vending machine and drank it as I walked. I was looking at the apartment building over the road when someone called my name from behind. Standing some distance away was Aida. I ignored him, and heard his irritated footsteps following me.

"Amazing, isn't it? As soon as I get here, I meet you outside your condo. There must be something between us after all."

He was panting.

"It's the other way around. Even though it's late, I was going out just as you got here. Just bad timing."

"I still caught you. Only just, though, right?"

He grinned, watching me intently through narrow eyes.

"So, what do you want? You said we wouldn't meet again."

He took out a photograph.

"This is you, isn't it? What's the story?"

It was me, all right, in a black coat, talking to someone. It was somewhere outside. All I could see of the other person was part of a hand, but I could tell from the wristband that it was Ito.

"Yeah, that's me. What about it?"

"That guy who's on the run, Kanzaki, he had this picture. The guy from JL. What does it mean?"

"That's what I'd like to know."

I realized that I was calm, probably thanks to the fact that Ito had warned me just before I came out.

"Don't tell me you're in JL?"

"Yeah right."

"Yeah, that's what I thought."

His stare grew more searching.

"I know you. At least, I think I do. You're a hard-nosed realist. You're not the type to join a group like that. My gut feeling tells me it's impossible. That's why I don't get this. What's going on?"

"I told you, I don't know."

I frowned, let out a long, slow sigh.

"Was this taken with a digital camera? Or a cell phone? Are you saying that everyone he's got a photo of is in JL? Anyway, that's me in the picture, but it's not focused on me. It's pointing further away."

Aida was still holding up the photo.

"That's not unusual when people are trying to take pictures without being seen," he said.

"Well, then, maybe he was trying to take a picture of something else and missed? Maybe of that woman walking behind me, for example."

"So you reckon it's just coincidence?"

"I'm just guessing. Anyway, I'm not interested in your affairs. You're a pain in the ass."

"By the way," he began, pointing a stubby finger at something over my shoulder. "What's that car doing there?"

A black car was parked at the corner of the condo, half its body sticking out like it wanted to be noticed. Mikihiko's private eye.

"Last time we met, that same car was following you and drove straight past us."

"Haven't got a clue."

"Sure you don't."

"Are you telling me that's a JL car? An expensive model like that?"

"You've got good eyesight. You can tell it's expensive? When someone's lying, their instincts are to say the first convenient fact that comes into their heads to back up the lie. They say one word too many."

At that moment my cell phone chirped to tell me I had mail. When I looked at the screen, it was from Azusa. She had just got into a taxi with Kaori. I breathed out slowly, my mind at ease for the time being.

"What was that about?"

"None of your business."

"Mind if I take a look at that email?"

"Of course I mind. It's from this woman. I gave it to her good yesterday, and she wrote to say she wants more."

"You really don't like talking to me, do you? But I've got some news for you. Yaeko passed away."

He continued to observe me closely.

"Is that so?"

"Actually I was going to tell you that first, but for some reason I ended up talking about the photo instead. I wonder why?"

"Beats me."

"I'm beginning to wonder if I do understand you after all. To be honest, I came here today to show you this photo and to give you that bad news, because I wanted to see how you'd react. And your reactions were just too natural."

A strong wind was blowing.

"Just like lots of really smart criminals I've met. Too natural."

I looked at him. He squinted back at me.

"So now I'm trembling with joy," he said.

"You're creepy, you know that?"

"See, that's the reaction I'm talking about."

We stared at each other for a long time. A noisy motorbike passed right beside us. He glared at me, unsmiling.

"We will meet again, after all. Now I've got my eye on you for a different reason. A different reason."

"You're wasting your time."

I squeezed past him, standing there like he was trying to block my way, and returned to the condo without glancing back.

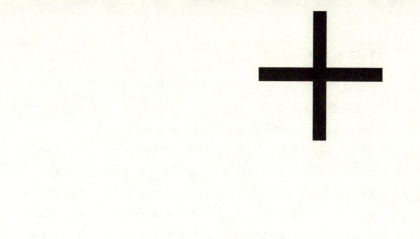

7

I OPENED THE curtain a fraction and peeked out the window. Mikihiko's private detective was parked outside, and had been there for several hours. I grabbed my phone and called Azusa Konishi. I was thirsty, so I sipped a glass of water while it was ringing, though she answered after a few seconds. I knew it was a bit rushed, but today was my only chance.

"I want you to call the cops right now, tell them there's been a strange car sitting outside your apartment for a long time. It's been following you, lying in wait for you all day. Give them my address."

"Okay. What color is it?"

"Black. The driver is a man in his fifties."

I hung up and called for a taxi. Then I put on my coat and looked out the window, smoking.

After about ten minutes a green taxi turned up, but I kept watching the black car, waiting for the police. Suddenly, however, the black car took off and disappeared around the corner. A minute later, as I was wondering what was going on, a patrol car arrived, its siren off. The timing, like it had been pre-arranged, gave me a bad feeling. Leaving the lights on, I took the elevator down, went outside and got into the cab, acting like I didn't see the black and white, which was still prowling theatrically. At that moment, though, I realized the cop was staring right at me. Pretending to be looking at my cell phone, I told the driver my destination. I checked the reflection in the side mirror several times, and as we went around the corner I sneaked a glance behind me. The patrol car didn't seem to be following.

I switched taxis at a shopping mall, and then again outside a railway station. Finally I got out in a residential area I'd never seen before. It was gradually growing dark, and the tall apartment blocks seemed to loom over me. I passed the watery lights of a gym, the harsh glare of a convenience store. I turned into a claustrophobic alleyway, and a cat emerged from the shadow of an abandoned bicycle. As I approached the condo, I buttoned up my new coat, pulled a large beanie down over my ears and put on a pair of sunglasses and a white paper mask, as though I had a cold. The scrawny cat stared at me. I entered the building, conscious of the weight of the bag I was carrying.

Just as the detective had said, there was no sign of any security cameras. Inside it was new but poky, and totally silent. I pushed the button for the seventh floor and the elevator doors slid closed. The building was full of tiny rooms that rich people rented for various reasons, no questions asked. Surrounded by apartment blocks, it was apparently used for storage and secret gang meetings, and women were also often seen coming and going.

I pressed the doorbell. There was no answer. I'd come prepared with lock-picking tools, but when I tried the handle the door opened. I noted that it was a lever type. My throat was dry, my fingers clammy inside my gloves. Putting the hat and sunglasses back in my bag, I moved along the cold hallway to another door. When I opened it I could see an orange light casting a feeble glow. In the middle of the room, Mikihiko Kuki was slumped on a couch, drinking. Bile rose in my throat, and I forced it back down. There was a strong smell of a woman's perfume. Walking slowly, I went and sat on the opposite sofa, facing him. He must have seen me, but he gave no sign of recognition. I placed the bag carefully on the floor.

"I've been waiting. I thought you'd come here. My private eye told me he'd lost you."

I kept my face blank.

"Anyway, you turned up at just the right time, because I was planning to meet you soon, and I can't get my secretary to bring you here. This place is secret, and my wife's bribed him to keep an eye on me. Stupid."

He took a mouthful of whiskey. The way he poured it

slowly into his mouth bore an almost sickening resemblance to Father.

"I bet you're plotting something. Unfortunately, though, I'm not remotely interested in your schemes. Something to drink?"

"I'll have the same."

I needed a drink—there was no way my tension would thaw out without one. There was no woman in the room, but I suspected there had been until a few minutes ago.

"I hear you've got in touch with Kaori. Good. I don't mind giving you the privilege of ruining her. Go and destroy her completely."

I drank my scotch. My throat grew hot, and then a warmth spread through my whole body.

"She looks a lot like her."

Suddenly he looked at me with a taunting expression. The temperature in the room dropped sharply. His limbs were as relaxed as ever, but his gaze grew sharper.

"You know you killed her, your mother?"

It felt like someone had stabbed me in the heart. I sat there, right in front of him, staring at his face. He smiled faintly.

"Well, sort of. Didn't you? She died giving birth to you. What? You didn't know?"

The only thing I could see was his mouth moving.

"The old house has a room hidden under the cellar, like this secret room here. The room where you killed Father. Yeah? But there's another room below that, an even smaller one."

He took a slow breath.

"That's where all your mother's belongings were. Did you

know that? The clothes she was wearing, some odd keepsakes like the glass she was drinking out of, locks of her hair and so on. Why? Because your mother was the only woman that Shozo Kuki, our monstrous father, ever loved. Apparently he tended to become fixated on mementos. The only people who know about that are me and the housekeeper Tanabe."

He was tapping his glass with his fingernails.

"I've already found Father's body, you know. When I heard that he'd gone missing, I thought he'd killed himself. Buried under relics of his dead lover. I visited the estate, called Tanabe, who'd been dismissed, and got her to open the underground room. Father had drunk the poison he carried on him. It appeared to be suicide, but it wasn't. There were strange scratches on the door handle, and it looked to me like he'd been locked in. Tanabe thought so too. She also found a child's footprints in the dust. She suspected you, but I wasn't sure, because you were still just a kid. Could you have done something like that? But as soon as I saw the torment in your face as you lay in bed, I was certain. I thought, 'Wow!' You looked absolutely identical to him, as though you'd murdered him and taken on his features. Last time we talked I told you it was the first time we'd met, but actually I watched you when you were having a nightmare way back then."

I was finding it hard to breathe. I forced myself to look at him. He laughed.

"What happened to Koichi Shintani? You had some kind of scheme in mind when you walked in here, didn't you? Don't say you've forgotten? Well, it must be hard to keep up the act when you're faced with the truth. But don't worry, Tanabe got rid of the old man's body, along with all your mother's stuff. The suicide of the chairman of the Kuki Group would have been too much of a shock for the affiliated companies. Even worse if they found out that he was killed by his own son. It's better to leave it unclear, whereabouts unknown, just treat him as dead. Like he had an accident while he was enjoying a hike in the mountains or fishing in a river somewhere. Tanabe was Father's mistress, and mine too. She hated your mother, so she burned all her things. And she was devoted to Father, so she dealt with his body as well. Cleaning up your mess."

He kept drinking his whiskey. His eyes were glazed with alcohol, and the smell was gradually drowning out the lingering scent of perfume. I couldn't keep up with what he was saying.

"Kaori looks like your mother. Not so much her face, just her general aura. I saw her once, and that's what I thought. I haven't been able to find out who her parents were, no matter how hard I looked, but I'd say they had some loose connection to the Kukis. Because Father was attracted to her, and so am I, even though she's not all that good-looking. She doesn't look anything like my mother, but somehow she's got under my skin. I'll tell you a story."

He stood up and took another bottle from the liquor cabinet. He couldn't be bothered getting ice, so he poured the lukewarm scotch into the glass just as it was.

"Several years ago, in Shinjuku in Tokyo, there was a traffic accident."

He slouched heavily onto the sofa again.

"Just a typical accident, and the person who died had

nothing to do with us. An ordinary collision between a car and a cyclist. The driver hurt his wrist slightly and the woman on the bike was killed instantly. The driver took his eyes off the road, just for a second, distracted by his cell phone, which he'd tossed on the passenger seat. Hundreds of accidents like that happen every day. But when I looked into it, some eerie facts came to light."

His thick lips twisted at an angle, though whether he was smiling or grimacing I couldn't tell.

"The driver's ancestor and the cyclist's ancestor came into contact once, a long time ago, during the war with China in the 1930s. The man's grandfather was a soldier. The woman on the bike was Japanese, but her relatives on her mother's side were from China. The driver's grandfather was in the Japanese army and during the war his unit was ordered to attack a particular Chinese village. Pillage, slaughter, they did it all. The man himself didn't actually take part in the looting, but since he was the youngest member of the platoon he couldn't put a stop to their folly and just had to endure it. And the cyclist's grandparents were caught up in the massacre and lost their lives. In other words, many years later the descendant of the man who had witnessed the carnage in China ended up killing the descendant of two of the victims, here in Shinjuku. This sounds like some kind of fate passed down through the generations, but there are four things about the story that are quite creepy."

The ceiling fan started turning uncertainly.

"One is that this traffic accident wasn't some kind of ancestral revenge tragedy. The perpetrators were still the perpetrators, the victims still the victims. The second is that the ancestor was present at the massacre but didn't actually join in. Third, the accident was not deliberate on the part of the driver. A moment's inattention, as it were, a simple mistake. And the fourth thing is that the driver received a slight injury to his wrist, but the soldier, tormented by his memories of the atrocities, in later life attacked his own wrists several times with a hatchet. What do you think of that?"

He poured another drink.

"It's just a coincidence," I said.

"True, you can look at it that way too. But you do hear stories like that from time to time. Or you could call it 'karma.' Like the killer driving the car and the victim were suddenly, through their respective bloodlines, swept up in that flurry of violence, that massacre in the Chinese village, like some kind of time slip. Retroactively, the accident makes the driver's ancestor seem like a perpetrator as well. If the accident was really just negligence, perhaps that means that karma can manipulate people's unconscious minds, as though they are linked through the unconscious. In this world, I believe that there are many incomprehensible karmic threads that transcend time and space. I don't know what these threads are trying to achieve by repeating similar things in different times and places. Maybe that girl Kaori had some kind of connection with the Kukis. Maybe she's descended from someone who was killed by one of the guns we sold in World War One."

"That's absurd."

"Really? Or perhaps she's the great-great-granddaughter of some woman who was raped by a Kuki. Or the descendant of that dead woman's best friend. Don't you think the word 'karma' has a really Japanese ring to it?"

He laughed. The whiskey seemed to be seeping out through his eyeballs.

"Maybe the Kuki family's repeated acts of wickedness are leading somewhere too. At any rate, when I look at her I feel a definite attraction. She stirs something inside me. I bet it's the same for you, isn't it?"

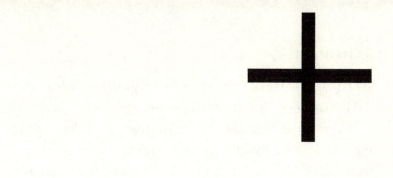

8

THE ONLY SOUND in the room was the tortured rumble of the fan heater. Maybe the place was soundproofed, because I couldn't hear a peep from the adjoining rooms. I took another mouthful of scotch in the gloom, felt the warmth slide down my throat. My cigarette smoke swayed lazily at the edge of my vision.

"It's going to be another long night," said Mikihiko, standing.

He scooped a small red fish out of the aquarium and dropped it in a dish, where it twitched convulsively. He watched for a while without expression, then deposited it on the counter behind him. It was still floundering, but he had lost interest.

"I'm so depressed. I almost killed this girl a little while ago."

He sank into the sofa in front of me again.

"Hurry up and spoil her. Defile the thing you value most in the world. If you pass through that violent whirlpool you can truly liberate yourself from the mundane and from your own life. Then come over to my domain."

The red fish had almost stopped moving.

"You're drunk," he said, smiling faintly. "This booze is strong. You look pretty slow-witted for someone who's up to something. But never mind. You're distracted, and I can bypass your consciousness and talk directly to your subconscious."

His eyelid was twitching slightly.

"You should be my sidekick. You'll enter my realm and be free. You'll be a perfect cancer, and I'll show you some wonderful sights. Since you killed Father and killed Yajima, you're the ideal person to be by my side. Here, I'll let you in on my modest goals."

I reached for more whiskey.

"But before I do, let me ask you this. If you were king of a country and you had no ethics or morals, what kind of citizens would be your ideal?"

He watched me. When I answered, my voice had gone hoarse.

"Ones who are easy to manipulate, I suppose."

"That's right."

I thought he might smile at that, but he didn't.

"Citizens with no doubts about anything, who will trust their king like children no matter what he does, who will get fired up as a single, unified body in support of war, who will turn a blind eye to corruption, who will swallow all his propaganda. Simple people, you could call them."

The fish behind him was completely still.

"These days, in fact, when people are readily susceptible to images and impressions, it's fairly easy to manipulate them with information from the government or the government's proxies. There are lots of ways of doing it, some of them visible, some not. If you don't believe me, just look at the screwed-up logic that was used to justify the Iraq War. The intelligentsia call this populism. They say that the public are stupid for being fooled by the government's lies. But that's not strictly true."

He smiled faintly.

"Why did the simplistic logic of the so-called War on Terror end up prevailing, despite being widely criticized? Why does a politician's popularity change because of images on TV? When three Japanese nationals were taken hostage in Iraq, why did the harsh phrase 'individual responsibility' become so widely accepted in Japan? Why is public opinion swayed by primitive images rather than by the complex reality of events? The answer is that people are busy. There are other reasons as well, but that's the main one. Everyone is busy with their daily lives, their worries, their work, their search for happiness, and you can't blame them for that. Who's going to take time out from their busy life to think about a dispute in some tiny country in Africa, let alone the business interests behind it? Do you think they're going to go beyond the mass media and examine the real meaning of the information the government is feeding them? Do you think that when some criminal is presented as an absolute villain, anyone is going to wonder if he's been falsely accused and actually go out and do their own digging? Do you think anyone will look into whether a TV commentator has got close ties to a particular political party? Hardly anyone will do that. Most people are too busy. And by working away behind the scenes, we're planning to provoke North Korea. We're planning Japan's Nine-Eleven."

He continued to study me, his face giving nothing away.

"Imagine a missile hitting Japan. Public opinion would change in an instant. The Peace Constitution would be thrown out of the window. As the number of victims was reported, as the grief of their families was reported, the whole country would be filled with pity and seethe with hatred towards North Korea. When people believe they have a good cause, the violence within them bursts forth unrestrained, as if their good angel has given permission for it to escape. Basically, that's how wars are started. The public executions they had in the old days worked on the same principle. Hardly anyone realized that they served any purpose other than punishing criminals, and even if they did, their voices were drowned out by the boiling violence of righteousness. People have enough on their plates just going about their day-to-day lives. Japan would agree to war, and our profits would be beyond our wildest dreams. The state would use taxes to buy the weapons we manufacture. Transport planes, the whole lot. And then after North Korea was defeated there'd be a construction boom. Obscene people flock to obscene money, and after millions of deaths there'd be even more obscene money swirling around. War is the best business model there is."

His mouth opened in a swallowing motion.

"At first I thought it would be okay if the missile missed the target, with only a few casualties. In that case there wouldn't be a war, but the defense budget would skyrocket and new markets would open up for us. That would certainly be entertaining to watch, but now I think we can go further than that, because I'm already ruined, and of course the object of a plan born from ruin will be more ruin. I don't care how many missiles rain down on central Tokyo. The country will be thrown into chaos, America and China will get involved, and the whole munitions industry will come along for the ride. That's part of my plan too. American arms manufacturers will be delighted, at any rate, because Japan will buy more weapons. This is all several years down the track, but I've got it all planned out."

He blew out a puff of air and rubbed his eyelid, as if the twitching was bothering him.

"It won't go that smoothly," I said. I could feel the corners of my mouth curling in a faint smile. "Even if people like you make your plans, humans don't always react as you expect. Sure, we're busy with our own problems, and it's hard to pay much attention to contracts for rebuilding in Africa. But you're carrying out your plan in Japan, right? I can't see the Japanese public acting like you think they will."

"That's right. You're not dumb, are you?" His voice grew stronger. "In fact, after we set things up, I think people's reactions are likely to be even more extreme than we anticipate. We'll just provide the catalyst, but the wave will pass through that human maelstrom and burst out in unexpected directions. Look at history. Before the Second World War, when

Japan walked out of the League of Nations, the forerunner to the UN, Japan's elite didn't expect their stupidity to be greeted with wild applause by the public back home, did they? Even World War Two itself, which unleashed Father's violence, the people supported it sincerely, fanatically. In other words, their frenzy provided the foundation for his violence. Do you think that the highest-ranking officials thought right from the start that the general populace would cooperate so eagerly with the war effort? They even continued to feed the public lies in order to manipulate them. But the people were busy and narrow-minded. They believed that they should slaughter foreigners to protect their friends and families. Their excitement and violence, rooted in a good cause, rose like a flood. It's a fever, get it? That fever, that's what I want. That fever, that flood, heading for doom."

By now he was almost shouting.

"Everything fits together as part of the system. That JL group that's active right now, their aim is probably to undermine authority. They're trying to bring it all tumbling down. But even their attacks on authority are ultimately part of the system. Thanks to JL, people are far more security-conscious, and at the moment my security firms are making a killing. Burglar alarms, everything, they're selling like crazy. Share prices are rising too, so the shareholders are making more money. The more they stir up trouble, the more money us rich people make. That's how the system works. You see? They probably don't even realize it themselves, but we actually provide some of their funding. This world is a monster."

He laughed and his eyes grew wider.

"Now that I would love to see. All the buildings collapsing, the fortress of people's happiness collapsing because their closed-up nature allows wars to break out and they get caught up in them. All that violent karma flying through space and time, converging on a single point. Wouldn't that be a sight? For warped specimens like us? As I looked on the ruins of the earth, with my dying breath I would mutter, 'Construction boom.' If the human race dies out entirely, then beauty and morality will disappear too. If that happens, even the gods who have neglected this world for so long will scowl with displeasure—if gods have eyebrows, that is. The human race, that failed experiment, will take revenge on the gods through their own downfall. Revenge on their father. Maybe the gods will come to stop it partway through. If they do, humans will be able to see them in person for the first time. Wouldn't that be amusing? It can all go to hell. In my dystopia, it can all just disappear!"

Suddenly he started to tremble, eyes blazing. I had a sinking feeling in the pit of my stomach, but I couldn't tear my eyes away from him.

"Ah, here it comes! Now!"

He clamped his lips tightly together, sweat pouring off him, still staring into space. His hands fumbled under the table, searching for something.

"Right. How about it?"

His hands came out holding a knife. Slowly, carefully, he placed it on the table like some precious object.

At some point the heater had stopped blowing out warm air, and I was getting cold. He took his hand away from the knife and sat rigid, as though turned to stone. His eyes remained unblinking, like a man possessed. I remembered the exalted state he had been in last time we met, similar to this. His gaze bored into mine, and I couldn't break free.

"Look!" he whispered in a choked voice, as if afraid of being heard. "Don't you see? Look! Now's your chance . . . look, do it, don't miss it. What are you waiting for? Look, here's my throat. Like this, like this."

He was making stabbing motions with an imaginary knife, as though teaching a child how to use one.

"This person called Mikihiko Kuki, he's already way past breaking point. Now's the perfect opportunity, don't miss it! Don't let it get away. Yeah? Quick! Before the moment passes. Quick, it's slipping away!"

He forced the knife into my hand. I couldn't move.

"Now is the time. This is what you see at the limits of depression. Death isn't the end, it's just one part, it's just one component. Give me that part, while I'm in this state, the epitome of evil, then my depression will break through, it will be complete, I will attain my true nature. Touched by death, the pleasure of extinction, at that instant I'll overflow, I'll become myself. I'll become my true self, death itself, the end itself, perfectly, perfectly, in that single second. It will all soak right through me. I'll join every other death, the pain and death of every person in every age, I'll savor them all. Every nerve that runs through my body will experience an unbearable delight as that huge, final wave washes over me. That's the moment. That's what my life is about, to go there, to experience that feeling. Everything yearns for oblivion. No matter how hard people struggle, all things are just waiting for death, trembling with joy. That's the reality of the world. It's here, the end of everything, it's really coming, subverting and perverting our innate energy."

He squirmed in his seat, speaking coaxingly, as though whispering words of love.

"Quick! It's all right. I've turned into this gigantic, grotesque monster before your eyes. You will be forgiven. The murders you've committed, they will all be forgiven. All your sins will disappear, by destroying an evil like me, by saving the lives of tens of thousands of people."

The knife started to shake in my hand.

"I'm right, aren't I? If I die, it will all be over, and I can become my true self. Kaori will be yours. Here's my throat, one second will solve everything, the depression that's holding me back, the revelation of my real self. Right here, right now. I can feel it coming."

I couldn't breathe. His soft, fat neck was right there in front of me.

"Do it quick. Yes, like that . . . Humans have always done this. They've always solved problems like this, by killing people they think are evil, by killing people who threaten their well-being. A man like me, who wants to destroy humanity, I'm an abomination, aren't I, for all those people who want happiness, even for the gods? Aren't I?"

Suddenly he began to shout. His mouth opened so wide I thought it would split and his bloodshot eyes bulged. In his exposed throat the thick veins stood out clearly.

"Quick! Everything will be forgiven. The gods and history are watching."

He stretched his neck even more, staring at me. My hand clutching the knife was soaked with sweat. I saw my father, twitching and convulsing with hunger in that tiny room.

"I can't."

"What?"

His face contorted.

"I'm too tired," I said. "Tired of this feeling."

He looked at me, mouth sagging.

"What a weakling! You've already killed two people. I expected better of you."

Gradually his expression regained its former blankness, as though something had passed. All that remained were the beads of sweat on his forehead. Once again his face revealed no emotion at all.

"You're pathetic. Really. Here's what will happen if you don't. I'll ruin that girl Kaori, and there's no way you can stop me. I'll keep her alive, but I'll destroy her, and I'll make you watch. I'll finish what Father couldn't. Perhaps that echo will alleviate my depression a little."

He picked up his whiskey again. I took out my pen.

"I've recorded all of this. The whole conversation."

He looked at me impassively.

"Since you're the Number Two in the Kuki Group, that could make life difficult for you. That you're helping JL, and all your crazy plans."

He laughed softly.

"Were you just pretending to be drunk, coming up with a feeble trick like that? What a loser."

From my bag I removed the bundle of documents and the compact disks.

"These contain proof of some of the things you've done so far. Even a recording of you killing your own daughter in this very room."

"Yeah?"

"Your secret discussions with a certain politician. Your illegal exports of large numbers of weapons, including centrifuges that could be used to develop nuclear weapons and helicopters that can be converted for military use. Even proof that you killed two prostitutes."

He regarded me with a bored expression.

"How did you get these?"

"Your own father was checking up on you the whole time. He always had reservations about you. He suspected that one day you'd be a danger to the Group."

"That detective?"

"I can't say. But your father had lots of other investigators apart from him. In terms of keeping tabs on people, he was way ahead of you. He compiled this material when you started going off the rails, as a threat to make you stop."

"I got someone to search his room after he died, and there were no records."

"He was careful."

I gripped my knees to stop my hands shaking.

"People like you, until your evil takes over completely, you pile up one crime after another. It goes without saying there's going to be a record."

I glanced at the knife on the table.

"Now even if you shoot me or something, it won't do you any good."

I looked at my watch. It was five to one.

"These are copies. In fact, I made multiple copies, and at one A.M. a friend is going to send them all off to the metropolitan police, the public prosecutor, the newspapers and TV, foreign corporations whose interests are opposed to the Kuki Group, and to the shareholders of every company you own. The cops will be knocking on your door any day now. You'll be caught and you can tell the police whatever you like, I don't care anymore. I hope you fall into the arms of the law, into a media storm, into the frenzy you were just telling me about."

To my surprise, he grinned.

"So the old man didn't love me after all."

The smile stayed on his face. Images of Father's missing ear, of the farming village in the Philippines that was the trigger for his explosion of violence, floated through my mind. Mikihiko sighed.

"Not bad. But you don't understand the first thing about me."

He took another gulp of scotch.

"Those things don't work on me. Do you really think I care about stuff like that? You're a real disappointment."

I took the explosive device out of my bag, the one that Ryosuke Ito had given me for safekeeping.

"This is cheap and simply made," I said, "but it'll blow away everything in this room. Now it's switched on."

I pressed the button on the cell phone that I'd modified and connected to the wiring. His face betrayed nothing.

"If you want to stay alive, it's easy. All you have to do is turn off the phone. You've got thirty minutes."

I got to my feet.

"I hope you get scared for your own life and turn this thing off. And think about all the people you've killed, all the people you were going to kill."

He gave a short laugh.

"Scared for my life? You're a cancer, aren't you?"

"I was just playing my small part, while evil monsters like you and Shozo Kuki took the leads. All I did was tie Shozo's malicious inquiries to your evil. And besides, Fumihiro Kuki is dead. My name is Shintani."

I put on my gloves. I didn't have any fingerprints, but I gathered up the knife and glass anyway, conscious that they might show palm prints. On the cell phone's display the tiny numbers were counting down.

"You don't understand a thing," he said quietly. "That won't affect someone as powerful as me."

"That's what you think."

"You're wrong." He gave a sigh of exasperation. "Just suppose that the world really worked the way you want it to. You'd still never get me inside a courtroom. The status quo will never change, because that's just how it is."

He continued wearily.

"Nothing will touch me. Unfortunately. Nothing can touch me. In the end, nothing will change. I'll just keep on living, just as I am now, whether I like it or not, wrapped in my own despair. And you will lose the girl."

"You'll never get your hands on Kaori," I said.

Our eyes locked for a few seconds. My gaze wavered, but his dull eyes didn't move. The timer on the bomb continued to count off the seconds.

"And while you're scared for your own life," I began, but he cut me off.

"You really don't have a clue. Nothing will change. Nothing can change. That's not what I want. Scared for my own life? What the hell are you talking about? Is that what you want?"

He was still lying deep in the sofa, wooden as ever, as though he was planning to sleep there. His face darkened.

"Are you telling me to cling to this ridiculous world? To life?"

He spoke lazily, sipping his drink.

"You must be joking."

I turned and walked away without answering. I could feel his presence at my back, but nothing happened as I left the room. I went down the hall, putting on my mask and beanie. Opened the front door, closed it gently behind me, lit a cigarette and headed towards the elevator. Not a sound came from Mikihiko Kuki's room.

9

"I THINK THE danger to Ms. Kaori has passed for the time being. They've started a full-scale manhunt for that JL suspect, so he'll probably be caught before long. At the moment she's at Konishi's place, and her building has tight security, so even if the guy does turn up she'll be safe."

The detective took a mouthful of hot coffee. I'd offered him tea, but he'd opted for coffee as usual.

"Okay, what about the media?"

"They'll handle it very carefully, because the dead man is Mikihiko Kuki, the second-in-command of the Kuki Group, and because he died while they were still checking whether the information they received was reliable."

On TV every station was running the story of Mikihiko's demise, of the explosion at his apartment, though they were saying they couldn't confirm if it was suicide or murder.

"When I looked at the material you gave me," I said, "it felt like a great weight had been placed on my shoulders. Mikihiko was raised by Shozo as a cancer. His father got tired of him partway through and let him go free, but by then it was already too late. Maybe, however, he believed that the discontinuation of his education was a sign of his father's love . . ."

"That seems unlikely."

He put the cup down quietly.

"His life was tragic. He looked like his spirit was broken. I . . ." I hesitated, then went on. "The estimated time of death was one thirty A.M."

"Yes."

"The same time the bomb went off. In other words, during that thirty minutes he didn't leave the room or take his own life. He just sat there the whole time."

Mikihiko's last minutes were really bothering me. His delirious ranting about death—I couldn't get it out of my head. I wondered if he was in that state of exaltation again at the moment of the blast. Did he feel everything soaking through him, feel himself becoming his true self? While he was sitting lethargically on the sofa, watching the numbers on the bomb growing smaller, did he feel it? Did he see the flash of the explosion?

"I don't know if this is a good outcome or not."

"I guess no one does," he replied.

We were meeting in a room at the same hotel, where the

detective had some kind of connection. A plane passing the window was just a shadow against the sun behind it. Perhaps the room was soundproofed, because there was no noise from outside.

"But I think you managed to change the course of events," he said suddenly, "whether you wanted to or not."

"What course of events?"

"I don't know. But in return, you've been badly damaged."

A banner was scrolling across the TV screen, saying that the body of a man who appeared to be the JL member wanted by the police had been found on the street. The cause of death was unknown.

"The press are having a field day, aren't they?" the detective muttered. "I wonder what happened to him?"

"Who knows?"

I watched the broadcast, sipping my coffee. It didn't taste of anything. Everything seemed to be passing me by without touching me.

"But I had nothing to do with that."

"I guess they have their own story, even though they've been taken advantage of by people like Mikihiko Kuki."

The presenter started reading the news flash out loud.

"But even assuming, for the sake of argument, that Mikihiko and his cronies planned it all, can people really be manipulated like that? Surely it can't be that simple?"

"I don't know. But there's a rumor that pretty soon several politicians and government officials are going to be under the microscope over those illegal arms exports, based on that information. That might put the brakes on them for a while."

The room was spotlessly clean. The heater was on, but my breath was coming out in white puffs. I stood up and started to walk away, but my legs went weak. I thought I was going to fall over.

"What are you . . . ?"

From his tone I sensed that even from behind he could tell I was unsteady.

"What are you going to do next?"

I debated whether or not to turn around, but realized I had nothing to add.

"I don't know, but for now, could you please make sure that Kaori is safe?"

I knew this was redundant, since the JL guy was dead and he'd just told me she was in no danger. But I couldn't think of anything else to say.

I WENT HOME and took off my coat. Pulled out a chair at the table, then went and sat on the bed instead. My pulse was uneven, so to take my mind off it I opened the fridge, took out a bottle of mineral water and drank. My heartbeat still wouldn't settle. I switched on the TV, but they were still going on about JL. I turned it off again and stood up. My bag was still lying on the table, as though I'd left it there on purpose. Inside was the bottle of cyanide.

I hadn't given it to Mikihiko because I figured that the bomb on its own would be enough. Though maybe that wasn't the real reason. Maybe I'd held onto it and brought it home so I could use it myself. I realized that I was staring at the bag, forced myself to look away, but I could feel my eyes being drawn back to it. It would be so easy. All my suffering until now—my heartbreaks, my depression, my regrets—all I had to do was drink that poison and they'd all disappear.

I hunted for a distraction, found my cigarettes and lit one. Just like the coffee I'd drunk at the hotel, it had no flavor at all. My pulse started to beat even faster and it hurt to breathe. I sidled towards the bag, took out the bottle and gazed at it for a long time. Just looking, I thought. It was cold to the touch. That chill felt right in my hand.

Remembering my half-finished cigarette in the ashtray, I picked it up and took a drag. I couldn't take my eyes off the bottle. It was like it was calling me. I'll just take the top off and take a peek, I thought, my body trembling with indecision.

I drank more water, focused on its coldness in my mouth. I told myself to put the bottle away for now, replaced it carefully in the backpack. My eyesight was still contracted to a narrow circle. Suddenly I needed to use the toilet, but just as I was leaving the room my cell phone rang. It was Kyoko Yoshioka.

"What are you up to?" she asked in her high-pitched voice.

I remembered that I'd called her once when I was drunk. Letting her know my number by mistake.

"You could say I'm busy."

It sounded like she was outside somewhere.

"Oh, okay, I'll keep it short. Um, that movie I was watching at your place, with the story that didn't go anywhere, what was it called?"

I walked slowly back into the living room.

"*Nostalgia*. It's Tarkovsky."

"Ah."

She fell silent. In the background I could hear the noise of cars, the shrill laughter of other pedestrians.

"Okay, thanks. Sorry. Bye."

There was another long pause, and then she hung up.

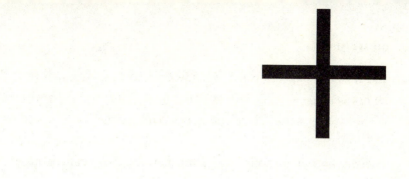

10

A DROPLET FORMED, slid down under its own weight, joined with other drops to become a trickle. The water reflected the lights. When I picked up my glass the drops seemed to cling to it, then quivered soundlessly on the table top as though unsure what to do next. I stuck a straw in my iced coffee, but it didn't taste of anything. I couldn't even feel its coldness on my tongue.

The man sitting at the table on my left, his head looked soft like a fruit. It seemed to swell and collapse in on itself. I felt I was suffocating. At that moment the door opened and Kaori walked in. She nearly bumped into the waiter, bowed and then turned towards me with a smile. I sipped my water and raised a hand to wave, but my gesture was too small to be noticeable.

"Sorry," she said. "Have you been waiting long?"

"No."

Seeming not to notice the state I was in, she called the waiter and ordered Darjeeling tea.

"I'm sorry about today. I know we were supposed to meet at the club, but . . ."

"Did something happen?"

"Yeah, there was . . ."

She looked down, as if reluctant to go on. I felt like the words were being dragged out of me. A customer nearby had put his briefcase on a chair, and for some reason I imagined that it contained a bottle of cyanide.

"I haven't had many customers lately, so Azumi suggested asking you to invite me out. It must be a pain. But even though you kindly agreed, suddenly there seemed to be some kind of trouble between the manager and the owner of the building, and the bar was closed for the day."

"Oh, well. I guessed there must have been a problem of some sort."

"I don't know, but I'm very sorry for putting you out."

"No, no, don't worry about it."

Beneath her white suit, her legs were sheathed in black stockings. Around her slender neck she wore a silver necklace. I couldn't bring myself to look at the supple movements of her body directly.

When I'd received her email invitation, I had immediately replied that I would come, but I had no idea what I would do

when I met her, what we would talk about. Everything I had
to do was already done. I had thought my life was already over
before I had the plastic surgery, when I was standing on the
roof of my condo looking down into the void without a thought
in my head. In spite of that, I'd kept on living. And now I'd
ended up here, and there was nothing left for me to do.

"Mr. Shintani?"

Kaori was staring at me with her big round eyes. Since it
wasn't a work day she wasn't wearing much make-up, and she
was so beautiful it made my heart ache.

"Are you all right?"

"Sorry?"

It didn't feel like we'd been there that long, but the café
had emptied out. The businessman with the briefcase was
still there, though. I couldn't shake the feeling that the bottle
of poison was inside.

"I'm sorry for dragging you all this way. You must have
better things to do."

"No, no, it's not that," I said.

I tried to smile to smooth things over, but the muscles in
my face wouldn't function properly.

"I'm just a bit tired from work."

"Sorry."

"Oh, it'll be all right. I'm on holiday at the moment, but I
still haven't caught up on sleep."

I finished my iced coffee, then reached for my cigarettes,
just to give my hands something to do.

"Is your work really busy?"

"No, well, no more than any other office job."

The waiter refilled my water glass with a smile. Kaori was drinking her tea. I hadn't noticed it arrive. Her lips were moist.

"What do you do?"

"Oh, just trading."

I remembered with a leaden feeling that I was actually unemployed.

"It sounds hard."

"Not really. Your job looks difficult too."

"Not at all."

She laughed. It brought back memories of her laughter as a child.

"The club isn't that busy. I guess it's nothing to joke about. At the moment we get a basic flat wage, but they're saying we could go to working on commission. If that happens I might have to quit."

"What would you do then?"

"Mm, who knows?"

She rested her arms on the table. Her slender fingers were moving slightly.

"When I was young, I thought about going to college and training as a nurse."

Her voice tailed off.

"You could still do that."

"No, it's impossible. I don't have the confidence. And I don't have much money."

I thought of all the money the Kukis must have sent her.

"But your job looks like it pays well."

"Mm. Well, I have money and I don't. I'd feel bad about using it."

"Feel bad?"

My pulse quickened.

"Yeah. I can't explain it very well, but a long time ago I was living with this rich family, and they gave me some money, but I caused them nothing but trouble."

I was about to object, but she continued.

"So nursing or anything like that is impossible, no matter what I do. Even going back to school is impossible."

"It's never too late," I said, but my words sounded hollow.

The waiter filled my glass once more, still with the same fixed smile. I looked at my watch.

"Oh, I'm sorry," I said. "I've taken up too much of your time, when you could be relaxing on your day off."

She gave a small shake of the head.

"No, you're the one who made time for me. If you don't have to rush off, maybe we could talk for a bit longer."

She looked out the window.

"It's a nice day. Shall we go for a walk?"

I looked outside too. It was chilly, and Kaori wasn't warmly dressed.

"But it looks cold."

"In that case, how about going for a drive? This is a pretty area."

And she smiled at me again.

KAORI HAD CASUALLY suggested a drive because she'd taken it for granted that I'd come by car, so she was very apologetic when I said I'd rent one, but I filled out the papers for a Prius at a rental agency in front of the station. She kept asking if I minded, and I replied jokingly that since she worked in a high-class club, it was peculiar that she'd get stressed about money. She took me seriously, however, and started apologizing even more profusely, so I had to explain myself. It was a bit windy outside, and the air felt dry. During our awkward exchange a junior high school couple walked past, holding hands with just the tips of their fingers. We got into the car.

Kaori's discreet perfume enveloped me. We were too close, and the whiteness of her clothes overwhelmed me. Even after I switched on the ignition I couldn't compose myself. The sheen of her stockinged legs was right there beside me. When I looked at them my heart fluttered, and I was painfully aware of her breasts as well. My entire happiness was sitting beside me, and I knew it would never be mine. The happiness that had turned up in my life once before like some kind of mistake, that had accepted me, and that had soon vanished into the distance. Memories of that time came flooding back, mingling with Kaori's immediate presence, more beautiful than ever. But she was really there, it wasn't a dream. Her warm body, Kaori herself, who had accepted without flinching my habit of collecting hair and toenails, was in the seat next to me. She was watching me curiously. Her face, too, was too close.

"Um, Kaori?" I said, gripping the steering wheel and staring straight ahead. "If you could, would you mind getting in the back?"

"Huh?"

"You're so pretty that having you sitting next to me makes me nervous."

She looked bewildered.

"What? I'm not that good-looking. And you're friends with Azumi."

"I really am nervous. Please?"

Clearly she found my request bizarre, but she got out and climbed into the back seat.

A silence fell over the car. At first she tried to hold it in, but soon she burst out laughing. I also smiled faintly, aware of the absurdity of our seating arrangements, of the whole situation.

"You're funny, Mr. Shintani!"

Maybe she really did think so. But perhaps romance is always absurd.

"Okay," I said. "Let's go. I haven't driven in a long time, so let's find somewhere without too much traffic."

"You look like a chauffeur."

We drove along the avenue. The trees were draped with cords for the New Year illumination, but since it was still daytime the lights hadn't been turned on. I wanted to find some quieter roads, but I didn't know Tokyo very well. It wasn't exactly rush hour, but we had to stop and start a lot. Kaori didn't seem to mind, though. She murmured that it was nice and warm, probably because the heater was on. She was watching me from behind, leaning forward on the seat.

"Oh, guess what? The manager I told you about, the one I don't like? He left."

"That's good."

"Yeah. But it looks like he was let go because sales are down, so at the same time I felt a bit sorry for him."

"Ah, I see."

Her voice touched my heart.

"Yeah, so on his last day we all bought a cake and gave it to him, as if we felt responsible. But one of the girls has a cat, and she dusted the cake with sand from its litter box."

I laughed.

"That's terrible."

"It must've been gritty when he took it home and ate it. It just looked like some kind of fancy powder."

"Yeah, really gritty powder! Women are scary!"

"Yes, especially when we gang up. But it's fun."

I turned left at the light for no particular reason and drove under a railroad bridge, thinking I didn't want to go too far. A couple in a red car waiting at an intersection were looking at us carelessly. They'd been shopping, and their back seat was piled with bags.

"Then the day before yesterday one of the girls—hey, the cake shop up ahead is good. Especially their cookies."

"After what you've just been talking about?"

"True." She laughed again.

"Okay, let's buy some."

"This time it's on me."

"No, don't worry about it."

I pulled up outside the shop and we bought some cookies. When we went back to the car and started eating them, crumbs scattered all over the upholstery.

"Look, we're making a mess," said Kaori.

"Doesn't matter, it's a rental."

"But look at it!"

"Yeah, you're right."

The cars started to thin out and there were fewer traffic lights. I made another random right turn on a road lined with apartment buildings. In the distance I could see the overpass of an expressway. I thought about listening to some music on the radio, then pulled my hand back, conscious of the possibility of hearing the news about Mikihiko. Until then things had been going quite smoothly, but for some reason the conversation stalled. I wanted to say something, but couldn't think of anything to talk about. Kaori's comment about feeling bad if she used the Kukis' money had stuck in my mind. She had it completely the wrong way around—it was the Kuki family that had caused her nothing but pain. I didn't know what she was apologizing for, and as far as I was concerned she should use whatever she could get her hands on to secure her future.

"Maybe you've heard this from Azumi," Kaori said, breaking the silence.

I was deep in my own thoughts, and her voice startled me. I realized she'd been speaking for some time.

"You know they're talking about that guy now, the one who died?"

Taken aback, I couldn't answer, and the atmosphere grew even more stilted.

"He's the son of the man who adopted me. I was astounded. I only met him once, though, when I was a kid."

The lights turned red, and I breathed a sigh of relief. I was finding it difficult to concentrate on the road.

"The money I was talking about, I got that when my guardian died. Then when I heard the news, I felt even more guilty."

"That's ridiculous," I said without thinking. "You've got nothing to feel guilty about."

Kaori was looking at my face in the rear view mirror.

"No, how can I put it . . ."

She dropped her gaze, staring at her feet.

"They're saying it might be suicide, aren't they? I'm not saying that's why, but I just thought, maybe my guardian killed himself too. Though he was already pretty old."

My throat was tight. I clung to the steering wheel, determined not to turn around.

"And he—" Kaori began, then stopped as though she'd remembered something. After a short silence she continued. "The old man who adopted me, he often used to weep in front of me. I was just a child then."

"What?"

The lights changed and I put my foot on the accelerator, but it was impossible for me to drive any more. I pulled over to the side of the road.

"The man who adopted you?"

"Yes. Um, Mr. Shintani?"

She was obviously wondering why I'd stopped. I couldn't utter a word.

"So, wow, how did we get to talking about this? Well, in that family, I . . . I had some problems, but the old man, he often got drunk and cried. It was really scary. Well, I found that pretty horrible, and I wasn't strong enough to handle it. But then the old man died, probably killed himself. And at the time I had this boyfriend, the same age as me, but I . . ."

"No," I shouted. "No. You mustn't think like that. Your . . . because Shozo Kuki was murdered."

"What?"

She stared at me. The silence seemed to grow even heavier. I went on, my throat hurting and my voice quavering.

"He was killed by a crime syndicate. There's proof. That's why."

"Mr. Shintani?"

The interior of the car was suddenly freezing.

"I . . . I know Fumihiro Kuki."

You could have heard a pin drop. Several cars drove by as we sat there on the shoulder.

"I don't think Azumi knows. I heard about you from Fumihiro. It's not that I was trying to keep it a secret, that I knew him. I just never got a chance to tell you. Azumi was talking about you, and when I heard the surname I realized you must be the woman he used to talk about. It's an unusual name. Fumihiro has always cared about you. If I ever saw you, he asked me to tell him how you were getting on."

"Fumihiro did?" she asked.

Kaori's voice, speaking my name.

"Yes, well, so, you don't have to worry about the Kukis anymore."

"What's he doing now?

Suddenly I was extremely reluctant to accept that I was no longer Fumihiro. I remembered that around the corner to the right there was the site of a demolished factory. I felt the dense air pressing down on me, felt something stirring inside. In the mirror I could see Kaori's lovely face. I couldn't move, as though I'd been seized by a powerful force. I gasped, realizing that what I was feeling was lust.

Maybe everything had been leading up to this moment, I thought. My chest thudded painfully and my eyesight dimmed. Mikihiko had told me that by eliminating all the people who were in the way, by setting up the right conditions, by meeting her again, I would destroy her. That I'd lay waste to the most beautiful, the most precious light in the entire world. And then that I'd transcend myself. By passing through an even greater shock than that of killing my father, I would change from a fretful human being into a monster. I would surpass my father and Mikihiko, I would wipe away the despondency that had shrouded me all my life, wipe away my regrets. I would change from Fumihiro to Shintani, and then from Shintani into a monster. I would cease to exist. In my madness, all my previous awareness would disappear completely. By dragging Kaori into the center of that turbulent vortex, my mind would change into a fierce flame and then vanish. From that point on I would never suffer again. As a monster cloaked in insanity, no memories or events would move me, because my previous self would perish. Then perhaps that violent, evil force would fly off somewhere else, like the traffic accident that Mikihiko had talked about. Maybe my whole life so far had been lived as that evil, for that evil. My heart was beating fiercely and I couldn't breathe. I looked at Kaori in the rear view mirror, but her eyes were too beautiful for me.

So beautiful that my existence, the reasons for my existence, lost all meaning. So beautiful that I was irrelevant.

Kaori's warmth, the joy of being with her day by day, certainly at one time it had been present in my life. I felt a persistent, overpowering pressure at the back of my neck. I couldn't destroy the me that possessed those joyful memories. Even if my consciousness was hard to bear, I never wanted to lose it, because that would mean losing my happy memories as well. No matter how miserable I might be, I wanted to keep those days inside me. I remained facing forward in the driver's seat.

"Fumihiro . . . he's happy now," I managed to say finally.

The windshield reflected my face back at me, the face of a killer, the face of a man who had lost everything.

"He's got a regular job at a company, he's married, he's happy. Working hard, and I heard he bought a house with a view of the ocean."

I still didn't look around.

"In the evenings he and his wife go for walks along the beach, hand in hand. She's quite cute, though not as pretty as you."

I knew I was just babbling.

"They've got one child, and he's doing his best not to pass his own depression on to his kid. When he argues with his wife, he's always quick to apologize. She often plays tricks on him, then laughs at his confusion. Pushes her beautiful eyes close to his and smiles mischievously. It's just an ordinary life, but for him . . ."

My eyes filled with tears and I could hardly carry on.

"But he says that he was really happy with you. Sure, it ended, but throughout his childhood he was able to keep on living because you were there, even with a father like that, even in that gloomy house. There were times when he thought about killing himself, but he managed to talk himself out of it thanks to the days he'd shared with you, because he knew you were out there somewhere. Because of you he was able to see a little good in this world. He could keep on going. His heart was filled with memories, and he never wanted to lose them. Those happy days really happened, and he wanted to keep them inside him forever. That's why—"

I couldn't prevent the tremor in my voice.

"That's why you must be happy."

The sun was slowly sinking. I couldn't turn around, but I could see Kaori in the mirror. I noticed for the first time that she was crying.

"This is so sudden. It's a bit of a shock."

Her words came out haltingly.

"When I heard he'd disappeared I was really upset, and I didn't know what to do. So Fumihiro is . . ."

The tears ran down her cheeks, but she didn't take out a handkerchief. I stayed motionless, my mind in turmoil.

"I thought that if I met him I'd get all messed up again and we'd both suffer, so I couldn't contact him."

Her words were like a hammer blow. It had never occurred to me that I lived inside Kaori in the same way that she lived in me.

"But still, just living is really hard, and not many good things have happened to me. But the time I spent with Fumihiro, that's been my salvation."

Vivid memories passed before my eyes, of us walking home together hand in hand as if we were checking the other was still there, of spending hours in my bed, giggling the whole time.

"I didn't know how he felt about me, but whenever I was having a hard time, I prayed that he was happy. If he was still alive somewhere, I could keep on living too. I could find some good in the world."

She faltered.

"Don't you think that's true? Because even people like us, we were able to be that happy, just for a short time. Because we were able to prove that such happiness exists. I always tell myself that no matter how difficult things are now, you never know what will happen in the future. And because I don't know, I've kept on living. That's how I've survived, because things like that can really happen. I'm so happy that Fumihiro is . . ."

Her arms and shoulders were trembling.

"Please tell him that I'm doing well too. And please tell him thanks."

I was shaken to the core. A warmth spread through my body, a warmth that I'd thought I would never experience again. I wiped my eyes several times with my right hand. Time flowed by and the sun sank even lower. Finally I roused myself, put the car in gear and drove off.

"For today, we'll . . . I'm sorry for bringing this up out of the blue. Please don't tell anyone. I'll take you home. You're staying with Azumi at the moment, aren't you?"

I tried to focus on driving. Azusa's apartment was close. I drove slowly down the narrow street, turning cautiously at the corners, past the shops and houses.

"Um," said Kaori softly, after a long silence.

She was watching me with troubled eyes, brushing away tears, as if trying to make up her mind. I grunted in reply, keeping my eyes on the road, feeling a sense of dread. We turned at an intersection and entered a residential area.

"Are you . . . are you really happy?" Her voice was low but I could hear her clearly.

"Yes."

I don't know how I managed to get the words out. My voice was still shaking.

"I'm married, so I probably shouldn't say this, but you really are beautiful, you're wonderful."

I could see Konishi's condo. The white building gradually grew nearer, and I stopped the car out front. I hardly knew if I was still crying or not, but I wanted to see Kaori one last time. Whether I was Fumihiro or Shintani, that no longer seemed important. I twisted around in my seat, taking in her eyes and lips, her thin neck and shoulders. She was as lovely as ever, so lovely that I wanted to find some good in the world, no matter what happened to me.

"I love you."

This was the second time I had made that confession to her.

"So it's probably better if we don't see each other again. Since I'm married."

I turned to the front again and unlocked the doors. She hesitated, but then started to move. I kept my eyes averted, and finally I heard her getting out. She walked around and stood by the driver's side door, peering at me through the glass, her figure lit by the setting sun. Dazzled, I wound down the window.

"Today," she started, "I, um . . ."

Her whole body was bathed with an orange light.

"I'm still a bit confused, but . . ."

I handed her a paper bag.

"Sorry, I forgot to give you this. It's a small present. A white hair-tie."

Kaori smiled weakly, her eyes red.

"Please use it from time to time, at the end of the day."

I took a breath. Tears welled in my eyes again.

"I'm really glad I met you."

I drove slowly away. I didn't know if she was watching me leave, but I knew that once I turned the corner it would be over. I searched for a place where I could pull myself together. After a few minutes I spotted a park. I stopped the car and got out, gently distancing myself from the lingering scent of her perfume. In a haze of tears I staggered to a bench and collapsed onto it. It seemed to embrace my crumbling body and spirit.

I sat there and wept. Perhaps from time to time I cried out. When I was finally able to stand, it was already quite dark.

11

THE RAIN THAT had started abruptly several days before had stopped, giving us a brief respite. A distant sun cast rays through gaps in the low, heavy clouds. Since morning, rain that couldn't make up its mind to become snow had formed countless puddles on the pavement, throwing random reflections of the strengthening sunshine. I'd stepped in several of these by accident and my leather shoes were soaked. The woman who doubled as receptionist met me as before, smiling and without make-up. When she ushered me into the reception room the doctor stood, looking at my face.

I sat on the white sofa and he pushed an ashtray towards me. As always, it didn't feel like a hospital. The surgeon was dressed in ordinary clothes, and his rigid smile was hardly a smile at all. The potted plants had grown a bit since last time, and the room seemed to be buried in soft foliage.

"I've decided to leave Japan for a while," I said.

He nodded slightly.

"I want to take some time to think things over. Everything that's happened. There's been too much going on."

The warm air gently stroked my cold skin. Without getting up, I took off my coat.

"But do you really have to leave to do that? And will you ever come back?"

"Maybe. I'm not sure. I just want to get away from it all for a while . . . think things over."

He nodded again, but I couldn't tell if he approved or not.

"I see," he said. "Well, I'll give you several months' worth of pills. They're just a precaution, but it's best if you keep taking them."

"Thanks."

The woman entered with tea. Steam rose from the white cups, hanging in the air for ages. She walked out again silently, her smile still firmly in place.

"I worked on her face too," he said, lifting the cup to his mouth.

The tea must still have been piping hot, but he drank it calmly without blowing on it first. It was as strong as ever.

"You two are mysterious," I said.

"You're pretty mysterious yourself."

I looked around the room, filled with green like a conservatory.

"What's your . . . ?"

He didn't seem surprised by my unfinished question.

"What kind of life she and I lead, how we got here . . . that's another long story."

He grinned and wiped the corners of his mouth.

"I'll give you three guesses, and I'll tell you which one is closest."

His smile seemed more definite than usual. I felt my own lips curving as well.

"Okay, how about this? You're at the end of a tragic love affair."

"So you're really going to play? Fine. You've got two left."

"The two of you killed someone precious to you."

"And the last?"

"You've used up your will to live. You committed some kind of crime and were persecuted by people, by society."

He slowly drank his tea.

"Perhaps all of them hit on part of the truth. But one thing's certain. This is the last refuge for both of us."

I gazed around the room once more. It was getting warmer.

"By the way, your face is looking good," he continued, turning a mirror towards me.

I saw my face, still glowing with cold from outside. My eyes were large, my chin tucked in, my cheeks slightly hollow.

"It's still new, but it already belongs to you. It's bonded to your own muscles and it looks truly yours. You've passed through something, am I right? I don't know if it was good or bad, but it shows in your face. I can tell because I'm a professional. It's better than it was before."

"No, that's not right. There's nothing admirable about what I've done."

My inner clock told me it was time to go. My body seemed to want to sit there forever, and I tried to make myself get up but couldn't. Just after midday I was due to meet Ito from JL.

"It's almost time for you to leave, isn't it?" The doctor stood. "I can always tell, even without people looking at the clock."

He gave another proper smile.

"Not because I'm a plastic surgeon, though. It's because I can often read what other people are thinking, what's bothering them. When I was a kid, my parents fought all the time. I'd get between them when it looked like they were about to start, and I grew up always conscious of their moods. It's funny that as an adult it seems to be a useful skill in life, one of my good points."

The doctor opened the door and I went into the corridor. He came after me.

"One last thing, though," he said softly. "If you've stumbled into a problem that can't be solved by humans, if you've taken someone's life . . . Overseas they have this concept of God."

The hallway was much colder than the room had been.

"People who believe in God, when they're suffering because they've killed someone, as long as they feel properly repentant, they can commend it to him. Thinking they can't be forgiven, that's just their own pride, because the only being in the universe with the power to absolve sin is God. Only God, far superior to humans, is able to forgive."

I said nothing.

"In some places in Africa, when young people who were abducted as children by guerrillas or revolutionaries and forced to fight as soldiers returned to their villages, they hold this ceremony. They tell them that if they go through this ritual, if they cross this line, they will be cleansed of the guilt that torments them, the guilt of murder. In fact, lots of young people have been saved that way."

He stood next to me as he spoke, studying my expression.

"Murder is beyond human judgment. For that, you have to turn to a concept greater than us."

I hesitated for a moment, then walked away. He followed me without a word. At the entrance I stopped to put on my shoes.

"I suppose that's one way of looking at it," I said. "We could seek redemption like that. Every killing is different."

I turned to face him again.

"But holding on to it, leaving it unresolved, I think that's right for me. I think I want to carry that perpetual burden, the knowledge that I've harmed others, I want to carry it for my whole life. I'm sure that's best for me."

He smiled serenely.

"That's why I like you, because you say things like that."

I GOT OUT of the cab, walked along a narrow street lined with rundown apartments and turned a corner past some shuttered-up shops. Opposite a prefab with a rusty traffic accident prevention sign on the wall was an empty factory. I stepped over the useless, twisted fence, and there was Ito. He was wearing the same gray beanie with a lightweight black coat and expensive denim jeans, sitting on a heap of scrap metal. When he noticed I was there he glanced at me briefly. Beside him lay a large backpack. For some reason I got a feeling of déjà vu.

"Are you sure you weren't followed?"

"I changed cabs, then walked the rest of the way. It's fine, I think."

On the ground, the puddles had largely dried up.

"The guy they were hunting is dead. Of the two who were on the run, he was closest to me. Did you know that?"

"It was on the news."

Ito was playing with the strap on his left wrist with his right hand. His cheeks twitched as though he was grinding his molars. Even when I lit a cigarette, he didn't look at me.

"The bastard's dead. All they said was that the body was found on the street, but it sounds like he jumped off a building. Still wearing his backpack with the evidence linking him to me in it. Stupid prick. Guys like that, they can dish it out but they can't take it when it looks like it's going to come back on them. They'll probably catch the other one soon too. JL will be finished."

He let go of his wristband, as though he'd finally run out of energy. His silver earrings glinted in the sun.

"Have you got the money?"

"Before that . . . have you really never killed anyone?"

Ito drew his brows together.

"Not yet. But don't get the idea it's because I'm chicken."

His eyes were slightly sunken and he looked thinner than before.

"It's just that it was too soon. That's why this has happened. We should have done the killing all at once, after we'd grown much bigger. Pull off one trick after another to cause the maximum confusion, and then do it all in one fell swoop. When they were told that what the prank they pulled with the TV commentator was lame, they just went crazy. Because they got such a big reaction from the media, they got an inflated idea of their own importance. Dickheads. What we were trying to do wasn't just about our own egos."

"But still, you should forget about killing."

Ito laughed derisively.

"What's with the preaching? Go fuck yourself."

"I'm Fumihiro Kuki."

"Huh?"

The sun was gradually sinking lower in the sky. A breeze touched my bare cheeks. Next to the scrap metal was a rusted steel drum. A few grains of sand, carried by the wind, hit the side of the drum with a faint noise. He was staring at me.

"I'm a cancer, same as you," I continued. "I changed my appearance. I murdered my father before he could finish my education, so I'm incomplete. Your first instinct was right."

He kept looking at me.

"When you kill someone, it leaves a feeling that you'll never be able to wash off. It stays inside you forever. It continues to affect your judgment and thinking. It narrows down your life significantly. You don't have to put yourself through that."

He didn't move, but he was still watching me. I remembered what we'd talked about before.

"What are you living for? I guess everyone has different reasons, but for me, it's because I've got memories that I don't want to lose. I don't know about you, but you never know, do you, what's going to happen in the future? You can't tell whether your life has been happy or unhappy until you're at death's door, through sickness or old age or whatever. There must be some warmth in everyone's life, in the long vector lines that stretch from the past to the future. The fact that you were thinking about killing in the first place, doesn't that prove that you're interested in other people? Because without other people you can't put your own thoughts and ideas into practice. Besides . . ."

I breathed in quietly.

"There are things that only people like us can do, that only people like us can think of. Right? Maybe I'm saying this to you because it's still hard for me to say it to myself—no one has to disappear. It's not necessary. If you can change your-self, it's okay to do it a little at a time. And if you don't want to change, then you don't have to. It doesn't matter if you're a useful member of society or any of that crap. You don't have to tell everyone what you're thinking, you can just qui-etly let your acquaintances know, if you like. Or you can just keep your thoughts inside your head. You can think calmly, can't you, without becoming desperate? You can brood about things, can't you? If happiness is a fortress, then it doesn't matter what you do. People who've got happiness to spare can give others a hand."

The sun had almost set.

"That's what I think at the moment, anyway. It's just because my life has been like this that I'm determined to sur-vive. And why shouldn't I enjoy what the world has to offer until I grow old and die?"

Ito looked away, staring at a patch of dirt. The slanting sun-light cast long shadows.

"You sure do talk a lot."

"Because with you, it's like I'm talking to myself."

Ito may have been exhausted, but he still seemed able to dress with care. Deliberately, he took off his beanie and tossed it to me. The breeze ruffled his medium length hair.

"I'll leave this with you until next time we meet. In return for your long speech. Until then, I won't do anything."

I held his hat in my right hand.

"Next time I'm planning something, I'll ask your opinion, because we're both cancers. And I'll pay you back the money some time too. I want to be even with you."

I passed him a paper bag full of cash and a page torn from a notebook.

"I'm leaving the country for a while. Use this email address to contact me. And if you need to change your face, I know a good plastic surgeon."

Ito put the money in his backpack, the paper in his pocket, and got to his feet. He started to walk off, then turned back and hesitated.

"I really never imagined I'd meet you like this."

"Me neither."

"Funny, eh."

With that he walked slowly away. I stayed where I was and lit a cigarette. The wind was growing stronger.

It would have been easier to catch a cab if I went in the same direction as Ito, but I headed the other way instead. I walked towards a main road, through the puddles drying on the pavement. In a small park a little girl was tearing around merrily, her mother watching and laughing. The child was running as hard as she could, but then stopped abruptly as though she'd found something. She pushed her face close to whatever it was she had discovered, studying it with a big smile.

I couldn't see what it was, a flower or an insect, but that instant of the child's rapt attention seemed to hold some special meaning. Though her intellect and reason were still unformed, her eye was drawn to things around her with friendly interest, as though they were drawing her in. Perhaps Kaori would have a baby one day too. That was up to her, of course, but maybe she would. Idly I imagined what her child would be like when it grew up. It would be nice if the world was a bit easier to live in then than it was now. I wasn't sure if I really hoped that but at any rate, when the idea popped into my head, I couldn't reject it out of hand.

The sun had almost disappeared below the horizon. Once again, the light began to give everything an orange hue.

12

YAEKO AND SAE Suzuki's graves were in a cemetery on a small hill on the outskirts of Tokyo.

Their headstones stood in the clear air and stillness. As I placed my flowers in front of them, I noticed that the ones already there were still fresh. I decided to give them some water. The detective, who had accompanied me, gave me a hand.

"You're not directly related to them, you know," he said quietly.

"I know, but I still thought I should come."

I lit a stick of incense with my cigarette lighter and then stood, looking at the graves in front of me. Silently I informed them that Koichi Shintani was dead too.

• • •

WE RETURNED TO the car without speaking, and the private investigator drove. The road to Narita Airport was fairly quiet, so we were soon on the expressway. A commercial was playing on the radio.

"But still," he said, hands resting on the steering wheel, "I think you did really well. For example, that JL guy who was on the run, I hear he was spotted near Ms. Kaori's condo. Maybe he was waiting for her to come home or planning to break in. You were wise to send her to Konishi's place."

I started to answer, then stopped, looking out the window. Below the expressway I could see acres and acres of sleeping houses.

"Takayuki Yajima too," he continued. "I think you had no choice but to do that. Of course, that's assuming you put more value on Ms. Kaori than on society's opinion. Even if you'd turned him in for drugs, as a first offender he'd have got probation, not jail time. And if you reported him for fraud it would have been difficult to prove, because the victims are usually reluctant to come forward. He was a textbook example of a marriage fraudster, because even if he was exposed, he could still put on a real performance and ingratiate himself with the ladies. Romantic attraction is a powerful thing, and he was very adept at using it. Plus he used drugs. When I was talking to his victims, I was often surprised that almost all of them still can't forget about him, even though they know he lied to them. They'd all gone through a stage where they wouldn't listen to anyone's advice. Even though they'd been reluctant to do drugs at first, eventually they became dependent, so they were ashamed and couldn't accept help from others. Drug addiction's a nasty business."

I stared off into the distance.

"And he was persistent. He never gave up, no matter what obstacles were placed in his way. Even if you'd asked the police to protect Ms. Kaori, it would have been difficult for them to do much. He wasn't stalking her, and basically the police can only act after a crime has been committed. There've been lots of women who've reported their stalkers to the police and still been murdered. To keep Ms. Kaori completely safe, dealing with him as you did doesn't seem unreasonable."

We drove straight as an arrow along the empty highway.

"That's if you care about what society calls 'morality.' Practically, if you consider how dangerous he was, the fact that you didn't stand to benefit personally, the peculiarity and urgency of the situation, you'd probably get about five years in prison for his murder. Mikihiko Kuki, well, that was his own choice. And as for that earlier event, you can't be charged with anything, because offenses committed by minors aren't treated as crimes."

I wanted to look at him, but just kept staring at the road spreading out before me. At his mention of that "earlier event" an image of my father's scrawny frame came back to me. I still didn't know what I should have done. Even if I could have gone back in time to do it over, I'd probably have done the same. But that didn't mean it could be forgiven, that I could forget about it, that it was a simple matter of black and white. Whatever the reason, I'd never forgotten the feelings

I had when I did it, and I had a responsibility to hold on to them. I pretended to shrug off what he'd said about my father and talked about Yajima instead.

"I'm not planning to reveal everything. Putting aside how many years I'd get, I'm thinking about turning myself in for Yajima. I want to take my time to think it over, decide what to do, the best course of action. I don't feel much of anything about him, but apparently I'm having nightmares about it. Sometimes I wake up covered in sweat and think, ah, I must've had another one. My weird dream with those chairs lined up in front of me, that's caused by what I did to Yajima, too. My body is blaming me for killing him. It's a tough burden to carry. If there are other people who are thinking of doing what I've done, I want to tell them not to. It ruins your life, and they should think of a better way. The only reason I managed to do it was because back then I felt I was already a dead man walking. If you think about wartime, hundreds of thousands of people end up living with that feeling."

"Haven't you worked it out yet?" interrupted the detective. "It may not have been one hundred percent certain, but there was one way you could have protected Ms. Kaori from Yajima that would probably have succeeded. That was if you'd become her boyfriend. All his skill at seduction would have been useless, because con men like that don't target women who already have a partner. In fact she was single, and even though she'd been warned about dating customers, she quite liked him already. But if you were going out with her, she'd have ignored him, and he could never have gotten close to her in the first place. Right? I guess with Mikihiko Kuki behind him he might still have tried to muscle in, but he probably wouldn't have got anywhere. Still, you didn't do it."

I said nothing.

"I think you did really well. The only thing that didn't go smoothly was your love life."

A truck loaded with timber raced past us. Cars were streaming by on the other side of the median strip, heading towards their various destinations. The radio started playing a gentle guitar melody.

"But you look a bit more solid now than you did before. When I met you earlier I had this rude thought. I imagined you were an old man on the verge of death, mumbling to God that at least you hadn't killed yourself."

He grinned. I smiled back faintly.

"You've really helped me a lot," I said. "You don't know how much."

"It looks like Azusa has genuinely made friends with Ms. Kaori. I'll keep an eye on her a bit too, but Azusa being her friend, that's got to be good for her, doesn't it?"

He hesitated for a second before continuing.

"The first time I met you, you asked me about the investigations I did for Shozo Kuki, as a test. Of course one reason I didn't hand them over was my sense of professional ethics, but I also thought about the enormity of the consequences if they came to light, and I couldn't give them to you. Actually there are still more. But I guess you've had enough of the Kukis, haven't you?"

We left the expressway and came out on a wide road. For some reason the passing cars and the houses, the traffic lights and the pedestrians, all seemed dazzling. When we reached Narita the detective lifted my suitcase out of the car for me, and I thanked him. Then he looked me in the eye and spoke.

"I saw you once, at the estate."

We walked past a row of waiting taxis. I noticed for the first time that he was a little taller than me. I looked straight back at him to show that I understood the significance of his words.

"You were about six or seven. I visited the house in Nagoya to report the results of an investigation to Shozo, and I saw you in the corridor, really skinny, with some toy blocks in your hand. I'm sure you don't remember it, but at that moment our eyes met. Your eyes looked like they were starved of love, like you were longing for some warmth, some affection, from the bottom of your heart. The same eyes I had when I was a child."

I watched his weary face for a few seconds. It was deeply lined but it was resolute. Several people walked past us on the way to the terminal. I stuck out my right hand and he shook it.

"Thanks for everything," I said.

"Let's go for a drink together sometime, nothing to do with work."

AFTER I'D COMPLETED the ticketing formalities, I buttoned up my coat and walked off, pulling my suitcase behind me. Even though I had plenty of time, I went through the baggage inspection, checked in my luggage, passed through passport control and headed towards Boarding Gate Twelve. The waiting room was still almost empty. I went to the smoking area, had a cigarette and then returned to the gate, thinking that I should have checked in my carry-on bag as well.

And there was Aida. He rose slowly from his seat, looking at me.

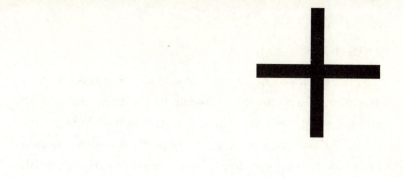

13

HE WALKED SLOWLY towards me. I ignored him and sat in a nearby chair, but he lowered himself into the seat next to me. We sat there side by side in the departure lounge in front of Gate 12. I stared blankly at the bag in my lap.

"Obviously," he said softly, "this isn't a coincidence. I've been waiting for you."

I kept my eyes forward, not looking at him. For some reason he adopted the same pose.

"You know about the cult Rahmla, that took over a nuclear power plant twenty-four years ago."

His voice was still low, his face averted. The empty, sterile waiting area seemed to spread out before us.

"They'd caused quite a bit of trouble before then. As a detective, I was involved several times when there were problems with people who'd left the group. When they seized the power plant, failed to blow it up, and committed mass suicide, one man left behind a posthumous statement, you could call it a suicide note. 'The seeds of evil, the mud that never dries, will squirm and grow at every corner of the globe, through humans' unconscious mind and karmic echoes.' Judging from the handwriting, it was written by Ryokai Ito, a highly placed member of Rahmla who was enrolled as a grad student at Tokyo University. Of course at the time the media didn't mention the fact that he was related to the family that controlled the Kuki Group. But those words have always fascinated me, so much so that whenever I caught a criminal I started investigating his links to Rahmla. Why? I don't understand it myself. I guess I was hoping for something. Naturally it would be terrible if a nuclear plant was really blown up, but still, I wanted something to happen. I wanted to know the answer. Looking at the media frenzy back then, there were probably lots of people who thought the same way. When Rahmla all killed themselves, I felt a bit let down. It's probably similar to the feeling I get when I arrest someone. Of course I've got a strong sense of justice, so I can't stand criminals, but at the same time I know there's another side of me that feels most at ease dealing with them, when I'm close to them. Maybe I've even hoping for something from them."

He still didn't look at me.

"When JL became active, I immediately thought of Rahmla.

I thought there must be some kind of connection there. Some kind of echo. I had another look at Ryokai Ito, but I got the same result. His wife was dead, and there was no record of any kids."

I remembered that Ryosuke Ito's birth had never been registered. Ryokai had kept his son's existence so secret that I didn't know of it until I looked through Father's papers.

"At the time of the Rahmla case, the police and Public Security were secretly checking up on the Kukis. That is one weird family. They've got this custom of breeding children for specific purposes. I also looked at Ryokai's father, who was born as a result of this custom. But then I got interested in this one man. His name was Fumihiro. Shozo Kuki's son, born when the old man was sixty. He'd disappeared and I thought he might have become a member of JL. I talked to my superiors, but of course they took no notice. Well, there was nothing I could do about that, and of course it was simply my imagination anyway. Also, the police weren't too keen on crossing swords with the Kuki family—they were too powerful, and they ran a really big corporation that guaranteed cushy jobs for lots of retired cops and prosecutors."

I stared straight ahead. I don't know why, but a sense of tranquility came over me, and I didn't need to pretend to be calm.

"I couldn't track down Fumihiro, though, no matter how hard I looked. I gave up and concentrated on the relatives of the other leaders of Rahmla. Then the investigation stalled. Their stunts got bigger and the case was more or less taken over by Public Security. We were relegated to deskwork.

Then one of my men asked my opinion about a case he was working on, and that's when I saw you. Takayuki Yajima's death. It brought back memories. I got in touch with Yaeko and found out that she was really sick. That's when I realized that I'm better at handling smaller cases, dealing with ordinary people's lives. I can tell you now, I wished you really had killed Yajima. With that faint hope, I visited your apartment. I thought if I could tell Yaeko that you'd been arrested for murder, that might give her some solace. But it was a difficult investigation. After it came out that Yajima shot up before he died, the regulars at the bar had probably all vanished, and even the staff had changed. No matter how many people we interviewed, no one admitted to having seen him. Still, I thought I'd stick with it. But when we found out that there was a member of JL in our precinct, we got really busy, and we didn't even set up an incident room for the Yajima case. For one thing, it was hard to identify the murderer because of how Yajima was killed. Then we found the room the JL guy on the run was renting, and we discovered your photo. I didn't know what to make of it. I thought that if you were connected to JL and were arrested, that would be good news for Yaeko, but she died first. More than that, though, you weren't the kind of guy who'd join JL in the first place. All my instincts as a detective cried out against it. And while I was puzzling over that, Mikihiko Kuki's death was splashed all over the headlines."

As he told his story, Aida remained completely immobile. In the distance a loudspeaker announced a plane's departure, but it wasn't mine.

"It looks like he was covertly funding JL, using hidden channels. He owned several security firms, and they were profiting from the scare. We still don't have any definite proof, but it's starting to look that way. But I didn't understand why the information about him had leaked just then, nor why he had been killed by a JL bomb when he was one of their secret financiers. Then something even more surprising happened— your picture turned up in Mikihiko's room too. What's more, there was a link between him and Yajima. Just before Yajima's death, you also went to the d'Alfaro. And someone else came out of the woodwork as well. Kaori Kuki."

I didn't turn around.

"I knew her name from the time I was looking into the Kuki family. I had this preconceived idea, though, that anyone who was actively involved in JL had to be a man, and I hardly paid her any attention. But we found hundreds of photos of her at Mikihiko's place. Yajima had pictures of lots of women, but Kaori was among them too. And finally, the JL guy who was on the run also had photos of her, and one of the sightings of him was on the street right next to her condo. We also learned that Yajima had been getting close to her."

He moved one arm slightly.

"That means I ended up putting the importance of the fact that Mikihiko had channeled money to JL, and how he'd done it, to one side and followed just one train of thought. That was that every single person who'd been planning to harm Kaori was dead—and all of them were somehow connected to you. Both Mikihiko and the JL guy had your photo, and you went to the same bar as Yajima. Then after Mikihiko's death, his secretary told us that he called you once to the hotel where he was staying. However, there was no connection between your life and his, and I couldn't find any link between you and Kaori either. I really didn't understand what was going on. But then I came up with a theory."

He took a deep breath.

"If you were Fumihiro Kuki, it would all fit together. Fumihiro and Kaori grew up together on the Kuki property, and since they weren't blood relations there was a good chance that they were intimate, and we received information confirming that. There were various unsavory rumors about Shozo Kuki and women, and he disappeared in mysterious circumstances about the time that Kaori entered adolescence. I'll say it one more time. Everyone who plans to hurt Kaori Kuki winds up dead. Someone like Fumihiro might also be interested in JL. And it would explain why you seemed so different when we met after all these years. But even though I had this theory, I couldn't be all that confident about it, because you look completely different from him—even down to the shape of your ears."

He turned to me, but I still didn't look at him. Various memories floated quietly though my mind, then vanished again. I laughed disbelievingly.

"It's all in your head," I said. "You've got no proof, and just saying it doesn't make it true. Maybe you're spot on, maybe you're partly right, maybe you're way off target. You can say whatever you want. They're just wild guesses."

I saw him stiffen.

"Maybe you're thinking of grabbing me and pulling out a

few of my hairs. Since my apartment has already been swept clean and re-let, that's the only way you can get my DNA."

Aida didn't move, but continued to watch me intently. I remembered Ito's gray knit cap, stowed in the suitcase I'd checked in earlier.

"But you're wasting your time," I said. "Because if you don't know where Fumihiro is, you can't check my DNA against his, so you've got to check it against someone else in the Kuki family. But even if you get lucky, if you get a match, all that proves is that Koichi Shintani is half-brother to one of the Kukis. In other words, all you'd be left with is the fact that the Shintani who was dumped outside an orphanage when he was a baby was the child of Shozo Kuki's mistress. All that would get you is a few raised eyebrows. You've got no evidence pointing to any suspects in the Yajima case, and both Mikihiko's death and the JL guy's death are being treated as suicide, so the grounds for your theory are really flimsy. And one more thing."

I took a breath.

"At the time of Sae Suzuki's accident, your suspicions of me bordered on obsession. You were friends with her mother and with Sae herself, and people on the force know that, right? So they'd think you were trying desperately to pin these murders on me because of your own personal vendetta, just like you were determined to pin it on me last time as well. No one would take your nonsense seriously. Your fantasies would come up against a brick wall."

"There's always your confession."

"I'm not going to confess."

People were starting to straggle into the departure lounge, but it didn't look like there were going to be many passengers. There were still no more than a couple dozen or so. I got slowly to my feet.

"We've known each other for so long, and we'll never meet again, so I'm only listening out of politeness."

Aida remained seated, looking up at me.

"I don't know how to put this," I went on. "You've been a real pain in the ass, and you've really pissed me off, but I never disliked you as a person. Look after yourself."

"What will you do now?" he asked softly.

For some reason the harshness seemed to have faded from his eyes. People were trickling towards the gate.

"I'll go on living."

With this I picked up my bag and followed the others towards the entrance. I could feel him staring at my back, but I put my boarding pass in the machine and went into the gangway leading to the plane. Little by little the feeling faded.

Halfway down the passage I stopped, thinking I'd like another cigarette before boarding, but in the end I gave up on the idea because Aida was probably still there. A few other passengers overtook me. When I adjusted my grip on my bag and turned around to start walking again, Kyoko Yoshioka was standing in front of me.

"Huh?"

She looked at my face and laughed quietly. She was wearing a denim jacket and a tight black skirt, with a small bag in her hand.

"You were talking to that strange guy for ages. I thought maybe you were in trouble, but I guess it was okay."

"What are you doing here?"

"Another weirdo in a shabby suit came and told me you were leaving, handed me a ticket. He had the most penetrating eyes, and I was really suspicious, but it turns out it was true."

The detective, I thought. His saying about breaking the rules flashed through my mind.

"It's lonely, isn't it, going on a long journey by yourself? I also thought, how dare you just take off without telling me!"

"I was planning to email you after I arrived."

The white corridor was almost deserted.

"Hey, look, maybe I wouldn't be your first choice, but I'm not that bad, am I? And number two becoming number one, that's how life goes. Always demanding the best, that's a strange way of living."

"I don't deserve you."

I looked at her.

"I've got nothing, see? Even my money, I'm planning on setting up a charity. I've changed my face, I've even killed people."

"But you're here, aren't you?"

She stared into my eyes.

"And you'll keep on going, won't you?"

A boarding call came over the speakers. She walked off towards the plane, and I followed. When I caught up with her she started talking again.

"My life wasn't going anywhere, so I thought I should listen to my heart for a change."

"I might come back to Japan and turn myself in."

"You'd get a few years, right? That's what the other guy said. If that happens, well, I'll make sure I don't cheat on you."

After we took our seats, she said she was going to tell me her life story.

"Even if you're shocked," she said with a laugh, "we're on a plane so you can't escape."

We fastened our seatbelts and got ready for take-off. Then she glanced sideways at me.

"Before that, though, I'd like to hear yours."

She took off her denim jacket.

"True, I've never really told you, have I?"

The scenery below us changed rapidly as the aircraft gathered speed and left the runway.

"This is the first time I've ever told anyone. I'm not sure where to begin."

We continued our ascent. As I watched the city recede into the distance, I realized that it was filled with millions of lives. Soon the plane passed through a bank of clouds, as though gathering together a bundle of long threads. Above the clouds the sun was blinding.

"Okay, well, when I was eleven my father called me to his study, and this is what he said. 'Now I'm going to tell you . . .'"

The sunlight streaming in through the windows sparkled in her eyes, and the reflection seemed to shine on me as well. I told myself I had to remember those thin, strong beams forever.